P9-DYD-117

Berkley Prime Crime titles by Laura Morrigan

WOOF AT THE DOOR
A TIGER'S TALE
HORSE OF A DIFFERENT KILLER
TAKE THE MONKEY AND RUN

Take the Monkey and RUN

Laura Morrigan

BERKLEY PRIME CRIME, NEW YORK

BERKLEY
PRIME
CRIME

An imprint of Penguin Random House LLC
375 Hudson Street, New York, New York 10014

TAKE THE MONKEY AND RUN

A Berkley Prime Crime Book / published by arrangement with the author

ISBN: 978-0-425-28201-4

PUBLISHING HISTORY
Berkley Prime Crime mass-market edition / July 2016

PRINTED IN THE UNITED STATES OF AMERICA

10 9 8 7 6 5 4 3 2 1

Cover illustration by Maryann Lasher.
Cover design by Diana Kolsky.
Interior text design by Kristin del Rosario.
Photos: Pawprints-Dzmitry Haishun / Shutterstock;
Leopard print-zimmytws / Shutterstock.

Penguin
Random
House

Dad, this one's for you.

ACKNOWLEDGMENTS

Much heartfelt gratitude to: My editor, Julie Mianecki, for her unwavering patience and guidance.

Myra Van Hoose, who helped with all things NOLA and gave me a great idea for a twist at the end. Next time, the vino is on me!

My small but mighty writer's group. Ladies, you're the best!

Justin Pullen for not only providing insight into the metaphysical and esoteric, but also hauling me to New Orleans for a much needed shot of inspiration.

My loving family who supports and encourages me. Especially my sister, Elizabeth. Thank you for always being there to brainstorm and make me smile.

And my mom, Frances, for cracking the whip (nicely) and helping with everything from research to edits. I love you.

CHAPTER 1

She sat calmly, unaware of the killer waiting to strike. He'd been watching, I knew. Silently stalking ever closer. I also knew if I didn't do something fast, she was going to die.

Horribly. In front of a crowd of people.

She had no defense and no way to escape. The little dove's wings had been clipped—literally.

Her owner, a street magician currently wowing the crowd with his humor and sleight of hand, had probably trimmed the flight feathers of her wings for the bird's safety, never thinking a local feline would be so bold as to leap into the middle of his magic act.

Hunt!

The word popped into my head, all excitement and intent.

Crap.

I scanned the area. The New Orleans winter hadn't managed to strip many leaves from the trees in Jackson Square, leaving plenty of foliage to hide behind.

"Where are you?" I muttered, trying to home in on the mild buzzing coming from the animal's mind. I'd known I was looking for a cat before I caught sight of the big tabby, crouched under a hedge.

It's one of the things I can usually tell. Feline, canine, equine—they all give off a different vibe.

My ability to understand animals was the reason I was in the Big Easy. I'd been hired to help find a missing woman by talking to her cat. I was still sketchy on the details.

Before meeting my client, I'd had time for a walk. Which was how I'd ended up watching a street magician and now, looking for a way to thwart a murderous feline.

A casual observer might think the bird was well out of reach, but I could see inside the cat's head.

The section of fence he was crouched in front of was bent—maybe damaged in Katrina or some other calamity, or simply warped with age. However it had happened, the tabby knew there was a spot just wide enough for him to slip through. Once he was on the other side, it would be an easy leap to the table. The prize would be his.

The humans gathered around didn't bother him. Humans were slow.

Slow to react, slow to give chase . . .

Like his human, who had never managed to kill a single mouse, much less a bird.

He'd bring this plump white one to his human. And maybe this time she wouldn't squeal in alarm when she found it on the balcony.

I had to smile at the flood of thoughts coming from the big tabby.

The cat was trying to feed its owner, who was clearly the most inept hunter in the world—at least from the cat's perspective.

It reminded me of another cat I knew, Dusty.

Dusty belonged to Kai Duncan, whom I'd been dating since that summer. Our relationship had had a rough start, since Kai was a crime scene investigator and less than eager to accept the existence of psychic abilities without concrete evidence. Not to mention my habit of keeping people at arm's length. But things were going well now. I smiled every time I thought of him, which I figured was a good sign.

Not so good was that thinking about Kai always distracted me, and by the time I shook off the warm fuzzies brought on by thoughts of his bright green eyes and heart-melting grin, the cat was slinking through the opening in the fence.

I eased another step closer.

"Watch carefully"—the street magician's voice rose over the music of a neighboring performer—"as I, Marvo the Magnificent, make this dove disappear!"

Hopeful, I paused and shifted my gaze to the man. Maybe I wouldn't have to save the dove after all. The magician flicked his wand with a flourish and a second dove appeared next to the first, seeming to flutter into existence out of nothing.

Whoa.

The crowd cheered. The cat shifted his focus to the new, more animated arrival.

Catch!

The cat's excitement swelled as the crowd's applause died.

Oh no, you don't.

I knew shouting over the crowd wouldn't make a difference. I'd have to use my mind.

Hey! Cat!

I pushed the thought at the feline with enough force to make him fold his ears back. *Yeah—I'm talking to you, buddy.*

The cat's tail twitched. Then he gathered his hindquarters to spring onto the table.

Not today, pal! But it was too late. The cat had locked on to a target and was ready to launch.

In desperation, I did the only thing I thought would work—I hissed.

Like, really hissed. Loud.

Everyone, including the magician and the cat, stared at me.

Yep, I looked like a lunatic. It wasn't the first time and it wouldn't be the last, so I tried not to think about it.

Without taking my focus off the cat, I stepped forward and hissed again. This time, I ended the hiss with a warning growl.

I added an extra mental kick only the cat would feel,

projecting the dominance and ferocity of a big cat—something I'd picked up from a tiger I knew.

I staked my claim on the doves. *Mine!*

The cat flinched. Eyes wide, with pupils so huge they made his irises look almost black, he flattened his ears and hissed back.

But I would be the winner of this little contest. I knew even before he shifted his weight and looked away.

Sorry, buddy. I couldn't explain to the cat why he couldn't have these birds. Well, I could have but he wouldn't have cared that the old magician needed them to earn a living.

He was a cat. Socioeconomics didn't matter to him.

The magician looked from me to the now-retreating feline. Understanding shifted his features.

"Oh my. That cat . . ."

"Was about to snatch one of your doves." I nodded.

"My dear girl—" He turned to the confused audience and raised his voice. "This young lady just saved Naomi and Paloma." With a flourish, he produced a silk rose from the sleeve of his coat, bowed, and presented it to me.

Everyone applauded and I suddenly felt more awkward than when I'd been standing in a crowd hissing at a cat.

"What is your name, my dear?"

"Uh—Grace."

"Grace." He paused to kiss my hand with a dramatic bow. "I am in your debt."

"Okay—well . . ." I eased my hand away and set the flower on the table. "You're welcome."

Backing up, I hightailed it out of the spotlight before the Magnificent Marvo could make me a part of his act.

As I neared the St. Louis Cathedral, I thought of the would-be dove killer and hoped I hadn't wounded the cat's pride too badly. He'd only been trying to do the right thing— in his kitty-mind, anyway.

Humans aren't the only ones who sometimes do the wrong thing for the right reason.

I was distracted from that deep thought when a man dressed as a jester danced past me wielding a butterfly net and wearing a sign offering free advice.

So far, New Orleans was living up to its reputation as a colorful, quirky, strangely charming city.

Despite the crispness of the January day, the crowd was thick. Palm and tarot card readers had set up shop along the wide, slate-paved plaza in front of the cathedral. Their brightly colored tablecloths fluttered in the breeze and added to the festive atmosphere.

My phone vibrated against my hand in my coat pocket. I fished the device out and knew without looking at the screen that it was my sister, Emma. Not for any extrasensory reason. I'm not that intuitive. I knew it was Emma because when she'd given me the phone, she'd assigned ring tones to different people.

Whenever our mom called, it played Vivaldi. Kai was the chorus of "Hot Blooded." Our dad, who's a mechanic, had a car horn playing "Dixie," *Dukes of Hazzard* style.

Emma'd recently changed her ring to play Cyndi Lauper's "Girls Just Want to Have Fun," which suited her perfectly.

"How's the Big Easy?" she asked.

"So far, so good. Everything okay with you?" I tried not to sound anxious but shouldn't have bothered. She knew me too well. I'd left my wolf-dog, Moss, and our kitten, Voodoo, in my sister's care. Emma was certainly capable of caring for them but she and Moss tended to have . . . let's just call them "personality conflicts."

"Don't worry—everyone is fine. I just wanted to call and wish you good luck on your first case."

"It's not a case." We'd been over this. "I'm not a private investigator or a cop. I'm meeting with a client."

"Who wants your help finding her missing sister, using skills only you have."

"I'm not sure about that," I said as I passed a shop advertising tarot readings, palmistry, and divination.

Not that I can do any of those things—I can't. My ability is far more mundane. At least, it is to me.

"Come on, Grace, this is a milestone. And you get a free trip to New Orleans! How's the hotel?"

"Nice," I said, which was an understatement. The Hotel Monteleone was grand and elegant, yet cozy.

"Pet-friendly, too, right? Have you made any friends?"

"As a matter of fact, I met a nice poodle as I was checking in."

"Yeah? Toy or standard?" my sister asked with interest. We'd had a poodle when we were kids—they were Emma's favorite dog.

"Standard. His name was Beauregard and he told me they put treats on his doggy bed as part of the turndown service."

"Nice. Too bad you couldn't bring Moss on the flight. That sounds like the type of treatment he'd go for."

"Oh yes," I said, and had the fanciful vision of Moss, who looks like a large, white timber wolf, sprawled on his back with cucumber slices covering his eyes as someone painted his toenails. The thought made me smile, then made me miss my dog. "Give him a kiss for me, okay?"

There was a pause and I could almost hear my sister's nose wrinkle in distaste. "How about I give him a nice pat on the head?"

I sighed.

"He wouldn't want a kiss from me anyway."

She had a point.

"Did you have a chance to check out the bar?" Emma asked.

I knew she was talking about the hotel's famous Carousel Bar, which not only looked like a carousel, but actually rotated.

"I only had a quick peek, but it looks just like you described." Emma had been to New Orleans a number of times and, being Emma, knew all the trendy spots.

"You'll have to try a French 75 later tonight—they're fantastic. I wish I was there."

"Me, too."

"Yeah?"

"Of course. Who else would drag me out of my room tonight?"

"You better drag *yourself* out, little sister."

"Listen," I said, realizing I hadn't been paying attention to the cross streets as I walked. "I've got to figure out where I am before I get turned around and miss my trolley."

"Streetcar. You're in New Orleans, not Disney World."

"Aren't they the same thing?"

"It's *A Streetcar Named Desire*, not *A Trolley Named Desire*."

"Point taken," I said, stopping at an intersection.

"I've got an event tonight," Emma said, "but leave me a message and let me know how it goes—okay?"

Emma was a—scratch that—she was *the* event planner in Jacksonville. "I thought you were taking the weekend off to start your birthday week."

My sister believed in dragging birthday celebrations out for as long as possible.

"Starting tomorrow," she said.

"Sorry I'm missing it."

"No you're not." She chuckled. Emma knew I could only deal with so much social interaction before becoming over-whelmed. I was good with animals. Really good. People? Well . . . I was getting better.

"Just promise to have a cocktail for me," she said. "And kick butt with your case—maybe not in that order."

"Deal."

After hanging up, I tapped the GPS app on my phone. It took a second to zero in on my location, and then it indicated that I was two blocks away from the streetcar I was look-ing for.

I made it across busy Canal Street and onto the St. Charles streetcar just before it pulled away.

The car was packed with people, tourists and locals alike,

and I had to stand near the front as we trundled along. Okay with me—it gave me a great view.

One thing I noticed about New Orleans was that there were Mardi Gras beads everywhere. Everything, from cute picket fences to razor-wire-topped security gates, was draped in beads. They dangled from trees like some sort of sparkling, mystical Spanish moss.

I'm not sure how much time had passed, but by the time I made it to my stop, I was ready for a walk. Which was a good thing.

According to my GPS, it was at least a dozen blocks to Magazine Street, where I was supposed to meet my client, Anya Zharova.

The late-afternoon sun was bright, and it, along with my brisk pace, kept me warm despite the chill.

I'd almost made it to the rendezvous location when my phone chimed, indicating I had a text message. I started to glance at the screen but heard someone say my name.

"Excuse me. Grace Wilde?" The voice came from my left and though we'd only spoken on the phone, I recognized it as Anya's. The Russian accent was a dead giveaway.

I turned and saw a blond woman step toward me. I shifted my phone to the other hand so I could shake the one she offered.

"Thank you so much for coming."

"I just hope I can help."

"I'm sure you will." Her accent made the last word sound like *ville*. "Please, it is this way." As we were crossing the street, I got another text. I frowned at the message. It was from a blocked number and was a single word: *Boo*. There was only one person who would send me a text from a blocked number.

Logan, AKA the Ghost. Man of mystery, criminal, sometimes ally. I hadn't seen him in over a month. He didn't contact me unless there was a problem.

Before I could type a quick response asking what was wrong, another text came in.

XX

Two capital *X*'s?

I shot Anya a surreptitious glance. The woman was paying for my time, and I didn't want her to think I wasn't giving her my full attention. As I looked up, I noticed a bar across the street with a large inflatable Dos Equis bottle tethered to the pole.

My phone chimed again.

Miss you. We need to talk. XX

I looked at the Dos Equis bottle and noticed the bum standing next to it. He seemed to be staring at me from under his dark hoodie. When he saw me looking he turned and went into the bar. He didn't shuffle or stagger. His movement was graceful and efficient.

"Grace, are you okay?" Anya asked, noticing I'd slowed to a stop.

"Yes. I'm so sorry," I said with an apologetic smile. "I just realized I really need to use the ladies' room. Too much coffee and a long ride in the streetcar. I'll be right back." I didn't give her a chance to object. Rushing across the street, I ducked into the bar.

The interior of the narrow tavern was dim and had that strange hushed hollowness that some nightspots have in the light of day.

There was a scruffy-looking bald man seated at the counter with his eyes fixed to the mounted television. I didn't see a bartender or a bum so I walked toward the back and stepped through the saloon-style doors into a small graffiti-coated hallway.

I paused for a moment. Had I actually just followed a bum into the deserted back room of a bar?

"I've lost my mind," I said on a whispered breath.

The space seemed deserted. At the opposite end of the hall was a door marked PRIVATE. I started toward it and was stopped abruptly when someone grabbed me and dragged me into a room to my right.

My scream never had a chance. As soon as I'd sucked in a breath, a hand clamped over my mouth.

I twisted and slipped away, only to be pinned with my back against the wall. Somehow the hand had stayed over my mouth the whole time.

"Shhh. Grace, it's okay. It's me." I blinked at the bearded face, then narrowed my eyes as they locked on to his.

Logan.

I shoved at his chest and, when he dropped his hand, hissed, "Get off me. What is it with you? Always giving me a freaking heart attack."

Logan might have been an enforcer for the mob, a guy so scary criminals were frightened of him, but that didn't stop me from getting angry at being manhandled.

"We don't have time to chat," he said in a harsh whisper. "Listen, you can't trust them."

"Them? Them who?" So far, I'd spoken only to Anya.

"You'll find out soon enough."

"Damn it, Logan, cut the cloak-and-dagger crap and just tell me what's going on."

"Right now all you need to know is you can't give them what they want."

"What am I supposed to do?"

"Lie. Even better, embellish. Add details that aren't true. You can't let these people know what you can do."

"How do you know what I can do?" I'd never told Logan about my ability.

"I'll explain everything later," he said.

"Logan—"

"Do you trust me?" he asked.

I hesitated, a little taken aback. The quick answer was *no*.

Trust didn't come easily to me. And I'd have to be nuts to trust an enforcer for the mob—and yet . . . it wasn't that simple.

Did I trust Logan? Not really. Did I think he would hurt me or let me be hurt? Probably not.

There was something in his expression. I couldn't quite interpret it. That's what happens when you spend more time talking to animals than to people.

"Grace—"

I pressed my lips together and, with some reluctance, gave him a quick nod.

"Good. Then trust that I'll explain everything later—" He broke off suddenly and looked over my shoulder almost as if he could see through the wall into the bar.

He pivoted, leaned into the stall, and flushed the toilet, then turned the handle on the faucet of the small, wall-mounted sink and mouthed, "Wash."

Bewildered, I put my hands under the running water.

After a few seconds, Logan turned the faucet off and touched his fingers to his lips. In the quiet, I could hear the light *click-clack* of heels on the wood floor, followed by the creak of the saloon doors as they swooshed open.

Logan punched the button on the ancient hand dryer. It sighed to life, wafting tepid air over my fingers.

"Watch yourself." The words were muttered so quietly in my ear, I almost didn't hear them.

Almost.

So great was the impact of those words that when a soft knock sounded at the door, I jumped, only barely managing to swallow a yelp.

Logan canted his head, indicating I should go.

I pulled the door open. Anya stood in the hall, blinking at me.

"Sorry." I shook excess water off my hands. "That dryer is worthless." I walked past her to the bar and grabbed a couple of paper cocktail napkins from their holder.

Anya trailed after me as I headed outside.

The unexpected run-in with Logan and his cryptic message had caught me off guard and made me jumpy.

I suck at small talk, especially when I'm nervous, and being accosted by Logan hadn't helped. I tried to hide my nerves by asking typical touristy questions, but quickly learned Anya didn't live in the city.

"I am only here to find Veronica," she said.

We rounded the corner and started down a narrow street. A slender man wearing glasses was waiting near a gate in a privacy fence.

"Grace, I'd like you to meet Dr. Barry Schellenger."

"Dr. Schellenger." I took the man's hand. His fingers were warm but his grip tentative and loose.

"I'm glad you could come, Miss Wilde. Please, call me Barry."

So, it was a "they," as Logan had said.

The man's eyes didn't dart but were never really still. He angled his head and studied me in a way that reminded me of a chicken who'd just caught sight of a particularly juicy bug.

Even without Logan's cryptic warning, the guy would have given me the creeps.

I tried not to let my trepidation show as I looked from him to Anya.

"Barry is Veronica's psychiatrist," she said. "I asked him to meet us. He is more able to explain my sister's condition."

"Condition?"

"Veronica is mildly schizophrenic."

"Oh?" Was there such a thing as mild schizophrenia?

"Do you have the text, Anya?" he asked.

She nodded, took a smartphone from the pocket of her coat, turned it on, and handed it to me. The screen displayed a text message to Anya.

It read, *I'm sorry . . . I can't stay here. I couldn't wait for you and couldn't find Coco. You remember where I got her? That's where I'll be. Get Coco and come as soon as you can. Don't tell anyone where you're going! Remember.*

"I'm not sure I understand," I said. "Is this from Veronica?"

"Yes," Anya said, taking the phone back.

"What's she talking about? What does 'remember' mean?"

"It means," Barry said, his tone grave, "that Veronica has most likely stopped taking her medication."

"How long has she been missing?"

"At least three days," Anya said. "That is when I got a call from her landlord."

"And the Coco she mentions?" I asked, though I thought I could guess the answer.

"Coco is her cat."

"So, you believe the key to finding Veronica is discovering where she got Coco."

"Yes," Anya said. "Unfortunately, she never told me."

"I'll be honest—zeroing in on such a specific detail is going to be tricky. If I can do it at all."

"Any insight you can give would be welcome," the psychiatrist said.

I glanced at him and almost flinched. He was looking at me with that weird chicken/velociraptor gleam in his eyes again.

"Please," Anya said, drawing my attention back to her. "I understand what I'm asking is difficult, but I will do anything to find her."

As I studied her face, I was reminded of the real reason I'd agreed to take her case. I'd asked myself, what would I do if Emma were missing?

Anything.

Just as Anya had said.

I'd hire a truckload of psychics, pay anything, *do* anything if my sister were in trouble.

Now, I had to wonder, was it all an act? Judging from Anya's expression, I'd say no. She looked worried and desperate. But worried and desperate for whom?

The psychiatrist gave me the willies. Maybe he was coercing Anya to help him.

If that were the case, Anya's concern might be for her own hide.

"Veronica is a danger to herself," the psychiatrist said. "The sooner we can make sure she's okay and gets the proper care, the better."

"Well then, let's get started," I said.

I'd ask Coco what she knew, but had no plans to tell them what I discovered. At least not until I heard what Logan had to say.

Barry opened the gate in the privacy fence and we walked into a small yard with a set of wooden steps leading to the upper floor.

At the top of the stairs was a small landing. The door to the apartment looked old but solid, except for the small cat door cut out of the bottom panel. An exterior lamp hung on the faded blue clapboard wall. Under it, a utilitarian plaque marked APT 4 was affixed to the siding.

Anya used a key to open the door and we stepped inside.

Veronica's apartment wasn't small—it was minuscule.

The ceilings were high but the floor space was no bigger than most hotel rooms. Even so, the area was organized and tidy, not at all like I imagined the living quarters of a schizophrenic would be.

"There's no bed," I said. Not that it mattered.

"It is there." Anya pointed up to what I realized was a sleeping loft.

A window had been added to the gable and Veronica had attached a kitty hammock to the sill. I knew it was occupied even though I couldn't see from where I stood.

I didn't reach out to the cat with my mind but I could feel her.

"The cat is probably up there, too," Anya said. "We have kept the cat door closed."

I nodded, then turned back to Anya. "I need a photo of your sister. Something to use as a reference when I talk to Coco."

"A reference?" Barry asked. "What do you mean?"

"Not all animals know our names. I can ask about Veronica, but it's better if I can use a mental picture."

"Interesting," Barry said. His glinting eyes narrowed in thought.

"Here is a photo," Anya said, moving into what one might optimistically call a kitchenette. Attached to the fridge was a picture of two young women. I looked at the photo—neither of them looked much like Anya.

She pointed to the woman on the right.

"Is it a recent photo?" I asked.

"Probably taken in the last year, I am guessing."

I looked back to the loft. "It might take a few minutes to get Coco to come down. I'll have more luck if I'm alone."

From his expression, I could tell Barry didn't like that. But Anya nodded and said, "Of course, we will be outside. Take your time." She ushered Barry out and shut the front door.

I turned back to Coco. Now I could see the tip of a tabby-colored tail hanging over the edge of the kitty hammock. It twitched back and forth.

Something in a nearby tree had caught her interest, though I didn't know what. I kept my mind shielded from the animal's thoughts. Before I started asking questions, I wanted to take a quick look around.

I hadn't had time to process much of what Logan had said, but if Anya and Barry couldn't be trusted and they planned to use me to find Veronica, I wanted to know as much as possible about her.

I started in the kitchenette. There was another picture on the fridge, a snapshot of Anya that was secured by a magnet featuring the famous cathedral and statue I'd seen earlier in Jackson Square. It was next to the photo of Veronica and her unknown friend. Though I noticed there were no pictures of Veronica and Anya together.

I didn't see anything else of interest in the small space and had decided to move on to the bathroom when a soft *meow* sounded from a few feet away.

Coco, moving as only cats can, leapt from the loft to land on the back of the sofa, then hopped down and walked toward me.

I opened my thoughts to the cat and knew an instant later what she wanted.

Dinner?

Though I could tell she wasn't very hungry, I obliged. Finding her food in a cabinet, I filled her bowl and knelt to give her a pet.

I ran my hand down her back and smiled. It was as if I'd kick-started a motorcycle, the purrs were so loud.

"Hey, Coco," I murmured, figuring I'd go ahead and chat with her now. She was calm and only mildly distracted with eating.

I hadn't been lying when I'd told Anya it can be tough to get specific information from an animal. I can't just access their mind in a way that lets you scroll through their memories like you can do with photos on your phone. Something has to trigger it. Finding the trigger is the hard part.

As I watched the cat eat, I was hit with a flash of inspiration and decided to try something I hadn't done before.

Clearing my thoughts with a couple of slow breaths, I pressed into the cat's mind.

Coco was munching away happily. I used the contented feeling of a full belly as a guide. I thought of warmth and safety and tried to conjure up the idea of family. Thinking of my own mother's hugs helped.

Suddenly, I felt like I was in a pile of purring fur blankets and realized Coco was remembering her littermates.

Who else is there? I asked.

Mamere, the cat answered.

I was going to need more than that.

Can you show me?

She did, though it wasn't the most detailed or helpful series of images.

I saw a pair of worn bedroom slippers. Bunny slippers,

actually. A section of wrought-iron fence. Tall, bright green blades of grass.

I could hear the buzz of an insect and the muted sound of a woman's voice.

I started to push for more but Coco's mind had jumped to Veronica. I saw the young woman smiling down at the cat.

"She's beautiful, Mamere," Veronica said in the vision.

Suddenly, there was another abrupt shift. Coco's thoughts leapt out of the memory and landed in the present. I blinked the room back into focus and glanced around to see what had distracted her, but saw nothing obvious.

"What?" I asked, looking back at the cat.

She didn't answer. Ears twitching, Coco's attention was zeroed in on the far upper corner of Veronica's living room.

Cats will do that sometimes—stare at nothing. Almost as if they're seeing ghosts, and who knows, maybe in some cases they are, but usually their attention is drawn by something more tangible—a moth fluttering against a window or the scrabbling of a rodent in a crawl space. Difficult for human hearing to detect, but for a cat?

Easy.

Sometimes my ability gives me an advantage, even over cats. Coco knew something was in the tree outside—she just wasn't sure what it was. I knew exactly what was creeping closer to the apartment, and I can promise you one thing—it was no rodent.

"What the . . . ?"

Frowning, I stood and moved to the wall, like I'd suddenly developed X-ray vision and could see through it or something.

After a moment, I stepped back and looked through the high window at the branches of a tree.

A little face peered back at me.

A monkey.

A capuchin, if I know my monkeys—and I do.

"Where did you come from?"

I refocused my thoughts and gently reached out with my mental feelers to get a read on the animal.

Skittish. But not upset or frightened. There was something odd about him. Or, more accurately, his mind.

It seemed to be pulsing. The hum of his brain fluctuated like the rise and fall of an ocean wave.

Interesting.

I wondered how long the little guy had been hanging around—pun intended.

More important, I wondered if he'd seen anything of interest regarding Veronica. I pulled an image of the woman to the front of my mind and presented it to the monkey.

The oddest thing happened. The mental picture of Veronica I'd shown the monkey flickered and froze. Then everything went blank. Another image flashed in my mind, too quickly to make out what it was.

It flickered and stabilized, but I still couldn't make it out. After a second, I realized why. The scene was polarized— like a 35 mm film negative.

The reversed colors made it hard to make sense of what I was seeing. I could make out two people, one male, one female.

Then, as abruptly as it had changed before, the colors went back to normal.

I pulled in a sharp, surprised breath. Because not only did I recognize Veronica, but I also knew the man. Shocked, I tried to absorb what the monkey had shown me.

Veronica being grabbed from behind by a tall, powerfully built man. I might not have recognized his bearded face had I not seen it less than an hour before.

Logan.

CHAPTER 2

"Logan." I growled the name, not sure if I was more angry with him for jerking me around or myself for trusting him.

My sudden spike of temper startled the monkey, and the scene disappeared in a flash of white light so bright I instinctively squeezed my eyes shut, which, of course, did no good.

The light was in my head. There was no escaping it.

Hissing out a quiet curse, I turned when I heard the front door open.

"I was just finishing up," I said, straightening.

"Are you all right?" Anya asked.

"Fine. Just a headache." I sensed the monkey was moving away. I really needed to follow him. For one, it was too cold for a capuchin to be overnighting outside and I wanted to make sure he got home. For another, I wanted to dig more into what he'd seen.

When had Logan grabbed Veronica? What more had the monkey witnessed?

"I'm very sorry," I said, trying not to sound as shaky as I felt. "But I don't have anything to tell you."

"You mean you couldn't communicate with Coco?" Barry asked.

"Not in the way I needed to. I'm sorry, but Coco couldn't tell me where Veronica found her."

"Maybe you could come back tomorrow and try again?" Anya asked.

"You're here through the weekend, after all," Barry added.

The tone of his voice made it clear what he thought of my services.

Fine by me. I just wanted to get out of there.

The monkey was still moving through the tree. I had to go before he was too far away for me to follow.

"I could come back," I said as I eased toward the door. "But I don't think I'm going to be much use to you. Coco might recognize where she came from if she went there, but getting that from her without more to go on is going to be very hard."

"If we find more information, would you be willing to try again?" Anya asked.

I didn't want to agree, but a part of me felt guilty. Not because I wasn't offering any helpful information. I wasn't sold on the idea that Anya was really Veronica's sister. But she had paid for my flight and hotel.

"Let me think about it. If I can come up with another angle that might work I'll let you know."

The gleam I'd noticed earlier in Barry's eyes turned into a cold glint.

"Let me give you a ride back to your hotel," he offered.

"No thanks. I'll enjoy the streetcar ride."

"Are you sure? It's not safe to wander—you could end up in the wrong neighborhood."

"I can take care of myself." I kept my tone light but knew I was projecting a pretty clear "back off" vibe.

I'm not the greatest martial artist—that's my sister's forte—but my get-lost-or-lose-an-appendage look has worked on both man and beast. In my experience, the only people who ignore the warning are too crazy to notice or too cocky to care.

I was pretty sure I knew where "Dr." Barry fit.

The guy was nutty as squirrel poo.

I wasn't hanging around to see just how deep his crazy went. "I fed Coco, so you don't have to worry about that," I said as I walked out onto the landing. "I'll call if I think of anything more."

I rushed down the stairs as quickly as I could, but the monkey had me at a disadvantage.

Which is usually the case. At least if you're trying to catch a monkey with nothing but your wits and charm in an area full of huge trees.

Something had caused the monkey to speed up. In fact, he seemed almost frightened.

Two-hundred-year-old live oaks are like monkey super-highways. The little guy was out of sight before I managed to make it out of the gate.

The odd, pulsing hum of his mind began to fade. I ran faster. The thick soles of my boots clapped hard against the concrete. If I didn't pick up the pace, I'd lose him.

It wasn't so much that I couldn't keep up, more that we were traveling on different planes. The monkey zipped through the trees, unhampered by things like fences and buildings. He cut through backyards and zigzagged over houses, while I had to pause, determine a direction, run, change direction. Pause. Repeat.

The only hope I had to slow the mad monkey dash was to get close enough to form a mental connection. I was pretty sure I could calm him down if—

Honk!

A car screeched to a stop a few feet away from me.

I blinked at the gesticulating driver, stunned at my own stupidity.

Running after an animal was nothing new to me. But running out into traffic? I needed to get my head on straight.

I waved an apology at the driver, who had decided to lay on the horn again.

Of course, by the time I reached the sidewalk and gathered my wits enough to look for the monkey, he was long gone.

Crap.

No monkey and, thanks to the fact that I hadn't been paying attention, no clue where I was. At least I could remedy the latter problem.

I reached into my coat pocket for my phone and its trusty GPS, but came up empty. I searched the other pocket. Nothing.

Had my phone fallen out somehow during the chase? I patted the back of my jeans and, finding nothing, slid my hand into my right-hand coat pocket again, which was the last place I remembered putting the phone. My fingers brushed over a stiff piece of paper.

I felt my teeth clench in frustration. I knew what the piece of paper was before I pulled it out to look at it.

A card, blank except for a phone number printed on one side. I glared at the paper.

Logan.

Another perfect example of why I shouldn't have trusted him.

He was a pickpocket.

I remembered he'd promised to explain everything. But what good was a phone number if I didn't have a phone?

Flipping the card over, I found a time—seven p.m. that night—and an address written on the other side by hand.

Okay, so he'd slipped the card in my pocket to tell me where and when to meet—but why would he take my phone?

How was I going to figure out where I was?

"Calm down," I muttered to myself. People had managed to survive without smartphones until very recently. I myself had only acquired my iPhone in the last few months.

How quickly man is hobbled by technology.

Squeezing my eyes closed for a moment, I pulled in a slow breath and tried to relax my shoulders as I let it out. I was just going to have to make do without a phone until I met up with Logan.

If I met up with him. For all I knew he was setting me up to kidnap me, like he had Veronica.

Okay, like he *might have* kidnapped Veronica. I only saw him grab her. I didn't see what had happened next.

With a final calming breath, I pushed thoughts of Logan out of my head. I had one source of information on what had happened to Veronica—the monkey had seen something. To find out what, I had to find the monkey.

I looked around the street, but before I could decide on a direction, I noticed a flyer stapled to a light pole. On it was a black-and-white photograph of a capuchin monkey.

At first I thought it was an "if found" poster, similar to the ones you might see for a dog or cat, and thought I'd be able to contact the monkey's owner, but when I got close enough to read the text, I found it was more like a wanted poster.

It read: HAVE YOU SEEN THIS MONKEY? REPORT SIGHTINGS TO THE AUDUBON ZOO.

A phone number was listed in bold letters. I reflexively reached into my pocket to retrieve my phone, then cursed inwardly when my finger touched Logan's card.

The bottom of the flyer was fringed with tear-away tabs printed with the phone number. I peeled one off and put it in my pocket.

At least I could call later.

I wondered if the zoo were merely assisting with the efforts to catch the monkey, or if he had actually escaped from the park.

The question reminded me of something I'd seen on the streetcar's local-attractions map—the Audubon Zoo was in Uptown, probably not far from where I was. Maybe even within walking distance.

I looked around for some indication of where I should go and noticed a sign for a Laundromat across the street. The place was busy and I figured the patrons would know the neighborhood, so I jogged over to ask for directions.

As soon as I stepped inside, I stopped in my tracks. Now I understood why the place was so busy. There was a full bar to one side and a pool table and dartboard to go with the washing machines.

"Not used to seeing a bar in a Laundromat?" someone asked from my right.

I turned to see a woman with a basket of clothes wedged under one arm.

"Uh, no."

"It's kind of a local thing." She shrugged and took a sip from the bottle of beer she held in her other hand.

"You're from the neighborhood?" I asked.

"Sure am."

"Could you tell me how far it is to the Audubon Zoo?"

"It's right up the road. Keep going that way." She pointed with the bottle. "You'll run right into it."

I thanked the woman and was happy to discover she was right. I made it to the zoo's entrance in less than fifteen minutes.

Following the map I'd been given at the front gate, I headed toward the monkey exhibits. Even in January, the zoo's landscaping was lush and green. Palm trees ringed a giant water fountain featuring life-sized elephants spraying water from their trunks.

It made me think of a Disney World ride I'd been on when I was a kid. All the animals were statues made to look lifelike. As you can imagine, it confused the heck out of me.

Back home in Ponte Vedra, where I shared a condo with my sister, I often walked on the beach to clear my head. I also took walks around the Jacksonville Zoo.

I didn't have time to indulge in a relaxing stroll today, though. I needed info on a monkey. Soon, the map brought me to what I was looking for.

Primates. A small troop of capuchin monkeys lounged in the last rays of the setting sun.

Looking around, I cast my senses around the area, but found no trace of the little escapee.

Focusing on the small troop of monkeys in front of me, I considered the best way to inquire about the capuchin I'd seen, but couldn't think of a way to phrase the question. I hadn't gotten a good enough look at the monkey back at Veronica's to use his image to ask if he'd escaped.

I settled for scanning their emotions and thoughts and looked for signs of distress, worry, or longing—anything that might indicate a member of their troop had gone missing—but found nothing more than a mild case of indigestion.

I can't say I was very surprised. There was something about the little monkey that didn't jibe with this group.

For one thing, the monkey I'd been following had a distinctly different feel to his mind. Which was interesting. I rarely encountered such a pronounced difference in the same species. It was something I'd have to ponder later. Right now the bigger question was, if he hadn't escaped from here, where had he come from?

With a sigh, I turned away from the capuchins and started to wander.

Believe it or not, being around a large number of different animals fills my mind with a gentle, white noise. It helps me relax and think. Which was exactly what I needed to do. I decided to try to put everything that had happened in perspective. Unfortunately, I didn't enjoy much time to reflect because before I'd reached the next habitat, a man's angry voice sounded from the path to my right.

"As a representative of the Fleur-De-Lis Homeowners' Association, I demand an answer."

"I just explained to you, sir," a woman answered, sounding exasperated.

I eased around the corner to see an old man, vibrating with indignation. He reminded me so much of my crotchety neighbor, Mr. Cavanaugh, that I had to blink a few times to make sure it wasn't him. They shared the same pinched, wrinkled, liver-spotted face and perpetually affronted attitude.

The petite woman who was unfortunate enough to be the

recipient of his ire had dark hair and a sweet-looking face. She motioned to a stack of papers in his hand.

"You can see from our files that—"

He cut her off by waving the paperwork in her face. "You're telling me the wild animal marauding our properties came from elsewhere?"

The zookeeper sighed. "Sir, that's exactly what I'm saying."

"Hogwash."

"Sir, we're doing everything we can to help catch the monkey."

"I am the president of the Fleur-De-Lis Homeowners' Association, and we will not stand for this!"

The woman planted her hands on her hips, clearly at her wits' end.

I felt for her. Dealing with unreasonable, self-important people had to be one of the circles of hell.

I decided to intervene, or try to, and rushed toward the two.

"You work here, right?" I asked the woman with feigned wide-eyed breathlessness.

"Yes. What is it?"

With a dramatic sigh, I placed my hand over my heart and pointed down the path. "I just saw someone tossing candy to the baboons."

Lips thinning, the zookeeper said, "You'll have to excuse me, sir." Without waiting for his reply, she turned her back to the man and walked away.

He sputtered, clearly outraged, and looked at me.

I gave him a farewell nod and, without a hint of sarcasm, said, "Have a good day, Mr. President." Then hurried after the zookeeper.

"Hey," I said quietly when I caught up to her in front of the baboon exhibit. "False alarm. Everyone's safe."

Frowning, she looked at me, then into the enclosure.

"I thought you needed a break from that guy," I explained.

Still frowning, the zookeeper studied me. "I did. Thanks."

"I guess there's an animal on the loose and he's blaming the zoo."

"You from out of town?"

"Got in earlier today."

She nodded, as if that explained everything. "The papers have been calling him the Mystery Monkey. He's been sighted all over but mostly in Uptown."

"In this cold?"

Her expression went from annoyance to concern. "We haven't had a freeze yet—but it's on the way."

"Poor little guy." I pursed my lips, not wanting to think about the little capuchin huddling all alone on a freezing night. "Any idea where he came from?"

"None. It's illegal to own a primate in the city of New Orleans, but people break the rules all the time."

"I'd like to help. I'm Grace, by the way."

"Marisa." She shook my hand and I fished a card out of my jeans pocket and offered it to her.

No, the card doesn't say I'm a telepath. I'm not quite ready for that, but it does give me the title of behaviorist and lists my website, which is filled with testimonials.

"I know this sounds a little crazy but I'm very good at what I do. You can go to my website and check the references. I've done a lot of work for the zoo back in Jacksonville."

"Okay." She spoke the word slowly and without much conviction.

"Anyway," I said because it was clear the woman thought I had a screw loose, "what I'm saying is you can call me if you find him. I can help catch him."

I could also ask him more about Logan.

"Actually," I said, remembering I didn't have a phone and cursing Logan again, "my phone isn't working at the moment, but I'm staying at the Monteleone. You can leave a message at the front desk."

"Sure," Marisa said, slipping my card into her pocket. "Look, the park is going to be closing soon."

"Right. I'll head out." It was getting close to the time Logan had written on his card, and I still had no clue where the place was.

I was going to meet Logan if for no other reason than to give him a piece of my mind and demand to know his role in what was going on.

"And if he doesn't give me my phone, so help me . . ." I muttered as I walked toward St. Charles.

My threats were all empty bravado, of course. I had no power over Logan.

Unless . . .

Logan was a wanted man. I could call the police and tip them off to where he was going to be in the next thirty minutes.

I knew it wouldn't work. Logan was known as the Ghost by cops and criminals alike. He'd earned the name for two reasons. One—no one knew who he was. Two—he possessed the almost supernatural ability to appear and vanish at will.

Logan always managed to escape the long, grasping arm of the law. Always.

He'd get away and I'd never get answers.

It was fully dark by the time I reached a busy-enough street to find a cab. The driver plugged the address into his GPS. I watched longingly as it zeroed in on the location and plotted a route.

I'd gotten too dependent on my phone.

By the time I arrived at the address—which turned out to be a divey little bar—I'd almost convinced myself to forget about my smartphone and simply carry around a Jitterbug.

Almost.

The bar was small and almost empty so I picked a barstool toward the back, where I could see the side and front entrances.

Aside from the large flat-screen TV, the place looked like it had been transplanted from 1981. There was a Pac-Man machine and on one wall I spotted a poster of Cheryl Tiegs in a bikini signed, *To Lenny—great grilled cheese! XXX*.

Ashtrays were large and readily available.

The bartender, a woman with dark eyeliner and a frothy nimbus of blond hair, asked, "What you need, honey?"

I was so mesmerized by the woman's resemblance to Stevie Nicks that it took me a second to answer.

"I'm waiting for a friend, so, water for now."

"You want it out of the tap or something fancy?" Stevie asked.

"I've had a long day, so let's go for fancy."

"One fancy water—coming right up." She turned in a swirl of fringed cloth and returned with a bottle of Perrier and a glass garnished with a lime wedge.

I sipped the water and pretended to watch ESPN, only half listening to the sports commentators debate the merits of playoff teams and make predictions about the Super Bowl. A clock next to one of the TVs read ten past seven.

Logan should already be here.

The side door swished open. I dropped my gaze from the TV to the mirror behind the bar. A trio of women scuttled in out of the cold. The door bounced closed. No Logan.

There was an abandoned *Times-Picayune* newspaper on the adjacent stool and I picked it up. The headline read:

MYSTERY MONKEY ESCAPES CAPTURE

Apparently the little capuchin had made a name for himself outside of Uptown.

After reading about the Mystery Monkey sightings and numerous escapes, I skimmed over a few more articles. One highlighted a fire in an abandoned warehouse where a body had been found. The police hadn't identified the body but had determined the cause of death was not related to the fire.

I caught myself wondering what type of forensic analysis was being used in the investigation and almost laughed.

See what happens when you date a crime scene investigator? Kai was rubbing off on me. Thinking about him made me want to call and see what he was up to. Which, of course, I couldn't do.

Where was Logan?

Bartender Stevie walked past holding a platter of chicken wings and a basket of fries. My stomach grumbled.

Mostly, I'm a vegetarian, though I confess to eating a scallop or two and eggs on occasion. My favorite food, aside from pizza, is salad. Recently, I'd been introduced, via one of my sister's caterers, to kale salad with sliced almonds, sunflower seeds, and dried fruit, topped with some sort of magical mustard vinaigrette dressing. It was by far one of the most delicious things I'd ever eaten. I didn't think I'd find it here.

I located a menu tucked between the salt and pepper shakers.

Stevie noticed and swished over to ask, "You need anything?"

"This says your grilled cheese is world famous."

"Sure is."

"Then I'll take one. And another Perrier."

The grilled cheese was delivered a few minutes later, but Logan still hadn't shown. I was about halfway through the sandwich when I heard a phone ringing behind me.

I turned to see a pay phone affixed to the wall next to the men's restroom.

"You have a pay phone?" I couldn't remember the last time I'd seen an honest-to-goodness *working* pay phone.

"We do. And it's probably the oldest and crappiest one in all of Louisiana."

A thought occurred to me as the phone continued to ring. Logan might have chosen this place so he could call me. I slid off the barstool, thinking I'd had a eureka moment, but hadn't made it more than a step when a man wiping his hands on an apron scurried out of the kitchen and lifted the receiver.

I watched him for a few seconds. The call was obviously for him.

Sitting back down, I tried to muster some enthusiasm for the greasy grilled cheese, but couldn't do it.

I looked at the clock—it was getting close to nine. It was time to call a spade a spade and realize Logan wasn't late. He'd stood me up.

I wasn't sure whom I was more aggravated with—him, for being a no-show, or myself, for waiting this long.

After paying my tab and getting quick directions to my hotel from Stevie, I bid her good night and stepped out into the night.

In the hours I'd sat in the bar, it had gone from cool to cold. The wind tugged at my hair and made me wish I had a scarf. I took a second to button my coat up to my neck, got my bearings, and started toward the hotel.

The New Orleans winter seemed to be a lot like North Florida's. The heat of the sun made the days mild but high humidity let the cold cut right through you on windy nights.

Shivering, I quickened my step. I thought about the little capuchin and hoped he'd found a warm place to bed down for the night.

Waiting had given me plenty of time to think and become a little paranoid. Even though it meant going out of my way, I decided to turn and walk down Bourbon Street. Safety in numbers, right?

The cold didn't seem to bother the partygoers. Shouts and laughter mingled with every type of music imaginable. I even passed a place with a polka band.

By the time I made it to the cross street leading to the Monteleone, I'd decided on plan A. Get a good night's sleep and call Kai in the morning.

The number to the Jacksonville Sheriff's Office was easy enough to look up—I could reach him at work and ask him to look into Anya and Dr. Schellenger. Kai would also be able to give me law enforcement/cop advice on what to do.

I was about to round the corner onto Royal Street when I saw him.

The only reason he didn't spot me was because I'd paused to tighten the belt of my coat before turning onto the windy street.

As I huddled against the building's corner and fumbled with the knot with cold-numbed fingers, I glanced up and noticed Dr. Barry Schellenger walking past the opposite corner.

I eased back farther into the shadows.

What was he doing here?

He was headed toward the Monteleone. My gut told me to stay put and watch where he went.

A gust of wind howled down the street, making the lower part of his coat flap open like the wings of an unsteady bird. He hastily pulled his lapels together but not before I saw what was holstered at his waist.

A gun.

Crap!

Okay—looks like plan A is off the table. Time to go with plan B.

In case you're wondering, plan B for me usually boils down to one thing—*run.*

CHAPTER 3

Hoping the sound of the wind-tossed leaves skittering over the sidewalk would cover my footsteps, I turned and fled.

I didn't know if he'd spotted me and I didn't stop to look back.

Thanks to my dog, Moss, I was used to running in sand. A cobblestoned sidewalk, uneven as it was, was much easier. I'd sprinted halfway down the block before Barry would have made it across the street.

The question was—where was I going?

Head to the noise and crowds of Bourbon Street? Circle the block and try to find a second entrance into the hotel? I nixed that idea as soon as it came to me.

Heart pounding, I turned onto Bourbon Street and immediately ducked into a small, dimly lit bar. Without pausing to look around, I scurried to a dark corner by a window. Taking a moment to catch my breath, I scanned the street for signs of Barry. When he didn't materialize after a few minutes, I allowed myself to relax.

Maybe, by some miracle, even though I was wearing a recognizable bright red coat, he hadn't spotted me, which meant he was probably still watching the hotel.

"Buy you a drink?"

I glanced over at the businessman who'd come up to stand beside me. He hadn't slurred the question, but both his glasses and tie were askew.

"No thanks."

"You sure? Absinthe is the house specialty." He raised his glass and swirled it for emphasis.

I'd never tried absinthe, and might have been tempted, if I hadn't just been running from a guy with a gun.

"No really, I'm fine."

"Come on—just one. If you don't like it I'll drink it." He gave me a wink that was probably meant to be charming.

Great.

Seemed like tonight was my night to be pursued by weirdos, one way or the other.

My wooer motioned toward the bar, where I saw several large, fancy glass urns filled with clear liquid. Each had dainty taps protruding from the bottom at glass height.

I watched as the bartender positioned a goblet of what I assumed was absinthe under a tap. Across the rim of the goblet, he placed an odd flat spoon with what looked like a sugar cube on top. The liquid dripped onto the spoon and into the glass.

I couldn't help but ask, "What's in the big urns?"

"Ice water. They have to cut the absinthe, otherwise, it's too potent. Makes people crazy." He grinned. "But I know the bartender. He'll give it to us straight if you're feeling frisky."

Oh good grief. I was tempted to ask the guy if his absinthe lines ever worked, but decided I didn't want to know. I was about to tell the guy to get lost when out of the corner of my eye I caught sight of a familiar figure walking along Bourbon Street.

Barry scanned the faces of the revelers as he walked slowly by.

I eased away from the window. Predictably, the absinthe

aficionado followed, still trying to sell me on the fun we'd have if I'd give it a try.

From where I stood—especially with the drunk guy blocking the window—I was pretty sure Barry couldn't see me, even if he happened to look through the window.

Still, I didn't want to make a scene and attract any attention, so I waited until Barry was out of sight before telling the guy to take a hike.

He told me to come find him if I changed my mind, and wandered back to his friends at the bar.

"You shouldn't let him turn you off absinthe," an older man seated at the closest pub table said.

I looked at the glass in his hand. "Doesn't it make you hallucinate?"

"Not that I've noticed. But this is New Orleans—hard to know if what you're seeing is real or . . . magic."

He snapped his fingers and, suddenly, he was holding a rose.

I blinked at him. "Magnificent Marvo?"

In the dim light, without the top hat or tails, I hadn't recognized him.

"Our paths cross again—it must be fate. Please join me."

Keeping one eye on the window, I accepted the invitation. Marvo signaled to the cocktail waitress and a few minutes later, a glass of absinthe was placed in front of me.

I took a tiny sip and made a face. "Tastes like licorice with a kick."

"It's the kick you have to be careful of," he said with a wink.

"So I've been told," I said, checking the window again for Barry.

"Everything okay?"

"Fine," I said, lifting the glass of absinthe. "Cheers."

He tapped his goblet to mine and we both took a swig. I can say this—I wasn't feeling much of the cold anymore.

It turned out Magnificent Marvo had lived all over the

world. He spoke several languages fluently and had called the Big Easy home for thirty years.

"You keep looking out the window," he said after we'd been talking for a while. "You sure everything's okay?"

"Depends on your definition of *okay*."

"Using my mystical powers of insight, I'd say you're looking for someone—and not in a good way," he said.

"Yeah . . ." I paused to think about what to say. I liked the old guy, but I didn't want to go over the whole story. Heck, I didn't even know the whole story. "There's a man I'm trying to avoid."

"I see," he mused, stroking the white hair of his pointed goatee. "Not something you can go to the police about?"

I lifted my absinthe, peering at the cloudy green liquid. I had considered contacting the police, but didn't know if that was the best idea. They'd want to know the whole story—which included Logan. Add a wanted criminal into the mix and the waters got muddy as the Mississippi, quick.

Taking a sip of my drink, I allowed myself to wish I had my phone so I could call Kai. He'd know what to say to the cops.

"I'm not sure the police will be able to help," I told Marvo. "Maybe you could teach me how to disappear?"

"You know, I might be able to do just that." He turned, rummaged through his bag, and placed what looked like a wadded-up ball of paper held together with a piece of masking tape on the table.

"What's this?"

"A smoke bomb. With some added flash for show. You need to get away—this will give you a chance."

"How does it work?"

"Just throw it on a hard surface. The ingredients inside mix and, *poof!*"

I gingerly lifted the ball and squinted at it. "Is it dangerous?"

"Not really. It requires a bit of force to work. Just don't sit on it."

"Thanks." I slipped the smoke bomb into the inner pocket of my coat.

"It's the least I can do. You saved my doves, so if there's something else you need, say the word."

"Well, I no longer have a place to stay while visiting the city. Any recommendations on a hotel that might have a vacancy?"

"No, not a hotel, but I do happen to know someone with a bed-and-breakfast. Belinda will take care of you. But it's on the other side of the Quarter. A bit of a walk."

"I don't mind walking."

He seemed to be considering something. Then his eyes drifted toward the door.

I glanced to where he was looking. A beautiful, curvaceous blonde had entered and was weaving slowly through the crowd, smiling and making eye contact with as many patrons as possible. In her left hand she carried a tray. On it was a clear, plastic rack containing two rows of what looked like test tubes filled with colored liquid.

Marvo caught the girl's eye and waved her over.

"Evening, Shay, how you doing?"

"Freezin' my fanny off," she said, and shot a wink at me.

It was no wonder—she was dressed in a pair of skintight gold leggings that didn't appear to be insulated, a low-cut top showing lots of cleavage, and a black velour hoodie.

"Slow night?" Marvo asked.

"I've had better."

"Is your husband working tonight?"

"Yeah, Michael's with his brother at Oz."

Marvo dipped his head in my direction. "This young lady is headed to Belinda's, but there's a man looking for her and trouble."

Shay's lovely dark eyes narrowed. "Give me a sec," she said, pulling a phone out of her hoodie's pocket. "I'll text the family."

I raised my brows at Marvo.

"Shay's whole family works in the Quarter. Shot girls, dancers. Her husband, Michael, is one of twenty-plus kids."

"Seriously?"

"Okay," Shay said, stuffing her phone back into her pocket. "I've got Sheba and Judith coming. We'll walk you to Oz. Michael and Gabriel will take it from there."

Before I knew it, two more lovely shot girls flanked Shay.

"Come on, baby," Shay said. "We'll get you where you need to be."

• • •

They got me *almost* where I needed to be.

At my insistence, Michael and Gabriel—who wore matching rainbow Speedos, suspenders, and not much else—stopped at a corner and stepped close to a wall to get out of the wind.

"I can find it from here, guys, really," I told them.

"Belinda's is across from the church," Michael said, pointing at a building down the street.

"You can't miss it," his brother added.

I thanked them and the shivering young men hurried back to work.

I was glad I'd let Emma talk me into wearing my fleece-lined boots. They hit me just below my knees and had been a pain at airport security but were proving to be an asset on the cold, cobbled streets. Despite the boots, gloves, and coat, I was half frozen and ready to get inside.

I found the church easily enough—it took up an entire corner. Across the street, I saw two businesses: a place advertising psychic readings and a real estate office. Neither was open and neither was a bed-and-breakfast.

Damn.

I heaved out a long sigh. For some reason, the cloud of fog produced by my breath made me feel colder and suddenly defeated.

Maybe I was on the wrong side of the street? I turned and

scanned the area but saw nothing bed-and-breakfast-like. In fact, the area was pretty deserted. It was quiet but for the soft *click-clack* of heels on the pavers.

Glancing in the direction of the sound, I made out the figure of a tall woman walking toward me, with two tiny dogs in tow.

Pomeranians, I thought, though I couldn't be sure until they reached the circle of light cast by the closest streetlamp. As the trio grew closer, I saw I'd been right about the Poms, but not their owner.

Clad in a long, elaborately embroidered kimono, marabou-trimmed sandals or not, the Adam's apple was a dead give-away.

She was definitely a he.

He was well over six feet tall, had dark skin, and was wearing the kind of head scarf I'd seen my sister don when removing particularly heavily applied makeup.

"There you are!" the dog walker said with a wide smile.

I knew he was talking to me, as I was the only one on the street. Still, the familiar greeting threw me. "Um . . . hi."

"Ain't it somethin'." The voice—a husky contralto—went with the shoes. My brain kept wanting to refer to him as her, so I went with that.

"What am I going to do with you?" she asked.

"Um . . ."

"Room or reading?" she mused, tapping a perfectly polished fingernail on full lips.

I glanced at the sign glowing in the window. It featured a crescent moon and other celestial symbols.

Still not sure I was in the right place, I asked, "You're Belinda?"

"In the flesh."

"In that case, I could use a room, actually."

She snapped glitter-tipped fingers. "I knew it. Come on, let's get you settled."

I followed her inside and found that the interior of the shop was as unique and surprising as its proprietor. Kind of Scheherazade goes on an African safari and has an estate sale.

There was fabric draped everywhere. A nook by the front window featured a small table with a set of tarot cards and a crystal ball.

"Thanks for opening up for me," I said as Belinda walked to a life-sized statue of Nefertiti.

"No problem, *cher*." Reaching around to the queen's back, Belinda clicked on a light, turning the statue's headdress into a torchiere.

"I guess I owe Magnificent Marvo," I mused.

"Who?"

"The magician."

"Marv? He told you to come? Huh. I haven't seen him in a coon's age. How's that old charmer doing?"

"Fine, I guess," I said, confused. "He didn't call and tell you to expect me?"

"Oh, I knew you were coming, *cher*. I always know."

Ookaaay . . .

I glanced at the crystal ball and it clicked. "You knew I was coming because you're a psychic."

"I am. And you're thinking—this queen is crazy. Don't deny it. I can tell."

"Well . . ." Had I been thinking Belinda was crazy? Not exactly. Different, yes. Unexpected, certainly. But crazy? No. I'd been called crazy too many times to point that finger at anyone. "I don't think you're crazy—I'm just a little overwhelmed right now."

"It's okay," she said. "Come on. You look like you need a bedtime snack."

My stomach rumbled at the suggestion.

The hall leading to the kitchen was lined with bookcases. Their shelves were clogged with not only books but all sorts of interesting photos, artwork, beaded African masks, and several oddities I couldn't identify.

I paused at what looked like some sort of altar decorated

with yellow and orange candles and a vase of peacock feathers. An assortment of odd items was scattered at the altar's base. Lipsticks and mini–perfume bottles, a dainty silver comb, assorted coins, and several photographs. Below it was a velvet cloth with an intricate symbol embroidered on it.

Belinda saw me studying the beaded cloth.

"For Oshun. Mother of Sweet Waters. She's a goddess of beauty and love. Like me." Belinda winked, then turned to motion to the opposite side of the hall and another altar. It was similar to the first but had blue and white candles and the vase held a trio of white roses. "This is Yemaya's shrine. She's a powerful spirit. A great protector of women and children. She takes requests. Just ask for her help and make an offering."

I'd never seen an honest-to-goodness voodoo altar. They were pretty neat. On a whim, I fished a coin out of my pocket and muttered, "Yemaya, if you can help me out with some protective awesomeness, I'd be grateful." Then I followed Belinda down the hall.

The kitchen, like the rest of the first floor, had soaring ceilings that made the place seem bigger than it was. A glass-fronted cabinet held a myriad of bottles, jars, and strange little odds and ends. Next to the cabinet was a tall chest with dozens of tiny drawers that looked like it belonged in an apothecary.

Belinda motioned for me to sit at the round table. As soon as I did, the blond Pomeranian hopped up to settle into my lap.

"That's Priscilla," Belinda said. "Elvis is the black one. He's my little helper, aren't you?"

"Yip!" *Little helper. The King!*

I smiled at the dog, then my host—or was it hostess?

Whatever. Her name was Belinda—I was going to stick with that.

This situation was surreal. Although, that morning, I'd boarded a plane hoping to talk to a cat about a missing woman, so maybe surrealism is subjective. But things had gotten weirder for sure.

I thought about Logan.

What the hell had happened to him earlier? Why hadn't he shown up for our meeting—a meeting he had arranged?

Belinda set a cup of steaming tea in front of me along with a small plate.

"Chamomile tea to help you sleep. And a piece of banana bread. My special recipe."

Whatever was in it, it was delicious. I washed the bread down with a sip of tea and sighed as its warmth melted into me. "This is great. Thank you."

"I aim to please."

"Is there anyone else staying here?" I asked.

"No. I kept this week vacant. I had a feeling."

"Like the one you had earlier?"

"I learned a long time ago not to fight the Tingle."

"The Tingle?"

"I get this little tingle along my left side. It always happens just as an idea pops up out of the blue. Take tonight, for example. I was getting ready to take off my makeup and thought, *I need to take Elvis and Priscilla for a walk*—right now. As soon as the idea hit me, I felt the Tingle. So out the door I went, and there you were."

Curious, I found myself asking, "What happens if you ignore it?"

"Ignore what? The Tingle?"

I nodded and took another sip of tea.

Belinda made a *tsk*ing sound as she shook her head. "I gotta respect the Tingle. I regret it when I don't."

"Well, I'm grateful to you and the Tingle."

"Like I said, I'm happy to oblige. Now, how about I show you to your room so you can get some sleep?"

The switchback staircase leading to the upper floors was so steep and uneven I wondered how guests managed it after a night out on nearby Bourbon Street. Heck, I wondered how Belinda managed the climb in the high heels. At least here my lack of luggage was a plus. It would be a treacherous climb toting a full suitcase.

Still, the place had a sort of careworn charm. The wood banister—wonky as it was—was polished to a gleam. The exposed brick wall, though chipped and dotted with holes and remnants of paint, gave the place warmth and character.

"Here we are." Belinda opened a door to a cozy room with a queen-size canopy bed. I might have sighed out loud when I saw the fluffy comforter and pillows.

"I'll send Elvis to check on you in the mornin'."

"Works for me," I told her as she shut the door. I was used to getting a wake-up call from dogs—and cats, for that matter.

Thinking of Voodoo made me wish she were there. I could always count on my cat to deliver a dose of purr-induced bliss that put me to sleep in a nanosecond. It turns out a night running around in the cold and drinking absinthe worked the same way.

• • •

I woke the next morning with an unfamiliar canine brain buzzing in my head. Even after I'd opened my eyes, it took me a second to remember where I was and what had happened the day before.

I'd gone from worrying about the repercussions of being more open about my ability to running from an armed weirdo. Thanks to Logan, I had no phone, no clothes, nothing. Except, it seemed, a persistent Pomeranian entreating entrance at my chamber door.

Elvis?

The King!

Thought so. Anticipation radiated from the little dog. He was soon joined by Priscilla, who let out a dainty yip.

Open!

Rubbing the sleep from my eyes, I rolled out of bed and crossed the room to open the door.

"Come on, you two."

Both puff-balls spun in delighted circles at my invite, then trotted into the room. That was when I saw the note. It was attached to Elvis's harness with a safety pin. He rose on his hind legs, one forepaw resting on my shin, and let out a quiet bark.

For you.

Thanks, buddy. I bent and retrieved the note.

Little helper!

You're the best.

The King!

Elvis promptly sat, obviously waiting for me to read the note.

I shook my head at his adorableness and unfolded the paper.

"Good morning! Come on down for breakfast when you're ready. Fresh towels and extra toiletries in the hall bath just across the landing. Coffee?"

Below the word *coffee* Belinda had drawn two boxes, one with a *Y* and the other with an *N*.

Smiling, I found a pen next to a notepad on the writing desk and checked the box for *Yes* then added a "thank you!" Because I was grateful and really needed coffee.

As soon as I'd reattached the note to Elvis's harness, the little dog trotted out of the room and bounded down the stairs.

"Pretty neat system," I said to Priscilla. "Why aren't you the messenger?"

Priscilla pranced in a circle and flopped onto her back to beg for a tummy rub.

Get the belly!

Gotcha.

Kneeling, I obliged and grinned as the little dog squirmed in delight.

Apparently, Belinda knew a note would get pulverized or torn off during Priscilla's joyful, supine squirmfest.

After a final pat, I stood and made my way to the bathroom.

In this ancient house I'd expected to find a claw-foot tub and pedestal sink but in keeping with the theme of encountering the unexpected, instead I walked into a small bath that reminded me of an upscale Asian spa.

Though the floors were the same scarred, wide, wooden planks as everywhere else in the house, the rest of the room was sleek and modern.

In the shower, I chose the Revive scented body wash, which, according to the label, was good for mental clarity and invigoration.

I can't say if it was that or the prospect of coffee, but by the time I started down the stairs, I was ready to take on the day.

Little Elvis, who'd heard me coming, pranced out of the kitchen to greet me and fulfill his duty by showing me where to go.

I followed him into the kitchen, where Belinda stood at the stove. She was decked out in head-to-toe leopard print, and wore a long wig in a shade of red nature reserves for scarlet macaws. Somehow it worked.

I must have been staring because she asked, "What, you don't like my hair?"

"No. I mean, yes. I was just thinking you look amazing."

She gave me a delighted smile.

"Well, you know what they say." She flipped a scarlet lock over her shoulder with a flourish. "You can turn it down, but you can't turn it off."

I smiled. "Is that what they say?"

She winked and turned back to the stove. "How'd you sleep, sunshine?"

"Like a dead rock."

"Good."

"It smells great in here."

"Coffee's still on, there are scones on the counter next to the mugs, and I'm making jambalaya."

"For breakfast?"

"Baby, it's almost eleven thirty."

"Really?" I paused in my coffee pouring to look out the window into the courtyard—it was overcast. Hard to tell where the sun was in such gloom. "What time did I get here last night?"

"Close to one."

My eyes widened. I rarely stayed out until one in the morning. "Must have been the absinthe," I mumbled.

Belinda chuckled. "Marv loves the green fairy."

"Weird. I don't have a headache or anything."

"Absinthe was originally medicinal. It's been used to treat all sorts of ailments. Stomach pain, inflammation—even helps with mild depression and stimulates your brain."

"Really?"

"Yep. A number of banned substances, like wormwood, which is the stuff in absinthe, hallucinogenic mushrooms, and the like, have been used for thousands of years as medicine."

I took a sip of coffee. It was perfect. Nice and strong, no trace of acidity. I took a second sip and decided I'd stick to caffeine to stimulate my brain for the time being. After several seconds of no big ideas, I gave up. I was going to have to become more caffeinated to come up with a game plan.

"Sit," Belinda said, motioning to the small round table.

I did as I was told and enjoyed a few more sips of coffee. Thinking of the sign I'd seen in the window the night before, I wondered if the shop was open for walk-ins and hoped Belinda wasn't missing business to cater to me. "How often do you do readings?" I asked as she set a plate in front of me and sat in the chair opposite mine.

"Every day. I'm the only psychic voodoo drag queen in the Quarter. Or so I'm told." She winked and I noticed the false eyelashes she wore were tipped in glitter.

"I'm not keeping you from clients, am I?"

"No, I'll hear the bell if someone comes in. Most of my bread is buttered doing special occasions, anyway. A surprise reading for the bride, that sort of thing."

Belinda had to be at least six-six in heels, and that wasn't counting the hair. I'm not sure the word *surprise* was sufficient.

"But enough about me—let's talk about you, *cher.*"

"I'm not sure where to start."

"You could start by telling me about the man you're running away from."

I blinked at her in surprise. "You saw that in a vision or something?"

She shook her head. "I've been around this old Quarter a few times and I know the look of someone who's been betrayed, and you had it last night."

"I did?"

"We can't always understand why people do what they do. Sometimes, you give someone your trust, they break it. But it's not your fault."

I shook my head. "I never trusted him."

"You sure? Because I was getting something else from you."

"You were?"

"It's a kind of hollow energy. Usually, I feel it when a person is disappointed and confused because someone they care about has hurt them and they can't understand why they would act the way they do."

"But . . ." I started to protest when it hit me. Belinda wasn't talking about Barry; she was talking about Logan.

Except I didn't trust Logan, either—did I?

The more I thought about it, the clearer the answer became. As angry as I'd been with him for stealing my phone, deep down I'd believed he'd show up and explain what was going on. I hadn't just been ticked off when he'd stood me up—I'd been disappointed.

It seemed I really had come to trust him. How the heck had that happened?

"You okay?"

I blinked over at Belinda.

"Sorry, what?"

"You look kinda mystified," Belinda said.

"I'm just surprised at myself for being so stupid."

"You can't blame yourself for something someone else does, *cher*."

Something about Belinda made me want to open up. I

couldn't tell her the whole story—it was too complicated and would take too long—so I went with the abbreviated version.

"So this Logan," she said when I'd finished. "You think of him as a friend?"

I winced. "Not in the traditional sense, but for the most part? In a convoluted way, yes."

"Do you think he stood you up on purpose? Maybe he tried to get a message to you but couldn't."

"Logan has always seemed pretty resourceful, but I guess I could call the hotel where I was staying to see if I have any messages."

She looked up the number for the Monteleone for me then handed me her phone.

The reception clerk put me on hold to check and came back on the line a minute later.

"No messages, Miss Wilde, but there's a package for you."

"Package? From who?"

"Let's see. It's not marked."

It had to be from Logan.

"I'll be by to pick it up soon."

"Be sure to have your ID with you."

That, at least, I had.

I thanked the clerk, hung up, and looked at Belinda.

"You need to go back to the hotel?" she guessed.

I nodded. The only problem was Barry and Anya. "I'm not sure how to get into the hotel without being spotted by the people Logan warned me about."

"Leave that to me, honey. Belinda is the queen of incognito."

It turns out Belinda and I have different definitions of *incognito*.

CHAPTER 4

I don't think I would've felt half as ridiculous had we not been on bicycles, but Belinda assured me it would be the quickest way to get to the Monteleone and pointed out that no one would be looking for a blonde on a bike.

You heard correctly. I was *blond*. And not just a run-of-the-mill, regular blond. I was sporting a wig that would put any Texas pageant queen to shame.

The outfit really wasn't that bad. I'd kept my blue jeans but traded my bright red, rather conspicuous, wool coat for a white, down-filled jacket that made me look like the Michelin Man. Though I don't recall the Michelin Man ever wearing angel wings and a halo.

"It's Twelfth Night," Belinda had told me.

"Meaning?"

"You know, the Epiphany."

"When the wise men went to visit Jesus?"

She'd nodded as she straightened my wings. "Everyone will be dressed up. There'll be angels, wise men, snowflakes, whatever."

"People dress up for the Epiphany?"

"Yes, baby. Twelfth Night is the first day of Mardi Gras."

"You're telling me Mardi Gras starts today?" I wasn't sure if I was excited or terrified at the idea of being in New Orleans during the infamous party season.

"We are going to blend right in," Belinda promised as she'd finished pinning the halo on my head. And wouldn't you know it, she was right—mostly.

You see, "blending in" when you're a six-and-a-half-foot-tall drag queen isn't possible. But it was a safe bet that, next to Belinda, nobody would notice me.

We parked our bikes across the street from the grand old hotel, securing them via a massive chain to one of the horse-headed hitching posts outside of Mr. B's restaurant.

Hustling across Royal Street, we blended in—again, I use that term loosely—with a bevy of tourists headed into the hotel. Once inside, Belinda guided me up a few steps and to a seat at the famous Carousel Bar.

At first, I was surprised to find the bar doing such a brisk business that early in the day, then remembered it was past noon.

"This place is popular," I said, looking around.

"The bartenders know what they're doing here, don't you, sugar?" She'd turned her attention to the older black man who'd stepped up to take our order.

"We do our best."

"In that case, give me your best milk punch. Actually, make it two."

I'll admit, I don't know much about cocktails, but putting milk and punch together sounded pretty gross to me. Before I could say anything, the bartender had turned away and started making the drinks.

"Milk punch?" I asked, almost afraid to know what was in it.

"Don't worry, we're not talking Kool-Aid. It's made with bourbon."

Not much better.

"Isn't it a little early to be drinking bourbon?" I asked.

"Never too early to drink bourbon in New Orleans. Besides, we got to blend in."

Blending in took one rotation of the carousel and a second milk punch, which turned out to taste dangerously like a vanilla milkshake.

By the time we determined the coast was clear, I wasn't worried about being spotted by anyone. Heck, I was a little fuzzy on why I'd been worried to start with.

"Okay," Belinda said. "You head to the front desk and get the package. I'll meet you in the lobby in five minutes."

"Got it." I slipped off the barstool and strolled, only a little more loosely than usual, to the reception desk.

"Hi, I'm Grace Wide—ah . . . Wilde." I blinked at the man behind the marble-topped counter and tried to act sober. "You have a package for me."

"You're a guest?"

"Yepper."

"Do you have your room key or ID?" I handed him my driver's license. He studied the photo, then my face.

"I'm an angel today." I pointed to the halo in case he needed clarification.

"Very nice." His smile seemed genuine, so maybe he meant it. "You're going to the parade?"

There was a parade?

Here's the thing—I don't like crowds or most people, but I love a good parade. Paradox.

"Hope so," I told the desk clerk.

"Here's your package, Miss Wilde." He handed me a padded envelope half the size of a magazine. I tucked it into my jacket and was turning to go when he asked, "Would you like your messages, too?"

"Messages? Um . . . sure."

"It's a voice mail. You can listen in your room or use the courtesy phone." He pointed to a phone at a cute little writing desk on the other side of the reception area.

Did I want to risk going to the room or try to hear over the echoing lobby?

"Can I listen to the message here?"

"Sure."

He handed me the receiver, pushed a couple of buttons, and after a few seconds, my sister's voice came over the line.

"I didn't hear from you last night so I'm assuming your phone either died or you lost it. In case it's the latter and you don't have access to your contacts, I'm going to give you my number and Kai's. Give one of us a call when you get this so we know you're alive."

There was an odd noise in the background and a muffled sound as she covered the receiver to speak to whomever she was with. The bourbon in my brain was not helping me think and she was already reciting her number when I realized I didn't have anything to write on or with. By the time I borrowed a pen and notepad from the concierge she was halfway through her number. Thankfully, I knew the area code and prefix so I was able to scribble the number down, along with Kai's.

I heard another shuffling noise over the message and my sister said, "There isn't room for you up here. Go on. Hugh, can you help me out here?" I couldn't make out Hugh's response but I heard the words *crazy* and *dog*.

Dr. Hugh Murray, exotic animal veterinarian, überflirt, and my sister's new honey, must have been helping Emma deal with Moss and his stubborn streak.

It didn't worry me—Hugh had plenty of experience with animals—until I heard a third person speak. The voice was too faint to tell who it was but my dog's reaction was loud and clear.

He growled deep and low.

A warning. What the heck was going on?

"Um . . ." my sister said into the receiver. "I've got to run. Call me later, okay? Love you."

Before she hung up I heard her say, "Moss, cut it out."

Okay, now I was a little worried, but I couldn't stand

there at the front desk and call her back. It was too much of a risk. I would have to hope she'd handled whatever situation had come up.

I thanked the desk clerk and handed him the phone. Even though I was itching to see what was in the package, I didn't want to hang around any longer than necessary.

I turned to look for Belinda. I spotted her posing with a couple of tourists next to the gigantic grandfather clock in the hotel's foyer.

I caught her eye and gave her a nod to say I'd gotten what we came for, then hooked my thumb toward the entrance.

After extracting herself from her admirers, Belinda sashayed to where I was waiting and we hightailed it out of there.

We bustled out of the gleaming glass and brass doors of the hotel and took a right—which was the opposite direction from where our bikes were parked.

"Where are we going?" I asked Belinda. "The bikes are that way."

"Leave the bikes. We're not going far."

Figuring she had a plan, I followed. The day remained chilly—which was a good thing. I needed the cool wind to blow the clouds out of my bourbon-fogged brain. Our hurried pace also helped.

Even in platform heels, Belinda was fast, and I struggled to keep up with her long stride. We walked past antiques shops boasting gilded furniture and glittering chandeliers and art galleries displaying bold modern paintings. At one shop, I spotted a large calico cat lounging in the front window next to one of those famous Blue Dog paintings.

Just past the marble steps of a beautiful judicial building we stepped into the welcome warmth of Café Beignet.

The place was hopping. Its tiny round tables were packed with customers waiting for the café's namesake treat. A waiter zigzagged through the crowd carrying a tray of the powdered sugar–covered fried dough, and suddenly I was hungry again.

"We'll never find an open table," I said to Belinda, realizing she hadn't attracted as many looks as I'd expected. Maybe this crowd was more local and used to seeing Amazonian-sized drag queens sporting angel wings and halos.

"Sure we will. Come on." Belinda led me out a side door into a courtyard and over to a small metal table.

"We should be okay here," she said as we sat. "Let's see what you've got."

I pulled the package out of my jacket and hesitated, glancing around. "You sure? We're only a couple blocks from the hotel."

"Whoever these people following you are, they ain't going to come here."

I followed the wave of her manicured hand to the building next door and saw what she meant.

Two police officers walked up the steps and crossed the portico. As they reached the door, it opened and a third cop exited the building.

"A police station?"

"Right next to a place that sells fried dough. Ain't that something? Now, the suspense has been killing me. What's in the bag?"

Before tearing the package open, I took time to inspect the envelope, but found only my name, handwritten in thick black ink.

The package contained two things: my phone and a card.

"Is that your phone?"

"Yes."

"So your friend gave it back?"

"Looks like it."

"Is there a note or anything?"

I shook my head. "Just this." I held up the card.

"Whose phone number is it?"

"Logan's, probably."

"Does that mean he wants you to call him?"

"I don't really care what he wants. I need to get in touch with my sister."

I opened my contacts and hit her number. It went to voice mail without ringing. I left her a message to call me back and hung up, frowning.

"I'm sure she's fine," Belinda said, reading my expression easily.

"It's not her I'm worried about." I explained what I'd overheard on Emma's message and my concern for whomever Moss had been growling at.

"Well," Belinda said. "You didn't have a second message at the hotel saying he'd mauled anyone, right?"

"Right." I relaxed a little at the logic.

"Check your phone."

I did. There were two missed texts from Kai. One wishing me luck on my "case" and a second from that morning, saying he was working a case and would be out of touch until that afternoon.

"Nothing about Moss," I said to Belinda.

"Then don't sweat it. You got bigger fish to fry."

I picked up Logan's card and dialed the number. After a couple of rings, a recorded voice told me the person I was trying to reach was unavailable and suggested I try my call again later. I shrugged and hung up.

"No answer," I said to Belinda. She huffed out a dissatisfied breath and leaned back in her chair.

"Well, damn."

My thoughts exactly. "Sorry. It looks like we went to a lot of trouble for nothing."

"Not nothing. You got your phone back."

She glanced at the screen and her eyes widened. "Is that the time? I've got to run. I've got a client coming in for a reading."

Out of her enormous bag Belinda produced a dark blue jacket, a colorful ski hat, and an extra-large Ziploc bag. She opened the bag and motioned for me to lean closer. With a few nimble plucks she removed the bobby pins holding my wig in place and moments later I was a brunette again.

Belinda slid the wig, halo and all, into the bag and zipped it closed.

"Anyone who saw you going into the hotel as a blond angel won't be looking for a subdued local. Trade." She held out the jacket. I shrugged out of the one I was wearing and handed it to her.

"I have appointments the rest of this afternoon but if you need me you call me." She handed me a business card and placed a set of keys on the table in front of me. She pointed one glitzy nail, first at one key, then the other. "Courtyard gate. Bike lock. The gate key also opens the side door into the kitchen."

"Thanks," I said with a smile and a small headshake.

"What?"

"I was just thinking you deserve that halo."

She waved the comment off. "Please. I'm only seventy-five percent angel sixty percent of the time. Oh, and take this." She fished a card out of her purse and handed it to me.

"A parking pass?"

"The lot is two blocks away from my place, on Dauphine."

"Why would I need a parking pass?"

"No idea. But you will."

"The Tingle?"

She winked and her glitter-coated lashes flashed like diamonds.

"Always listen to the Tingle."

She turned to glide away through the crowd, graceful as any ballroom dancer. It made me wonder if people would ever stop surprising me.

The thought reminded me of Logan. I picked up the card he'd left in the package and studied it.

What was going on with him? What was his connection to Veronica? Had he done something to her? They were the same questions I'd been asking myself since the day before. Not having any answers was becoming more frustrating by the minute.

Slipping the card back into the envelope, I tucked the package into the messenger bag Belinda had loaned me.

My phone began singing, *Oh, girls just wanna have fun!* And I snatched it off the table. "Emma?"

"Hey! You didn't lose your phone after all. Did you forget to charge it?"

"It's a long story. Is everything okay with you?"

"Of course. Why wouldn't it be?"

I picked up the slightest strain in her voice. "Emma, what's going on?"

"Nothing."

"Em—"

"Damn it. I was trying to surprise you."

"With?"

"Well, because you couldn't come to my birthday celebration, I thought I'd come to you."

"What?"

"Yep! We're on the way."

"We? You have Moss with you?"

"And Hugh and Kai."

"What?" I sputtered.

"Surprise! Don't worry—I've already contacted the hotel. They can accommodate us and extend your stay."

I was too shocked to speak for several seconds. Finally I managed to say, "Em, you can't go to the hotel."

"Why not?"

"It's not safe."

"Oookay." She drew out the word, then asked, "What am I missing here?"

"A lot. Listen, it's too much to try to explain on the phone. But there's something fishy going on. I was being followed last night so I couldn't go back to the hotel, and I'm pretty sure Anya is involved."

Kai's voice came over the line. "Where are you?" he asked.

"Safe. I'm sitting in a café next to a police station in the French Quarter."

"Stay there. We'll call you when we're ten minutes away." His voice was steady, but I thought I heard a trace of irritation in his words. Maybe it was worry. I wasn't very good at interpreting human emotions, which was why I didn't know what to say to people half the time.

"Okay."

"Be careful. We'll be there in a couple of hours."

If I had any hope of waiting that long, I was going to need a coffee and an order of beignets. I squeezed into the café and waited in the very long line.

Twenty minutes later, I was sitting back in the courtyard and washing down the sweet, fried confection with a hot café au lait.

A street performer who had set up next to the café to sing for tips kept me entertained. He had a great voice and inspired applause after every song. After a truly impressive version of "Will the Circle Be Unbroken," I got up and walked around the ornate iron fence to toss a dollar into his tip jar.

My reward for this moment of generosity was to return to find I'd lost my table. I didn't really mind though—the couple who'd claimed it had two little kids who would probably be hopped up on sugar in no time. But it left me with limited seating options.

The hum of a feline mind caught my attention and I glanced around to see if I could pinpoint the source. A moment later I caught sight of a large brown tabby cat as he emerged from the landscaping to slink over to a sizable bowl of food someone had placed under one of the concrete benches. I abandoned my search for a table and went over to have a chat with the cat. Might as well talk to someone while I waited for the cavalry.

After a few minutes of mostly one-sided conversation, the cat moseyed off to curl up for a nap in its warm kitty spot. The thought brought on a sudden acute awareness. I realized my butt was becoming colder than a well digger's toes where it made contact with the concrete bench. I considered trying to wedge myself into the café again, but after a glance through the crowded doorway, nixed the idea.

Abandoning the cold concrete bench, I stood and glanced at the portico to my right. Maybe I could warm up inside the police station?

I walked toward the station. As I climbed the white marble steps I noticed a sign advertising the sale of merchandise inside.

A perfect excuse to loiter. Maybe I'd get lucky and they'd have a scarf for sale. Making my way inside through the tall glass-and-wood doors I discovered the NOPD offered its wares in a unique way—with vending machines.

There were a number of items sporting the crescent moon and star logo of the department. T-shirts, ponchos, even drink koozies, but no scarves. I took my time deciding and had settled on a long-sleeve T-shirt when my attention was snagged by two words: "Mystery Monkey."

I turned to see Marisa, the zookeeper I'd met the day before, speaking to a tall, uniformed police officer.

"We've had a number of sightings reported to the hotline in the area," she said.

"Last time, it was a raccoon in a shed," grumbled the cop. "But we'll check it out. You want to meet us there in case this is legit?"

I tiptoed closer. Had someone caught the Mystery Monkey? Good news if they had. Not only was it too cold for a capuchin monkey to survive for long without shelter, but, if I could tag along, I might have a chance to talk to the little bugger about Veronica and Logan.

"Hi." I stepped up to the pair and offered my hand to the policeman. "I'm Grace Wilde."

A little bewildered, he took my hand and shook it. Before he could give me more than his name, I turned my attention to Marisa.

"I was just looking at a couple of gifts and couldn't help but overhear. Need another set of hands?"

"Actually, we might. Officer Green, would you mind bringing Miss Wilde with you?"

"You're with the zoo?" he asked, looking back and forth between us.

"She's a consultant with the Jacksonville Zoo. According to one of their veterinarians, she's very good at handling situations like this."

It seemed she'd called and spoken to Hugh.

"In that case, we'd be glad to have you."

As I followed the policeman to his cruiser I told myself Kai wouldn't be mad. Surely, I couldn't be faulted for leaving the safety of the police station if I was with the cops, right?

With that flimsy excuse firmly in mind, I slid into the passenger seat of the police cruiser and headed to apprehend the spunky simian. Fifteen minutes later we stopped near a small crowd of people who were blocking an intersection in—if I'd gotten my bearings—Uptown New Orleans.

"The monkey just slipped past the trap," a woman said as we approached the group. "I could've sworn we had him."

"It was like he knew right where to go," the man with her confirmed.

"He got away?" Marisa asked, her tone disbelieving and more than a little frustrated.

I looked in the direction the man motioned and focused on getting a bead on the monkey. It took some doing because of the weird, intermittent flickering of his brain waves, but I managed to zero in on them.

"There," I said, and pointed to the canopy of a huge live oak tree.

"You see him?" Officer Green asked, squinting at the tree.

"Yep." That wasn't 100 percent true. I couldn't really *see* the monkey. But I could detect his brain waves with my ability and home in on their source. It's really closer to hearing than to seeing, but in that moment, I figured it was better to skip those details and keep it simple.

Rather than try to pinpoint the animal's exact location, I

walked slowly forward. It was something I'd done before. Ninety percent of the time only a few people would notice or follow. Humans were not very observant animals. Unlike elephants, who almost always pay close attention to what you're doing. Such busybodies.

In this instance the only people who followed were the cop and the woman who'd told us about the monkey's narrow escape.

"I don't see him," the woman said in a low voice.

I paused to press my fingers to my lips, then whispered, "I only saw him for a second. He's in the tree. Maybe we can try to circle around and drive him toward the trap." I didn't really know what the trap was but I wanted to get close to the monkey and do so on my own.

"Okay, yeah. We'll flank him," the cop said. It was clear from the way he was gazing at the tree that he hadn't spotted his quarry.

"Good," I said. "You guys head around the tree. I'll stay here and keep an eye out for him."

"If you spot him again," Officer Green said, "give us a signal."

I nodded and waited for the two to move off before closing my eyes and focusing on the little monkey in the tree.

When our thoughts connected, I discovered the little guy was pretty calm for a critter who had just escaped capture.

Hey, buddy, come on down.

I extended the invitation with the idea of safety and friendship.

There was a rustle in the canopy and the capuchin came into view. He tilted his head and regarded me from on high, then leapt to a lower branch.

That's it. Come see me.

With his long limbs and prehensile tail, he made it to the lowest branch in seconds. After a series of curious squeaks, the little monkey stopped half a dozen feet from where I stood.

I lifted my hand slowly and extended my arm.

Here you go—

Before I could prompt him to hop onto my arm, a series of images fluttered into my mind's eye. For the second time in as many days I was taken completely off guard with what I saw.

CHAPTER 5

Me. The monkey showed me an image of myself holding a small paper tray of beignets.

Just as it had when he'd shown me Logan and Veronica, the scene lasted only a couple of seconds and, like before, the colors of the image were reversed at first then shifted back to normal. This time, most of what I was seeing was in muted duotone. The exception being the object the monkey was sitting on. It was glittering purple and looked like part of a Mardi Gras float. I saw myself step toward the float. Smiling, I held up the beignets.

I didn't get it. He wanted me to bring him beignets? It would be easy enough. *I'll gladly trade you a couple of pastries for info on Veronica.*

The image winked out the instant I thought of the missing woman. It was like the monkey's mind had gone blank. Then, suddenly I was hit with a surge of absolute, bone-numbing fear so strong I flinched away with a gasp.

What the . . . ? Before I could pinpoint what had caused the flood of emotion, the monkey's gaze settled on mine and the fear faded to confusion, then something close to frustration.

Struggling to get a grip on my own racing pulse, I pulled in a slow breath and said, "It's going to be okay, buddy." I focused on sending him reassurance and reiterated my desire to help.

Not buddy, the monkey told me. *Cornelius.*

I couldn't help but smile. *It's nice to meet you, Cornelius. I'm Grace. If you come with me, you won't have to be scared—okay?* I offered my arm as a perch. Cornelius studied my outstretched hand, considering, then eased forward.

"Come on." I gently murmured words and added calm encouragement with my thoughts.

The little monkey's eyes darted about, reminding me so powerfully of Barry's shifty gaze I couldn't help but think of him and his long coat. I tried to push the thought away before my feelings for the creepy man transferred to Cornelius, but failed. The monkey started, leapt to a higher branch, and bounded up the tree. In seconds, he'd scampered out of sight and out of range of my other senses.

"Dang," a voice from behind me said. "You almost had him."

I cursed inwardly and shook my head. Stupid rookie mistake. I could've kicked myself for losing focus.

"Yeah, that was really close," the zookeeper added as she came to stand next to me.

I glanced at the young woman. "Close only counts with horseshoes and hand grenades."

"Still, he was responding to you like he hasn't to anyone else. How long are you going to be in town?"

"I'm not sure."

"Do you mind if I call the next time we get a good lead?"

"Of course not," I said as we walked back to where the cruiser was parked. "My phone is working now so you can reach me at the number on my card."

"Thanks for trying to help," Marisa said. Her smooth brow wrinkled into a frown as she scanned the nearby treetops. "It's supposed to freeze tomorrow night. I really hope we can catch him before then."

"Me, too."

I climbed into the police cruiser and was so lost in thought as we rode along I didn't realize Officer Green had been talking to me.

"I'm sorry—what?"

"I think your phone is ringing."

"Oh." I fished it out of my jacket pocket and saw I had a missed call from Emma. I quickly called her back.

"Hey," my sister said. "We're pulling into the one-way cluster suck known as the French Quarter."

"Right." I looked out the window and tried to decipher how far away I was.

"You're still at the police station, aren't you?"

"Not exactly, but I'll be there soon."

I looked at Officer Green for confirmation. He nodded and said, "Five minutes."

"Who was that?"

"I got a ride from a nice policeman after helping them find, and then lose, the Mystery Monkey."

"The what?"

"Long story. I'll see you soon, okay?"

"Okay. Kai mapped the location of the police station on Royal Street. We'll meet you there."

"On second thought," I said. "How about meeting up at a parking lot?" I fished through the messenger bag to find the pass Belinda had given me and relayed the address to my sister.

"You want me to drop you on Dauphine?" Officer Green asked when I hung up.

I shook my head. "I have a bike a couple of blocks away from the station. Thanks, though."

He dropped me off at the corner of Royal and Iberville, and I hopped on my borrowed bicycle and headed to meet my friends.

• • •

There'd been no sign of Barry or Anya skulking about the Monteleone, but I kept a watchful eye out anyway as I rode.

I even circled the block before stopping at the parking lot. It was a countersurveillance trick I'd picked up not long ago. For a moment, I wondered if I should be worried about the fact that I'd gleaned such knowledge, but shook off the thought.

Knowledge is power, right?

After leaning the bike against a light post, I found a patch of pale afternoon sunshine and settled in to wait.

Turning my face to the sun, I closed my eyes and let the warmth wash over my skin.

Even without looking, I knew the moment my crew arrived. How? Easy—the familiar rumble of Bluebell's massive engine preceded her through the gates of the lot.

A 1975 Skyline Blue Suburban, Bluebell was big, loud, and—in that moment—a sight for sore eyes.

I know—it had only been a day and a half, but what can I say? Bell and I are close.

Hugh was behind the wheel. Kai, riding shotgun, was the first to climb out of Bluebell.

I watched him stretch and allowed myself a moment to admire the lean lines of his body before walking toward him.

Kai smiled when he saw me and, like always, I felt a tremor of warmth slide to my core. But this time, it didn't freak me out. Well, not as much as it used to, anyway.

"Surprise," Kai said as I approached. His smile widened to a toe-curling grin.

"Yeah." I grinned back, as tongue-tied as a teenager. There was something about the combo of his perpetually tanned skin, dark hair, and green eyes that always got to me.

I was spared having to come up with something to say because Moss chose that moment to burst out of Bluebell.

Using Emma's lap as a launching pad, he rocketed toward

me in a blur of white fur. My dog vibrated with energy and excitement and oddly, something close to surprise.

I got the vague impression that Emma, or maybe Kai, had told him he was on the way to see me, but Moss hadn't really bought it until he'd gotten close enough to sense my presence.

I dropped to one knee and braced myself for my dog's greeting.

Moss is no dainty canine. He's over a hundred pounds of muscle and white fur and stands almost as tall as a Great Dane. Being greeted by Moss without proper precautions could result in bodily injury and more than a little dog slobber.

Grace!

"Hi, big guy."

Grace—here!

"Yes, I'm here—ack!" As I spoke, I got a serving of wet dog kisses right on the mouth.

In the wild, pack mates greet one another with a lot of tail wagging and muzzle licking. For the most part, I've managed to convince Moss the licking isn't necessary, but on occasion he gets carried away.

It seemed today I was in for a face full of dog spit.

Okay, enough. I missed you, too.

I was grateful for the ability to communicate with my dog telepathically because, in that moment, I didn't dare open my mouth to talk.

As my sister and Hugh climbed out of Bluebell, I wiped my face clean, gave Moss a final pat to his flank, and stood to face the rest of the group.

I suddenly felt something else—a distinctly feline brain. One I knew.

Voodoo?

"Meow!" My three-month-old kitten, who was still tiny, leapt from Hugh's arms and bounced toward me. Her miniature leash flapped behind her like a kite tail.

The kitten would never be a big cat—sizewise, anyway.

Personality was a different story. Voodoo routinely bossed around a wolf-dog, plus every human she came into contact with. The instant her fur brushed over my legs, I felt a ripple of pure satisfaction zip through me. Looking up at me with huge golden eyes, the kitten squeaked out a *meow*.

Up?

I was moving to lift her off the ground before she'd completed the request—that's how cute she is.

I took a moment to snuggle the kitten. Her cashmere-soft fur tickled my nose as she rubbed her face against mine.

"I can't believe you rode all the way from Jacksonville with both of them," I said to the group as I got to my feet.

"Well, it wasn't the plan," Emma said drily. "That little one managed to stow away in one of my bags."

"She's lucky she didn't get crushed when we loaded them in the back," Hugh said with a wink.

Without cracking a smile I turned to Emma and asked, "Did they have to use a forklift?"

"All we needed"—Hugh lifted up his arm to flex his biceps—"was man power. Right, Kai?"

"That," Kai said, "and taking a few things out of Bluebell."

I followed the men to the back of the Suburban and I felt my eyes widen as Kai opened the back.

Typically, Bluebell's cargo area was stocked with animal carriers, a medical kit, a change of clothes, and other random supplies.

I could see my first aid kit, but it was buried under a pile of luggage.

"Don't worry," Kai said. "Everything's safe in my garage."

He'd read my expression correctly—I was worried, just not for the reason he'd assumed.

"What about my Glock?"

He frowned. "I didn't see your gun."

"I keep it locked in the box with my tranquilizer equipment."

"Then it's in the garage, too."

"Um, do you have yours?"

Kai carried his service weapon for work. I hoped he'd decided to bring it on the road.

"No. Do I need it?"

"Probably not."

"Does this have something to do with why we can't go to the Monteleone?" my sister asked.

"Come on," I said, handing the parking pass to Hugh to hang from the rearview mirror. "I'm staying at a bed-and-breakfast a couple blocks away. We'll talk there."

With everyone grabbing as many bags as they could carry we managed to haul the luggage, and my bike, in one trip.

I opened the gate to the small courtyard, then the side door into the kitchen.

"Let's head upstairs," I said.

"Don't we need to check in?" my sister asked.

"I'm pretty sure Belinda, our hostess, has rooms open. So, no."

"You're sure? She might have other reservations."

"She doesn't. It's kind of complicated," I said.

"So far," Emma said, "the only explanation you've given us about what's going on is that it's long and complicated. When are we going to find out the whole story?"

"I, for one," Kai said, "vote to hear it sooner rather than later."

Elvis bounded into the room, spun in a few quick circles, and let out a yip.

Little helper!

I smiled at the dog. "Hey, Elvis."

The King!

"Everyone, this is Elvis."

"Please tell me there's a Priscilla around here somewhere," Emma said.

I did a mental scan for the second Pomeranian. "Coming down the stairs, right now."

"Perfect," my sister said with a grin.

Priscilla pranced through the doorway a moment later and made a beeline for Moss.

Friends? Moss wanted to know as he sniffed the tawny puff-ball.

Friends! Priscilla flopped onto her back, tail wagging like mad.

"Yes, we're all friends," I said to the dogs.

Not that they needed my help understanding that. Elvis spun in a happy circle, barked, then ran to Moss. With a growl the little dog jumped up to nip at my dog's chin.

Play!

"Hang on." I handed Voodoo, who was watching the dogs and ready to join the fun, to Kai, and scooped Elvis away from his new friend.

"Moss won't hurt him, will he?" Emma asked.

"Nope. But I need this." I felt for and found the note pinned to his harness.

Good job, buddy, I told him.

Little helper!

I detached the note and set Elvis on the floor. Free to play, he zipped over to Moss and Priscilla to incite a game of chase. Which, given the size differences, consisted of the two Poms running around and through Moss's legs while he tried to catch them.

Play! Voodoo squirmed in Kai's arms.

"You can put her down," I told him.

When he did, the kitten trotted to the dogs, crouched low, and waited for the opportunity to pounce on one of her new toys.

"Now that we've got that settled." I sighed and unfolded the note. "Let's see what Belinda has to say. 'Second floor is vacant. Make yourselves at home. There's food in the fridge and a dumbwaiter next to the washer for the luggage.' Okay," I said, looking around at the group. "Let's get y'all to your rooms."

We used the mini-elevator to haul Emma's stuff up to the second floor and Elvis dutifully detached himself from his game to lead us up the stairs and show us to the empty rooms. Once everyone had deposited their things in the correct place, we assembled in the hall.

"All right, spill," Emma said. "How did Belinda know we were coming if you didn't tell her?"

"Belinda just knows things." Everyone waited for me to elaborate. I tried again. "We came in through the courtyard, but did you notice the sign for psychic readings in the window? That's her."

I'll say this for my crew—none of them seemed overly surprised to learn I'd met up with another psychic.

"You think she's legit?" Emma asked as we started down the stairs.

"Seems to be."

"Well," Hugh said, "this *is* New Orleans. There has to be an above-average number of psychics per capita in this city."

"Psychics and charlatans," Kai added as we gathered in the kitchen. "I'd say, more of the latter."

Emma shot me an inquisitive look at his comment. I shrugged. I wasn't surprised by his skepticism. Kai was a scientist. He believed in tangible evidence and hard facts. He'd eventually accepted my telepathic ability, but it hadn't been an easy sell.

Moss wandered over to sniff the Pomeranians' food bowls. Finding them empty, he moved on to investigate the nearby countertop. My dog is tall and smart enough to nick food from just about anywhere in a kitchen.

"Hey," I said. "No counter surfing. We're guests, so behave."
Hungry.

"Did you remember to pack his food?" I asked Emma.

Her eyes widened. "Um . . ."

"I did," Hugh said. "In my bag. I have some for Voodoo, too. I'll run up and grab it."

"I admit," Kai said, "I could use a meal."

"Agreeing with Moss? You must be hungry," Emma teased.

Moss is a little territorial. He tolerates Kai being around but isn't crazy about it. During the road trip, some of my dog's lingering animosity toward Kai must have surfaced. I remembered the message Emma had left and the mysterious growl from Moss.

"A Voodoo issue," Emma said when I asked what had happened. "Once we figured out she was in one of the bags we let her out. But we didn't want her to escape when we stopped for gas. Hugh found a harness in the glove box but when Kai was putting it on her she started squirming."

"Moss didn't like seeing Voodoo trying to get away from me," Kai explained.

"No, he wouldn't like that at all." I shook my head. Moss could be psychotically overprotective when it came to his kitten.

Hugh returned with the dog and cat food. He fed my animals while I pulled the pot of leftover jambalaya out of the fridge. There was enough to serve for dinner, but still . . .

"I feel kind of bad," I said, lifting the lid. "The four of us will probably finish off this whole pot."

"I can run to the store to grab some French bread and stuff for salad," Emma offered.

"Don't you worry about that, sugar." Belinda's voice carried into the room from the hallway. "This is an all-inclusive boutique establishment. Belinda does not let her guests go hungry."

Rather than turning to look at Belinda, who by now had stepped into the kitchen, I opted to observe the rest of the group.

It was the right choice.

Upon seeing our hostess, Hugh's jaw had gone slack. Kai, who, as a seasoned investigator, was pretty good at keeping his expressions neutral, actually did a double take.

My sister simply grinned like the Cheshire cat before

extending her hand and saying, "It is such a pleasure. I'm Emma. This is Hugh, and Kai."

Belinda shook everyone's hand and angled her chin at Moss.

"And who is this?"

"My dog, Moss." At the sound of his name, he walked over to stand at my side. "He's not as dangerous as he looks."

"Dangerous? I think he's gorgeous." She bent to stroke his head. "So soft and handsome."

Moss, gorgeous.

I rolled my eyes.

Voodoo slinked around Moss's front legs to greet Belinda with a soft *meow.*

"Aw, look. You have a kitty, too," Belinda cooed.

Moss gave the kitten a few licks. *Moss's kitty.*

"That's Voodoo," I said.

"Ain't that somethin'. Voodoo, huh? I like it." She glanced at me with a wink, then straightened to address the humans in the group.

"I heard y'all are hungry. So let's get dinner started. Grace, turn on the stove and get the jambalaya going. I'll be the one to run to the store for side dishes. It's time to close the shop anyway."

With that, Belinda headed out while the rest of us settled around the kitchen table.

"Okay," Emma said when we were all seated. "What's been going on? The last time I talked to you, you were headed to catch a streetcar to meet Anya."

I nodded. "I was. But before I could find her, Logan showed up."

"Logan?" Emma's brows arched in surprise.

"What's Logan doing in New Orleans?" Kai asked.

"He's Logan, so who knows? Whatever he's doing here, he decided to scare the crap out of me with a cryptic warning."

"Back up a second," Hugh said. "Who's Logan?"

"A criminal who works for the mob." Kai's answer, though accurate, was abrupt and seemed to be laced with a smidge of irritation.

"This guy's your friend?" Hugh asked, sounding more intrigued than anything else.

I wrinkled my nose. "I wouldn't call him a friend, exactly."

"If he's not your friend, why warn you?"

"He has a habit of doing that," Kai said, his expression unreadable.

I couldn't deny it. "Let's just say I'm pretty sure he wouldn't hurt me. Lie? Yes. Steal my phone? Yes."

"So that's what happened to your phone—he took it?" Emma asked.

"Yeah. He picked my pocket and left me a card with a place and time to meet, along with a promise to explain."

"What did he say?" Hugh asked.

"Nothing. He was a no-show. I waited for a while but finally gave up."

"So what was the warning?" Emma asked.

"He told me Anya wasn't who she claimed to be and that I should lie to them about my ability."

"How does Logan know about your ability?" Kai's question sounded more like an accusation.

"Wait," Emma said. "What 'them'?"

"When we got to Veronica's apartment, there was a man waiting to meet me. He claimed to be Veronica's psychiatrist, but I have my doubts."

"What made you think he wasn't on the level?" Emma asked.

"He was—I don't know . . . off."

"Would you have thought so without Logan's influence?" Kai asked.

"Yes. The guy gave me the creeps. He was overly curious about how I was going to talk to Coco. He had a lot of questions."

"Not surprising," Kai said. "I had a lot of questions about your ability when I found out about it."

"This was different. He was kind of aggressive about it."

"So he was pushy," my sister surmised.

I nodded. "Pushy and weird. I can't picture someone going to him for therapy. Plus, Veronica's apartment was pretty neat and organized for someone who's supposedly schizophrenic."

"Appearances can be deceiving," Hugh said. "Haven't you ever watched *Dexter*?"

"Did you see any medication? Prescription bottles, that sort of thing?" Kai asked.

"I really didn't have time to look."

"What about the cat? Would Coco understand something like mental illness?" Kai asked.

"She would. It depends on the circumstances, but animals can sense stuff like that. Honestly, though, I didn't think to ask her about it. I was more focused on trying to figure out if Coco could tell me where she came from."

"Why?" Emma regarded me with obvious confusion.

"Sorry, I must have skipped that part. Anya believes the key to finding Veronica is uncovering where she got Coco." I told them about the text message Anya had shown me.

"If Veronica sent her a text," Hugh said, "maybe they're really sisters."

"Actually," Emma said, "if we're going on the assumption that Anya is lying about who she is, then we should assume the text is also fake."

"You're right," Hugh conceded. "Texts are easy enough to fake. She could have sent the message to herself."

"But what's the point?" I asked. "Why bring me all the way to New Orleans just to ask me to find information she doesn't need?"

Everyone was quiet for a moment, then Hugh said, "Maybe Anya is looking for something else, and the missing-sister story is just a way to manipulate you."

"Bottom line," Emma said, "whether the text is fake or not, it seems clear that whatever Anya wants, whether it's Veronica or not, is located wherever Coco came from."

"We can't be sure about the text without looking at her phone's log," Kai said. "And we'd need to know Veronica's number."

"What did Coco tell you?" Emma asked.

"Not much. I know there was a place she felt safe when she was just a kitten. I could hear an older woman's voice. Coco showed me a nice view of a pair of bunny slippers. Oh, and wherever this place is, it has iron railings."

"Well, that narrows it down," Hugh said drily.

"I know, not exactly a unique feature in New Orleans. Just as I was about to push for more detail, the monkey showed up."

"Monkey?" Emma said.

"The papers are calling him the Mystery Monkey. No one knows where he came from, but there've been sightings all over."

"What kind of monkey?" Hugh asked.

"Capuchin." For Kai and my sister's benefit, I added, "Like the one in the *Pirates of the Caribbean* movie."

Emma shook her head with a half smile. "Only you could come to NOLA to talk to a cat and end up with a monkey."

It was a fair point.

"The monkey was sitting in a tree looking into the apartment. It's a perfect vantage point, so I thought I'd ask him if he'd seen Veronica."

"And?" Emma prompted when I paused.

"That's where it gets weird."

"Oh good." Hugh chuckled. "I was wondering when it was going to get weird."

I shot him a look. "Anyway, I asked him about Veronica and he told me"—I paused to think about it—"I'm not sure what he was trying to say. He showed me Veronica and Logan."

"Logan?" Kai asked.

I nodded. "More specifically, Logan grabbing her from behind."

"Wait," Emma said. "Logan kidnapped Veronica?"

"I don't know. Maybe." I looked around the table and realized from the blank and confused looks that I wasn't making much sense, so I tried to clarify. "What the monkey showed me was really strange. The colors were totally wonky. The whole thing flashed, kind of like a strobe. I saw Logan grabbing Veronica the same way he had me. And I mean exactly the same way."

"Logan grabbed you?" Kai asked.

I nodded. "From behind and yanked me into a bathroom in a bar."

"You were in a bar?" Kai's tone had shifted from interrogation to irritation.

"Right."

My sister nudged me under the table with her knee.

I glanced her way. I'm pretty inept when it comes to interpreting most people's facial expressions, but Emma I could read. Her look was telling me to tread lightly. I just had no idea why.

"Uh . . . anyway, the point is, the whole interaction was really weird. So, I'm not sure what it meant."

"It seems pretty clear to me," Kai said. "The monkey saw Logan grab Veronica. Could you tell where they were?"

"No. Like I said, it was weird." Everyone seemed to be waiting for me to go into more detail, but I wasn't sure how. I gave it a shot, working my thoughts out as I talked.

"When I was waiting for you to get into town earlier, I overheard a cop talking about a credible sighting of the monkey. I got a ride—with the police," I said, looking at Kai, "to try and catch him. Obviously, he got away, but while I was trying to convince the monkey to come to me, suddenly this crazy image pops into my head. Kind of strobe-y with odd colors, just like the one with Logan."

"What did he show you?" Hugh asked.

"Me. I was handing him beignets while he sat on a Mardi Gras float."

"Weird," Emma said.

"Very. And here's the thing—I had been sitting at Café Beignet forever, so I know I smelled like a giant, fried pastry. The cop I was with had just been talking about how they didn't need a Mystery Monkey on the loose with Mardi Gras coming up."

"So," Emma said, "you think the monkey was simply interpreting your thoughts? Why would he do that instead of the simple back-and-forth you can usually do?"

"I don't know. But his mind feels different."

"From?" Kai asked.

"Anything I've experienced."

"So it's possible the image of Logan grabbing Veronica was just a reflection of what you'd been thinking about?" Emma asked.

"I'd have to spend more time with the monkey to know."

"Maybe," Kai said, "you just don't want to believe Logan kidnapped an innocent woman and is warning you off to save himself."

I was spared having to come up with a response by Belinda, who bustled in through the back door, loaded down with almost a dozen grocery bags. We all scrambled to help.

"Woo! I may have gone a little overboard with the food, but I have a feeling it'll get eaten." Belinda's smile was wide. It seemed clear having a bunch of strangers to cook for made her happy. "Let's get this meal started."

Bustling about with the others in the homey, strange little kitchen provided a sense of calm I hadn't felt since I'd arrived in New Orleans.

Belinda donned a bright yellow apron declaring, HOT STUFF COMING THROUGH, and began assigning tasks.

Being the expert salad maker, I was given the produce and started chopping lettuce. My sister's a bit of a health nut so when Belinda started talking about using only butter from grass-fed cows and the benefits of going gluten-free, I knew she and our hostess would be fast friends. Emma looked at me with a wide grin. "Belinda is my spirit animal."

"I noticed," I told her.

We sat down to a great meal and it wasn't long before the questions started again. Belinda knew most of the story, except the bit about me being able to talk to animals, which was odd, considering how open she'd been with me about her own abilities.

Oh well, old habits die hard.

Before I could come up with a good way to tell her about my telepathic ability, Emma asked, "So, how did you get your phone back?"

"I wouldn't have, if it wasn't for Belinda."

We told them about the package recovery operation at the Monteleone.

"Girl, we rocked that mission: impossible." Belinda lifted her hand for a high five and I hit her palm with mine.

"You tried to call Logan?" my sister asked.

"I did, but he didn't answer."

"Where's the package?" Kai asked.

I got up and retrieved it from the messenger bag I'd hung on the wall peg next to the jackets.

"There's nothing on it but my name," I said, handing it to him.

Kai examined the envelope and frowned as he studied a smudge on the inside.

"What?"

"It's hard to tell for sure, but this looks like blood."

"Blood?"

"Let me see your phone."

I retrieved it from the messenger bag and handed it over. Kai popped the phone out of its case to inspect the sides and back and after a few seconds, nodded. "Definitely traces of blood."

"Does that mean Logan's hurt?" I sounded more upset than I'd meant to.

I noticed a muscle tighten in Kai's jaw. "I don't know. Given what he does for a living, it may not be his blood."

"Don't worry, *cher*"—Belinda gave my arm a reassuring pat—"I'm sure he's not hurt too bad. He wouldn't have been able to deliver the package if he was."

"I'm not clear on what made you have to leave the Monteleone in the first place," Hugh said. "Did Logan tell you not to stay there?"

I shook my head. "After Logan stood me up, I went back to the hotel and saw Barry sneaking around, *with a gun*. So"—I looked at Kai—"Logan or no Logan, I decided to get the hell out of Dodge."

"Which is how you ended up here," Emma said.

"Pretty much."

"Barry had a gun?" Kai asked.

"I saw it when the wind blew his coat open."

"What's his full name?" he asked.

I had to think about his last name. "Schellenger, I think is what she said."

"From New Orleans?"

"That was my impression, but who knows?"

Kai had taken his phone out of his pocket and was typing as I spoke. Full investigator mode: activated.

"What about Anya? What's her full name?" Kai asked.

"I'm not sure how to spell it." I looked at my sister.

"I have it in my appointments. Just a sec." She took her phone out of her purse. "Here. Anya Zharova." She held the phone out so Kai could see.

He added it to his notes with a nod. "She was a client of Emma's, right?"

I'd had a chance to go over only the basics with him before packing up and hopping on a plane.

"She was going to be," Emma said. "I only met her once. During our first meeting she got an urgent phone call about her sister. I could overhear everything Anya said because she only took a few steps away while she talked on the phone.

When she said something about her sister being missing and not being able to ask the cat what happened, I thought Grace might be willing to help."

"Emma called me and asked if I'd talk to her," I said. "We spoke on the phone, I told her about my ability, and she begged me to come to New Orleans."

"But the first time you met face-to-face was yesterday," Kai said.

"Right. It was all very rushed," I said. "Anya wanted me to leave with her as soon as I agreed to talk to Coco, but I couldn't drop everything—namely the newborn lion cub I was holding—so Anya made arrangements for me to fly in yesterday."

"And she knew where you were staying?"

"Yes, she handled everything. In fact, she was going to pick me up from the airport, but I got a call from her saying something had come up and she couldn't make it."

"Interesting," Kai said.

"What?"

"The whole thing seems like a setup, don't you think?"

I exchanged a look with my sister. "After everything that's happened—yes."

"I'm going to call Jake. See if anything comes up when he runs their names." Kai lifted his phone to his ear and a moment later I heard a faint "Yo," which meant homicide detective Jake Nocera had answered the call.

Kai made his request, listened to something Jake was saying, and flicked his gaze to me. "Yeah, you know how it goes," he said. "I don't think so but let me ask. Grace, do you have any more info on Anya or the psychiatrist?"

"No, I told you everything."

"I might be able to help with that," Belinda said. "If you're open to letting me do a reading."

I glanced at my sister, whose eyes had lit up with excitement. "Sure," I said. "Why not?"

CHAPTER 6

"Give me a second and we'll get started." Rather than leading us into the shop, where the small table was set in a nook, Belinda had gone and gotten her tarot cards to do the reading in the kitchen.

"Do you need to light candles or anything?" Emma asked as she and Hugh cleared the last few plates from the table.

Belinda waved the question away. "Please, the only thing I need is a sip of wine and this." She held up a small drawstring bag made out of colorful fabric.

"What is it?"

"Some people call it a conjure bag, or mojo bag. I call it a gris-gris. I filled it with charms and herbs and whatnot. It keeps my energy from affecting the reading."

"So if you're having a bad day," Emma said, "it won't bleed over and make it seem like she's having a bad day?"

"Exactly."

"Does that mean we should leave, too, so you don't get any stray vibes?" Hugh asked.

"No, we're the only two touching the cards, so everybody can get comfy."

The group settled around and Belinda nodded to me. "Okay, *cher*, let's get started."

She set the deck of tarot cards in front of me. "Go ahead and start shuffling. When you're ready, cut the deck into three stacks."

I did as asked, fumbling a little with the large cards.

"I do things a little different. In case you hadn't noticed—I'm not your average, everyday psychic," Belinda said with a wink. "When you get your three stacks, I'll start going through the deck. I'll be guided to stop at a certain card and flip it over. Sometimes I'll have a strong sense of the meaning of the card, but sometimes it's very general."

"Okay," I said, still focusing on not sending the cards flying with my sucky shuffling skills.

"The first card I'll draw represents the situation you're facing. I'm hoping we can use it to learn a little more about this Anya woman and her doctor friend."

"We'll learn more than we know now, right?" I said. Finished shuffling, I cut the cards three times as instructed. Belinda gathered them into one pile and began laying them, one by one, facedown on the table. After over a dozen cards, she finally paused and flipped one over. We all leaned in to get a look at the card.

I was no expert, but it didn't look good.

"That," Kai said as he angled his head to study the card, "looks bad."

The tableau depicted a dark-haired woman, blindfolded and bound. She stood surrounded by eight swords, which pierced the muddy ground around her.

"Well," Belinda mused. "It's not good news, but it's not altogether bad. The Eight of Swords is a card of temporary hardship. Conflict and treachery—which isn't much of a surprise. I'm also sensing a withdrawn or introverted personality involved."

"Like me?" I asked.

"You're not withdrawn," Emma said. "Maybe a little introverted, but—"

"Not Grace," Belinda said. "I'm sensing a male in connection with that energy."

"Barry?"

"Can't say for sure. But there's one other thing that's coming through. These ropes here"—she tapped the bindings on the card with a glossy fingernail—"ain't symbolic. Someone is being held against their will."

"Veronica?" I looked at Kai for his input.

"That would be my guess," he said. "You still have the card Logan gave you?"

I nodded.

"We're going to need to call him." Kai's face was tense, but the emotion driving the expression was hard for me to identify.

"Wait," Belinda said, drawing our attention back to her. She'd turned over a second card.

I let out a relieved sigh. This card didn't look nearly as foreboding as the last. In fact it was kind of pretty. It showed a woman sitting with a lion.

"That's not so bad, right?"

Belinda shook her head, frowning. "Strength," she said. "Usually a card of balance. An expression of mental and physical health."

"I'm sensing a 'but' here," Emma said.

"It's reversed, see? It's upside down. Which usually indicates a feeling of vulnerability and self-doubt, but I'm getting another vibe here." She looked up from the card to study me, confused. "It's you. You're the tamer of lions. Literally."

"It's true," Kai said. "Grace . . . ?"

He waited for me to explain, which I appreciated.

"I can communicate with animals telepathically."

Belinda's already arched brows shot higher.

"I thought you might have picked up on it," I told her.

"I only get what I get," she said with a shrug.

I nodded, understanding completely.

"But," Belinda said, touching the card, "this is more than your ability. It's you and only you. You're the only person who can stop this—"

She slid the first card forward.

I looked at the card. The bound woman, the swords, the marshy ground.

"Crap."

After the reading, the discussion jumped around a bit but it became obvious those who'd been on the road trip from Jacksonville were beat. Everyone, except Belinda, decided to call it a night and start fresh the next day.

I was a little disappointed at Kai's quick "See you in the morning" before he closed his door.

My sister's room was across the hall. I knocked and when she said, "Come on in," opened the door.

Emma's room was smaller than mine, but it suited her. Mainly because of the large armoire that dominated one entire wall. She'd opened its double doors wide and was busy putting her clothes away. The scent of cedar and lemon oil wafted through the room and tickled my nose.

"Need help?" I asked.

"Nope. I'm almost done."

I noticed she'd brought some of her favorite outfits and felt a pang of guilt. My sister had come all the way to New Orleans to include me in her birthday celebrations and we'd been talking about a kidnapping the whole time.

With a silent promise to make it up to her, I crossed over to the sleigh bed and ran my hand over the smooth wooden footboard.

"What was all the nudging about down there?" I asked as I sat on the bed and bounced a little to try it out. Comfy.

"I was trying to stop you from making Kai mad. Not that it worked."

"Mad?" He *had* seemed frustrated. "What did I say?"

"It was all the Logan talk."

"What about it?"

"Logan seems to come to your rescue a lot. And you seemed worried at the idea that he might be hurt."

"Only because I've been mentally bad-mouthing him since he took my phone. I'd feel terrible if something had actually happened to him."

"Well, you might want to tell Kai that."

"Why?"

"I think Kai might wonder what's going on between you."

"Going on?"

"If there're some romantic feelings."

I blinked at my sister in confusion. It was true, the first time Logan had decided to help me, Kai hadn't exactly appreciated it, but I'd assumed he'd simply been worried about Logan's status as a wanted criminal with ties to the mob.

After that, well, I thought I'd made that clear, hadn't I?

"Kai knows I'm not interested in Logan," I said, finally.

"You sure?"

Was I? It seemed obvious to me.

"You think I should say something?" I asked.

"Men can get protective over what they think is theirs, sweet cheeks."

I frowned. Being referred to as someone's possession aggravated me. At least it should have. But really, thinking that Kai felt possessive of me didn't bother me that much. On the contrary, I felt a pleasant warmth ripple through my chest.

That aggravated me.

"I know." My sister lifted her hands in defense. "You hate thinking about this sort of stuff. But you need to."

By "this sort of stuff," my sister meant anything with an emotional weight greater than a feather.

This was heavier. Being open meant being vulnerable emotionally with another human being.

"God, Em, I don't even know how to bring it up."

"Just say, 'Hey, I think I should reiterate that I don't know what's going on in Logan's head. I really don't think he has the hots for me but you should know even if he does, I have zero romantic interest in him.' That should cover it."

It sounded so easy coming from Emma. Somehow, I always seemed to mess up conversations like that and say the wrong thing.

"Do you love him?" my sister asked, gently.

The question took me by surprise. I blinked at her. "Do I—wait, what?"

"You heard me. Do. You. Love. Him?"

"Come on, Em, I don't even know him that well."

She crossed her arms and gave me a don't-BS-me look so reminiscent of our mother's, I almost laughed. "What?"

"You've been seeing each other for over six months."

"That doesn't mean anything. For all I know, Kai has a secret family stashed in another state."

"He doesn't. I checked."

"You did not." I knew my sister too well. Oh, I knew she was serious about checking up on Kai, but she'd had help. "You got Wes to do it."

"Of course," she said without a hint of remorse.

I rolled my eyes. Wes Roberts and I had been friends since we were kids. He'd grown up to become a fabulous attorney with lots of connections and almost as much sass as Belinda. He and Emma had a long history of conspiring when it came to what was best for Grace. I was used to it.

"Stop avoiding the question," my sister said.

I sighed and flopped onto the bed. Love?

"I don't know, Em. I'm not even sure I know what love is."

Yes, I loved my sister and my dog—maybe not in that order—but that wasn't the same thing as being in love with someone.

"Hmmm," Emma mused, coming to sit next to me. "Well, is he the first person you think about calling with news?"

"Good or bad?"

"Either."

"That depends on the level of criminal activity involved."

She laughed, but I wasn't kidding.

"Okay, how about this—does thinking about him make you smile?"

"Usually, but thinking about Krispy Kreme doughnuts makes me smile, too."

"Then it's settled," she said, laying on the sarcasm. "You must love him."

"Tease all you want, but I'm serious. I have no clue. Look at what happened with Dane."

Dane Harrington was the guy I'd fallen for in college. He'd completely swept me off my feet. Then dumped me on my rear the second he'd found out about my ability, so it couldn't have been the real thing.

"Dane was an ass."

"Yes, but I loved him. Or thought I did. So, how can you be sure? For all I know, my feelings for Kai are just as skewed as they were for Dane."

"You were, what, twenty-one? Come on."

"Okay, say I do love Kai. What if he doesn't feel the same way?"

"Then he's an idiot."

Thinking about all the possible complications of falling into the quagmire called love was making my head hurt, so I changed the subject.

"I think this town is messing with my ability."

"Because you're not vibing with the monkey?"

"I'm telling you, Emma, he's a weird little guy."

"Maybe you're just adjusting to new circumstances. It's happened before."

She meant it had happened when I was almost murdered by a lunatic several months ago. Before then, my ability was limited to a dozen feet or so. Something—the stress or maybe the panic—had led to a breakthrough in that area, and now my range, if you wanted to call it that, was much wider. I hadn't taken a formal measurement, but it had to be over three times as much.

"This doesn't feel like an adjustment, as you call it. It's as if his thoughts are disconnected. Like when he was showing me the image of the Mardi Gras float, I got this surge of . . . terror. It wasn't the monkey's fear, or at least I don't think it was. It was more like he was remembering someone else's pain and expressing it to me."

"That's happened before, hasn't it? With Roscoe?"

Roscoe was a papillon who'd witnessed his owner's murder. The little dog had had a flashback of the scene so strong I'd nearly panicked.

I shook my head. "This was different, I wasn't seeing anything traumatic. It was just me, holding some beignets, while he was sitting on a float."

"And you didn't hear or see anything that startled him? Maybe he saw the cop?"

"No, I have no idea what he was trying to tell me," I said.

"That he wants beignets and to ride in a parade?" Emma suggested.

"That's what I thought at first. I told him I'd give him some beignets if he'd tell me about Veronica. And just like that"—I snapped my fingers—"he freaked."

"So it was thinking about Veronica that triggered his response."

"Yes, but I wasn't really picturing her. Just saying her name in my head. It's too abstract a concept for Cornelius to have reacted to."

"Why? You ask Moss about people he knows."

"Exactly. It has to be someone he knows. If I say, 'Where's Emma?' he can tell me. But if I were to ask about Jake, who he's met but doesn't really know, without picturing him, Moss would have a hard time understanding who I was talking about."

"Well, there's your answer. The monkey and Veronica are more acquainted than you realize."

CHAPTER 7

The next morning I awoke in a more familiar fashion than I had the day before.

Giant dog at my feet. Tiny cat on my face.

As I attempted to extract myself from the pair, Voodoo squeaked out a yawn, stretched, and went back to sleep. Moss, on the other hand, hopped down and let out a barely audible *woof!*

"You need to go out?"

Potty, he confirmed.

I got dressed and decided to wear the loaner jacket from Belinda, figuring my red wool coat, though warmer, was still too conspicuous. With the ski hat and gloves, I was almost comfortable in the crisp winter air.

I ended up taking all three dogs for a walk, which was a little awkward due to the fact that the Pomeranians had to take at least four steps for every one of Moss's. We figured out a rhythm finally and made it back to Belinda's in time to help with breakfast.

Like the night before, Belinda, wearing her Hot Stuff apron, doled out tasks, and everyone got to work. Everyone except Kai, who had stepped out into the courtyard to take a call from Jake.

"Well," he said a few minutes later, when he'd finished the call. "Jake came up with zero information on Anya Zharova."

"Think she's using an alias?" Hugh asked. He'd been recruited to set the table and was placing an assortment of mismatched antique plates on the round table while Emma assisted by laying out napkins and silverware.

"What about Barry?" I asked as I sprinkled cinnamon and powdered sugar on the platter of French toast Belinda handed me.

"He was a lot easier to find," Kai said. "He is a psychiatrist. Until recently, he worked at a research facility doing something with brain scans."

"Here in New Orleans?" Emma asked.

He shook his head. "Outside of Atlanta. I called the research facility but they had no interest in talking about one of their ex-employees. They would only tell me Dr. Schellenger decided to go into private practice."

"Meaning he moved here and started seeing patients?" Again, I tried to picture Barry providing help to the mentally ill, but couldn't.

"It's hard to say," Kai said. "Jake couldn't find him listed as a psychiatrist in New Orleans or anywhere else in Louisiana."

"So he is a fraud, like Logan said." My sister gave me her I-got-your-back nod.

Kai didn't notice. "Not necessarily." He took his phone out of his pocket to check his notes. "Dr. B. M. Schellenger is a licensed psychiatrist in . . . five states."

"Okay." I tried to boil it down to the bottom line. "He's really a psychiatrist, just not Veronica's psychiatrist."

"That depends. He could have treated her somewhere else. We need to know more about Veronica. At the very least, we need a last name to go on. Jake tried Zharova—nothing came up."

None of us were surprised at that.

After a stout meal and lots of coffee, Kai leaned back in his chair. "Okay, here's what we're going to do," he said. "Grace, you and I will head back to Veronica's apartment. If we're lucky, we'll be able to take a look at her mail and come up with a last name. Hopefully, you'll be able to talk to Coco as well."

"Maybe you'll get extra lucky and the monkey will show up," Emma added as she cleared the plates. "You can find out how well he knows Veronica."

"If not, maybe Coco will know," I said.

"What are you two talking about?" Hugh asked.

I explained the theory that Veronica and Cornelius were closer than we'd first assumed.

"He isn't her monkey, though," Hugh said. "You would have noticed a cage in her apartment."

"I didn't look everywhere, so I don't know. You know, some people don't keep their primates in cages."

Hugh and I shared a look that said how stupid we both thought that idea was.

"It's illegal to have a monkey in the city," Belinda said. "Even if Cornelius is her pet, Veronica would hide him. Especially from her landlord."

"In any case, we can't count on his showing up," Kai said. "We'll have to track him down another way."

"You have an idea?"

He nodded. "I've been thinking that what Cornelius showed you was really specific. Maybe he was just reflecting your thoughts, but maybe he was asking you to meet him somewhere. Belinda, is there a way to look at photos of Mardi Gras floats? Maybe if we can figure out the exact float, we can find him."

"You could check the Internet, but that might take too long." She took a thoughtful sip of coffee and turned to me. "Grace, you said the monkey was sitting on a float. Was it inside or out?"

"Inside. I could see a dark wall and a window but no detail of the building."

"What about the float?" Kai asked. "Could you see any specific decorations or words anywhere?"

"No words. He was sitting on a rounded surface covered with lots of purple glitter." I thought about it. "There were also stars. Just a few of them, on the purple."

"Anything else?"

"Not with the float, but through the window I could see the sky. It was either sunset or sunrise."

"If it was sunrise you missed your date," Hugh said.

"I'm thinking the float has to be one of the Mardi Gras museums," Belinda said. "They're not really museums. More like big warehouses where floats and whatnot are stored and repaired. Some have workshops where you can watch the artists work on a new design."

"How many of these places are there?" I asked.

"Several, and they're big."

"Emma"—Kai turned to look at my sister—"can you check out Mardi Gras floats? There has to be a way to narrow the search down."

Belinda nodded. "I can help with that. Don't worry, we'll figure out where the Mystery Monkey is headed."

"One more thing," I said. "We're going to need to take Cornelius somewhere once we find him." I started to look through my jacket's pockets for Marisa's number. "Somewhere in here I have the number for that keeper at the Audubon—"

"Marisa. I'm on it," Hugh said. "She called me to check up on you, remember?"

"Ain't this somethin'?" Belinda said with a wide smile. "I feel like we need to put our hands together and yell, 'Go, team!' Y'all ever do that?"

Emma chuckled. "No, but we should. Maybe we need matching T-shirts."

"That say what?" I asked.

"Go Wilde, what else?" Emma grinned at me in delight.

"Ooh, yes!" Belinda linked her arm with my sister's and as they walked out of the kitchen I heard her say, "I know a guy who does the '80s-style airbrushing, with glitter paint . . ."

I shook my head and looked at Kai. "They're going to make T-shirts."

"Seems likely." He tried to hide it by taking a sip of coffee but I saw his lips twitch in a smile.

"You think it's funny?" I tossed my napkin at him. "You'll be wearing one, too."

"Proudly."

• • •

Thankfully, Moss was content to stay at the bed-and-breakfast with his new buddies and Voodoo. It would've been considerably more difficult to sneak into, well, anywhere really, with my giant white wolf-dog.

Moss tends to attract attention. Which he loves.

Magazine Street was clogged with all manner of traffic and I was glad we'd taken Belinda's advice and ridden the streetcar. I couldn't imagine finding a parking place for Bluebell on one of the brick-paved side streets.

On the ride over, I'd considered taking my sister's advice and telling Kai about my feelings, or lack thereof, for Logan. But the streetcar was crowded and Kai, being a gentleman, had given up his seat to an elderly woman.

I decided to wait for a better time.

Yeah, no avoidance issues there.

We got off the streetcar near Veronica's place. Something I'd learned recently was that a big part of getting away with something you shouldn't be doing is acting natural. Knowing this, I followed Kai's lead and nonchalantly mounted the stairs leading to Veronica's apartment.

I started getting nervous only when I stood by loitering as he flipped open the top of the mailbox to peer inside.

"Just a 'current resident' mailer."

"So . . . now what?" I asked.

Kai studied the door's lock, then turned to sweep his gaze over the landing, which doubled as a small balcony.

There wasn't much to see. Space was too limited for patio furniture or a grill, but Veronica had set a couple of potted plants in one corner.

One of the terra-cotta pots was nestled in a saucer. Kai lifted both and I shook my head when I saw a key gleaming in the morning light.

"You've got to be kidding," I said. "Who leaves their key in such an obvious spot?"

"You'd be surprised."

"I am."

Kai opened the door and we slipped inside.

As quietly as possible, we went through the tiny apartment.

Coco was nowhere to be found, which would have worried me if it weren't for the empty food bowl on the floor. That told me the cat had come home at some point in the last day and eaten.

Maybe the tabby would show up while we were there and I'd get a chance to talk to her.

"Well," Kai said after several minutes of searching, "I think you're right. Something's off with this place."

"It's too neat for someone who's supposed be schizo-phrenic, right?"

He shook his head thoughtfully. "It's not that."

"Then what?"

Kai didn't answer right away, but continued to look around. I could almost see the gears in his head turning as he analyzed the space.

"Too bad you don't have your field case," I said when he squatted to examine a scuff mark on the floor. Who knew what the CSI gadgets he used for work might uncover?

"I didn't think I was going to need it." He cut his eyes toward me with a wry expression. "Should've known better."

"Hey," I said, "I'm not always this unlucky." At least I hadn't been until I'd started coming clean about my ability earlier that summer. Since then, I'd been dragged into a murder investigation, stalked by a psychopath, and nearly shot.

Kai didn't comment—he'd stopped to study the two photos stuck to the fridge.

"A nice touch, don't you think?" I said.

"What?"

"That's Anya." I pointed to the photo with only one person in it.

"It is?"

I nodded. "I'm thinking she planted it to reinforce her claim of being Veronica's sister."

With the back of his pinky finger, he lifted the edge of the photo and bent to look at the back. Then took out his phone and snapped a photo of the picture.

"Interesting," he murmured. "You may be right. Which means this"—he pointed to the photo next to it—"is the only personal photo in this place."

I'd seen the picture the first time I'd been there. It was a snapshot of Veronica and an unknown girlfriend grinning at the camera.

"What's more," Kai continued, "both of the photos are stuck to the fridge with the type of magnets a tourist would buy."

"Okay. What's that tell us?"

"Not much on its own," he said. "But let's look at the whole picture."

He opened the cabinet under the sink and pulled out a caddy filled with cleaning supplies. "These have hardly been used," he said, lifting the basket to place it on the counter. "There aren't any pots or pans anywhere, and the only cutlery in the drawers are plastic."

"Meaning Veronica prefers takeout to cooking?" I guessed, though I was pretty sure it was the wrong answer.

"I would have thought so but there's no art on the walls

and the curtains are so new they still have creases where they were folded."

I finally got where he was going. "You think she just moved in? But there aren't any boxes anywhere," I pointed out.

"I'd guess Veronica only recently came to town and arrived with little more than what she could fit in a couple of suitcases."

I nodded. "I can see that. But it doesn't help us with her name."

"No, but this might." He pointed to the second photo on the fridge.

"How?" I leaned in to look at the photo.

The two girls posed cheek to cheek in front of what was obviously a bar. Besides coming to the brilliant conclusion that the two were roughly the same age and appeared to be friends, I was not seeing how it would help.

"This woman is the only link we have to Veronica."

"But we don't know who she is or where this picture was taken."

He studied the photograph. "There's actually a lot to go on in the photo. See the name tag on her shirt?"

I peered at it. "It's cut off."

"Not all of it." Kai opened one of the two kitchen drawers and found a pen, then started writing on his hand.

"There are three letters in the first name. The first letter might be an *L*, *J*, or *I*. Judging by the second letter, which looks like an *M*, I'd say her name starts with an *I*."

"The third has to be an *A*, right?"

"I think so."

"Ima?"

"Yep. The last name is totally cut off, unfortunately."

"Still," I said, "Ima is an odd name. Maybe it will help us find her."

"There's also a good bit going on in the background. If you know the bars in New Orleans, you might recognize the location."

"Assuming it was taken here and not wherever she came from."

"It's worth a shot, though," Kai said.

It was. "Belinda might have an idea." I knew she'd been in the city awhile, but even if she didn't recognize the bar, she could get ahold of Magnificent Marvo, or even the shot girls, Shay, Sheba, and Judith. They certainly knew the French Quarter well. "Let's head back to the B and B and ask."

Kai shook his head. "You can check with Belinda about the bar—I'm going to take this photo of Anya to the NOPD and see if I can get them to do a reverse lookup and get an ID from the DMV."

"Wow," I said, pretending to be impressed. "That was a lot of acronyms."

He ignored my comment.

"Come on," he said. "Let's go."

"Ten-four."

Kai shot me a look, but I just smiled. As I started to follow him out of the kitchen, it occurred to me I needed to refill Coco's bowl.

"Hang on. I have to leave some food for the cat."

Opening the cabinet where I'd found the dry food the day before, I paused when I saw the bag.

"Kai, I think someone has been here."

He came to stand beside me and looked at the bag of cat food.

I pointed to the brand-new, nearly full bag.

"The other day, there was another bag. It was almost empty and this one hadn't been opened." I looked at him. "You think a neighbor is coming by?"

"It's the most logical explanation if Veronica left with the intention of returning."

That would mean she hadn't been kidnapped by Logan after all. Not wanting to tread on the delicate subject of Logan's involvement, I simply nodded, poured food in Coco's dish, and set it on the floor.

I felt Coco's approach before she slipped through the cat door.

"Like magic," I said.

"What is?"

"The way cats can hear food being dished into their bowls from a mile away. I should have thought of that when we first got here."

With a happy *meow*, Coco trotted into the kitchen. She took a couple of bites of kibble before turning to beg for attention.

"I'm going to see if I can get more info from her," I told Kai. "Maybe we'll get lucky."

"You do your thing."

"Hi, Coco." Squatting, I ran my hand over her patterned fur and she began to purr quietly. Soft, relaxed waves of contentment rolled through me.

Nice. Pet.

You're a sweet kitty, aren't you?

Coco puff.

I smiled. *Does Veronica call you that?* I pulled the image of the cat's owner to the front of my mind and used the tendrils of our mental connection to present it to Coco.

The purrs intensified.

Where? Coco asked. She was clearly missing Veronica.

I don't know, Coco.

I asked about Veronica, but didn't get much. Coco wanted to know where her owner was as much as I did.

Usually, if an animal has seen something upsetting happen to a particular person, just asking about him or her would trigger the memory.

I spoke to Kai without looking up. "Whatever happened to Veronica, Coco didn't see it."

"Has she ever seen Logan around?"

I showed the cat an image of Logan, with and without his beard.

"Nope," I said to Kai. "Nothing with him."

"Try asking about Anya."

"You don't still think she could be Veronica's sister?"

"No, but, like Cornelius, they might know one another better than we realize. It might give us something," he said. "Like Anya's real name."

With a slow breath, I focused on thoughts of the tall, pretty blonde, then asked Coco, *Do you know Anya?*

The cat didn't connect with the name but she knew the face and accent. In a flash of memory I heard Anya's voice and the click of high heels on the wood floor.

It was early in the day and the bright morning sun streamed like a spotlight into the room.

From her kitty hammock in the sleeping loft Coco could see the woman pacing the length of the small apartment as she talked into a cell phone.

The cat wasn't really listening to what was being said. It wouldn't have helped, anyway. Anya was speaking Russian, which, as it happens, is one of the many languages I don't understand.

Hey, don't judge—at least I can speak whale.

Anya paused to look up at Coco, and I knew one thing. The woman was not a cat lover.

Oblivious to the contempt on the woman's face, Coco watched sleepily as Anya walked out the front door, and continued to observe from the window as she walked down the steps. Anya stopped to speak to a man at the bottom of the stairs.

With the slow blink of tired cat eyes the memory faded.

I didn't recognize the man Anya had spoken to but I knew it wasn't Barry.

Was there another player in the game?

"Grace." Kai's harsh whisper cut into my thoughts. "There's someone coming."

While I was still processing what he'd said, Kai pulled me to my feet and we ducked into the only place we could hide— the tiny bathroom.

The sound of rapid footfalls stopped at the door and were followed by the rattling *click* of the lock.

Kai clicked off the bathroom light and pushed the door partly closed. We huddled behind it and listened. A woman called out as the apartment's door swung open.

"Coco! Hey, kitty. You hungry?" The voice was gentle and carried no trace of the Baltics.

Coco responded with a *meow* of greeting.

Layla.

"You want foodies?"

Coco answered with another *meow. Pet.*

"Okay, let's get—hey—your bowl is still full. Come here. You feeling okay?"

I slipped into the cat's mind to get a look at her caretaker but she had lifted Coco into her arms and the only thing I could see was the view over the woman's shoulder.

"Let's make sure you have water." The woman set Coco back on the floor. From that vantage point, all I could see was a pair of well-worn tennis shoes and two jeans-clad legs.

I urged Coco to look up at the woman. But the cat was busy rubbing her face and scent along Layla's legs.

"You haven't been eating frogs again, have you?" Layla asked. "They'll make you sick."

I felt Kai move next to me and I abandoned the cat's perspective for my own. Kai had shifted to peer out into the apartment. After a few seconds he eased back behind the door.

A moment later, his hand found mine and gave it a reassuring squeeze. We waited while Layla took care of Coco's water and chatted with the cat.

"I still haven't heard from your mama. But don't worry, I'll take care of you until she gets back. All right, sweetie, I'm double-parked and I've got to go to work. Be good. No more frogs."

A few seconds later the front door opened, then closed. I could hear the woman trot down the stairs.

"Come on," Kai said, and we crept out of the bathroom.

"That was close," I said. "Though I guess we could've stopped her to ask about Veronica."

"I think we would have given her a heart attack. Plus, we're breaking and entering."

"Yes, but she obviously knows Veronica, so she might know where she is. Should we follow her?"

Kai had moved to look out the window. "She's long gone. I didn't get a good look, but I think she might be Veronica's friend in the photo."

"I don't think so," I said. "Coco called her Layla, not Ima. But maybe they're the same person? I can ask—" I was going to say "Coco," but in that moment I realized the cat wasn't inside.

"Ninjas!"

"You want to talk to ninjas?" Kai asked.

"No." I waved off the silly idea. "Cats. They're like freaking ninjas. Coco's gone. She must have slipped out the cat door."

"Well," Kai said, "we have more than we started with. Ima and Layla might know each other," he said as we walked out the door. "The more people we can talk to who know Veronica the better."

"If I can find the bar," I said as he replaced Veronica's key.

"It's how investigations work."

"I remember." Kai had made the point before. "You have to *collect* the dots before you can *connect* them."

I'm not a patient dot-collector.

We headed toward Magazine Street to try to catch a cab, and out of the corner of my eye I got a glimpse of a man who looked oddly familiar. I stopped and turned to look for him.

"What?" Kai asked.

"There was just this guy—he looked like someone Coco showed me, I think." Looking from face to face, I scanned the people in the area, but didn't see him again. "He's gone."

"When did Coco show him to you?" Kai said as we continued down the sidewalk.

"When I was asking about Anya. Coco was in the loft and

she could see Anya talking on her cell phone downstairs. When she left, Coco saw Anya meet up with this guy outside."

"Just a guy? Coco didn't know him?"

"It was hard to tell. The cat was dozing in the window, so she wasn't really focused on the people around."

"Could be a neighbor."

"Or he could be working with Anya and Barry."

"Or Logan."

"Possibly," I conceded. "Though Logan's kind of a loner. Not that I know him that well—it's just the impression I get," I added quickly.

"He's not that much of a loner. He keeps popping up to protect you."

"Not because I want him to." I took a deep breath and said, "Kai, listen. I don't invite any kind of attention from Logan."

Before I could expound on the point, a cab pulled to curb next to us and let out a rushed-looking man in a suit.

Kai waved a questioning hand at the cabby. The man nodded and we were on our way to the Quarter. I didn't want to talk about Logan in the cab, and hoped what I'd said was enough to get my point across.

It must have been because Kai asked the cab to wait while he walked me to Belinda's front door. He gave me a quick kiss before promising to call with any information on Anya.

I'm a little embarrassed to admit how much I enjoy moments like that. Strange how a simple kiss, or the brush of his hand down the back of my arm, can make me feel connected and safe.

I glanced around the shop as I headed inside. The curtains were pulled back from the nook where Belinda did readings and no customers were browsing the shelves so I called out, "Hello?" before walking toward the kitchen.

Voodoo was the first to answer my call. Sprinting down the stairs with a *meow*, she threaded between my legs at light speed—a move that nearly killed us both on a regular basis—and ran through the kitchen door.

Bubba! The kitten had seen Moss—whom she called Bubba—and informed him of my return.

Bubba! Grace here.

"Hey, y'all," I said as I entered the kitchen. My sister and Belinda were seated at the table, huddled together looking at Emma's laptop. Moss, who was under the table, swished his tail across the floor a couple of times but didn't get up. I bent over and saw why. Little Priscilla was curled on his front paws, fast asleep.

"She's in love," Belinda said, peering at me over the top of her cat-eyed, crystal-encrusted reading glasses. On anyone else the glasses would have looked ridiculous. But Belinda—well, she made it work.

"He's a heartbreaker," I said with a sigh.

Elvis poked his head up from Belinda's lap and yipped.

Hey, Elvis.

The King!

"I hope he's not jealous."

"He's happy to have my lap to himself. Besides, the King doesn't get jealous, do you?"

He answered by climbing up Belinda's chest to shower her chin with doggy kisses.

Voodoo ribboned between my legs.

Up.

I scooped her off the floor and came around to see what my sister and Belinda were working on. Mardi Gras floats, of course.

"Make any progress on the float ID?"

"We have a few contenders," Emma said, and clicked on a series of images she'd saved onto her computer's desktop.

I leaned over her shoulder to study them. "It's hard to tell. Cornelius was on the float, not next to it, so it's obviously a different perspective, but I'm going to say this one is closest." I pointed at the second photo of a float that featured a king. His cloak was purple and dotted with gold stars.

"That looks like a Rex float," Belinda mused.

"Rex?" I asked. "Is that a Mardi Gras krewe?"

She nodded. "One of the oldest."

"Can you find out where it's stored?"

"Yep, we already have a list." Emma tapped a piece of paper between them.

"I have another favor to ask." I pulled up the photos on my phone and opened the snapshot I'd taken of the picture of Veronica and her friend.

"I know it's a long shot," I said, handing the phone to Belinda. "But is there any chance you might recognize something in this photograph that can tell us where the picture was taken?"

"Mmmm . . . let's see." Belinda studied the image. "Oh, Erin Rose."

"Veronica's real name is Erin Rose?" I asked the question at the same time Emma said, "You know her?"

"No. That's the name of the bar—the Erin Rose. See the flower?" She pointed to a neon light over the bar in the shape of a red rose outlined with a green shamrock. "It's on all their shirts and whatnot. The place has been there forever."

"So it's in New Orleans." Finally, a break.

"It's in the Quarter. Just off Bourbon on . . ." She paused to think about it. "Toulouse, maybe?"

"Conti," my sister said, holding up her phone. "Googled it."

"Are they open this early?" I asked. It was well before noon.

"I'm not sure they ever close," Belinda said.

"It says ten to six," Emma said.

"A.m.? They're open until six in the morning?"

"Sounds about right," Belinda said.

I looked at Emma.

"Let the good times roll," she said, and turned to Belinda. "You coming?"

"I wish I could, sugar, but I've got a client coming in for a reading. You girls have fun, though."

"Where's Hugh?" I asked when I realized he wasn't around.

"He went to sweet-talk that zookeeper. She wasn't answering her phone."

"I don't blame her," I said. "The Fleur-De-Lis Homeowners' Association president has probably been calling her nonstop."

"Who?" my sister asked.

I explained my run-in with the grumpy, self-important man. "He reminded me of Mr. Cavanaugh—I swear they could be brothers."

"If that's the case, I wouldn't answer my phone, either." My sister had had plenty of run-ins with our crotchety neighbor.

"Is it okay if Moss stays here?" I asked Belinda. "He doesn't want to disturb Priscilla."

"What a sweet boy," Belinda said to Moss. "Of course you can stay."

"Hugh should be back soon," Emma added. "He can take all the dogs out when he gets back."

With that settled, Emma and I headed out to see if we could find Layla, who may or may not have been the friend from the photo, or, at the very least, someone who could tell us Veronica's last name.

CHAPTER 8

The Erin Rose is what I would call a dive bar, but in a good way. It was small, with what seemed like decades of bar decor layered on the walls.

There were only a few patrons sipping beers at the counter. The bartender looked up from the pint he was pouring and nodded a greeting to us as we walked in. There wasn't anyone inside who looked like the woman with Veronica in the photo.

"Check the back room." Emma cocked her head toward the rear of the bar. "I'll talk to the bartender."

With a bright smile my sister went to lay on the charm and get some info. I headed through a narrow hall into a small room with a tiny bar along the back wall. A mural depicting larger-than-life people in various modes of drinking had been painted around the room. The faces were so distracting that at first I didn't notice the blonde behind the bar.

She was busy wiping water droplets off freshly washed glassware and stacking the glasses on top of one another.

Bingo, I thought, smiling. I had found the girl from the photo.

"Hey, what can I getcha?" she asked when I approached.

I noticed her name tag, sounded it out in my head, and laughed. "Ima Loza?"

"My boss." She rolled her eyes. "He makes you wear it if you lose your name tag."

"But you're Layla, right?"

"Right," she said with a smile. "You need a drink?"

"No thanks. Actually, I was hoping to talk to Veronica."

She frowned for a moment, then asked, "You mean Ronnie?"

"Yeah, Ronnie."

"She's not here today. But I can tell her you stopped by when she gets back into town."

"That would be great. My name is Grace. Did she go back home?" I asked. Maybe I could find out where Ronnie was from.

"You know what, I don't know. She called me in a big rush a few days ago and asked me to feed her cat. I try not to pry into people's personal lives, so I didn't ask her."

"You don't happen to know Ronnie's last name, do you?" I asked, then quickly amended my question when she frowned. "I mean, what her name is now. I know it used to be"—I searched the bottles lining the bar behind Layla for inspiration—"Jameson, but I'm wondering if she went back to her maiden name, you know, after the divorce." I had no idea how I was coming up with this stuff, but it looked like Layla was buying it, so I kept going. "It was ug-ly."

"Really? Ronnie? She never mentioned being married. Bad, huh?"

"Oh yes."

"That explains a few things, I guess. Like, she said she was starting over here, but that's why a lot of people come to the city."

"Layla! Shake a leg with those glasses."

"Crap, that's my boss. Gotta run. But Ronnie definitely wasn't going by Jameson anymore. It's Preaux. One of the *possédé* Preaux, she says."

"What's that mean?"

"Some Cajun thing, I guess. You'd have to ask her." With

a parting smile, Layla picked up the stacked pint glasses and scurried back to her duties.

I walked out of the back room and nodded to my sister. One of the guys at the bar had bought her a shot that she was trying to politely refuse. When I gave her the thumbs-up, indicating we'd gotten what we came for, she regarded the shot for a moment, shrugged, and tossed it back.

The guys at the bar cheered. Emma gave them a slight bow and bid them farewell.

"I don't get how you can be so healthy in one second and do a shooter the next," I said as we stepped onto the sidewalk.

"Hey, that was Jägermeister. Which is basically herbs and roots. So technically, it's pretty healthy."

I thought about what Belinda had told me regarding absinthe and chuckled.

"It's true," Emma persisted. "I mean, it tastes awful . . ."

"I believe you. I was just thinking you and Belinda really are made for each other."

"I'm already making plans to come back and visit when things calm down. You're totally coming with," she said as we started down Bourbon Street. "I've already talked to Wes."

"I'm kind of surprised he's not here this weekend."

"He was going to come, but has a huge case starting Monday. He promised to make it up to me."

"I think I'm going to have to make that promise, too. You came all the way here and haven't done anything for your birthday."

She shrugged. "It's not exactly what I had in mind for a birthday getaway, but we're all together and you know that's really what matters." She looped her arm through mine as we walked. "But you're still going to have to make it up to me. Starting with buying me lunch. Come on, Central Grocery has a muffuletta with my name on it."

I called Kai as we walked, but got his voice mail.

While waiting in a considerable line at Central Grocery, my sister informed me that the place, which was just as

much a deli as a grocery store, though famous for its muffulettas, also offered chocolate-covered crickets.

Oh goody.

Kai returned my call, which gave me a reason not to listen
to my sister list any other weird "snacks" available.

"How'd the search for Ima go?" he asked.

"Better than I'd expected. It turns out Ima and Layla are
one and the same." I explained the gag name tag.

"What did she tell you?"

"Well, she didn't know where Veronica—known to her
friends as Ronnie—went, but I did get her last name. Ronnie
is Cajun. Last name, Preaux."

"Good. I can pass this on to the contact Jake hooked me
up with here and see what shakes loose."

"How about you? Any luck with your acronyms?"

"Nope. Louisiana doesn't allow you to use the DMV data
for facial recognition, which means I got nowhere fast trying
to do a reverse lookup with Anya's photo."

The man behind the sandwich counter shouted, "Next!"

"Where are you?" Kai asked.

"A place called Central Grocery. You want me to pick
up something for you?"

"Sure. You know what I like. Thanks. Hey, did you make
any progress with the float identification?"

"Possibly. There's one serious contender, but it's hard to
know with such a small piece of the whole to go on."

"We'll find the monkey. And Ronnie."

"I hope so. At least if Cornelius is in a warehouse, I won't
worry about him freezing. As for Ronnie—I think I'm going
to worry about her after that tarot reading."

"You really think Belinda has a psychic ability, like you?"

"No, not like me. But I get what you're saying. The
answer is yes. I think Belinda is hyperintuitive. Like I said
before, she just *knows* things."

He was quiet for a moment. "I can buy that," he said finally.
"But the card reading is harder to get my head around."

"I think that maybe she uses the cards as a way to focus. They're just a tool."

"Right." The word was contemplative rather than skeptical. I decided to let him come to his own conclusions in his own time.

"Next!" the muffuletta man called out again. Emma nudged me.

"I've got to put an order in. I'll see you at Belinda's."

We hauled four huge muffulettas—no crickets, thank you very much—back to Belinda's.

Hugh had indeed made it back and ended up not only taking the dogs for a walk but Voodoo, too.

He'd also gotten the okay from Marisa to bring Cornelius, when we found him, to the Audubon for an evaluation and temporary housing while we tried to figure out where he'd come from.

"Marisa loaned me a cage, too. It's in the back of your Suburban," Hugh said, unfolding the paper wrapping of his sandwich.

Belinda, who'd been pouring pomegranate-infused tea into everyone's glasses, set the pitcher on the table and said, "I narrowed it down to two places. The float you're looking for is in one of them. You have time to go through both."

"Good," I said, liking how much progress we'd made. "It can't hurt to be early."

I sat at the table. Before I managed to unwrap my veggie muffuletta from its paper, Moss appeared next to me.

"No," I said.

Bite?

No.

Please bite?

I pulled in a deep breath, then let it out slowly.

"Stop acting like a beggar."

He let out a high, pitiful whine.

Bite?

Shaking my head, I pulled my mental shield into place to

block out the pleas. Even though I couldn't hear his litany of requests for a bite of my sandwich, being seated at the table put his head level with my shoulder, which made his sad, I'm-starving face hard to ignore.

I gathered my sandwich and drink and moved to stand at the counter.

Moss was undeterred. Following me, he let out another whine, then licked his chops.

I tuned him out and unwrapped the muffuletta.

As soon as I'd taken the first, oily bite, my phone started ringing.

Annoyed, I set my sandwich down and almost choked when I saw the number on the phone's display.

"What?" my sister asked.

"It's Anya."

"Answer it," Emma said.

I forced down the barely chewed bite. "And say what?"

"Just see what she wants—play it by ear."

Crap!

I hit the green accept button and answered.

"Grace, this is Anya Zharova."

"Oh, hi, Anya, how's it going?"

Grace Wilde—smooth as a shark's backside.

"I'm calling to see if you have reconsidered speaking to Coco again. I realized today that I'd neglected to tell you something that might be important. Veronica mentioned that she had adopted Coco from a person, rather than an animal shelter. Perhaps that is helpful?"

I grabbed a paper napkin and scribbled the words *talk to Coco again*, added a big question mark, and looked at my sister.

"Well . . ." I stalled to give Emma time to read and consider. "I'm not sure . . ."

Brows knitting, she met my wide-eyed gaze and nodded firmly.

"I guess it might be worth a try."

"Good. I can pick you up at the hotel in an hour."

"Um . . . an hour?"

Emma lifted her shoulders. She made a monkey face—a pretty good one, actually—then tapped her watch and lifted her hands, palms up.

I understood her question.

Will it give us time to find Cornelius?

It would have to.

"I'm not at the hotel but I can meet you at the apartment."

"Fine, I will see you there."

I hung up and said, "Crap! I just agreed to meet Anya."

"You did what?" Kai asked from the doorway.

"If we hurry," Emma said, "we can set a trap."

"A trap?" he countered. "What do you think she's planning—a picnic?"

"The same thing," I answered, and looked at my sister. "He's right—it's totally a trap."

"Of course it is," she said. "But we have the advantage. She thinks you're alone. So when you don't show up and she leaves, we'll be able to follow her. Grace doesn't even have to be there," Emma said. I could tell by Kai's expression he was considering it.

"Okay. We're going to need everyone in on this. Hugh?"

"Yep."

"Don't forget about me," Belinda said.

"No." I shook my head. "We can't ask you to get involved."

"Really? I don't see anyone else here who's lived in this city their entire life, do you? I'm going."

"If anyone should stay here it's you, Grace," Hugh said. "I mean, haven't we determined that this is a trap? Why walk into it?"

"Let's look at this logically." I set down my sandwich and wiped oil from my fingers. "Anya goes to the apartment. She waits for a while. I don't show up. What's her next move?"

"Call you and see if you're running late," Emma suggested.

I nodded. "Right, she calls me. I can either answer and tell her I'm not coming or ignore the call. Either way, she figures out I'm going to be a no-show. What's her move after that?"

"She calls her partner," Hugh said before taking a bite of his muffuletta.

"Exactly. She calls Barry and tells him I stood her up."

"Unless he's with her," Emma said.

"That would be even better." I glanced from face to face but was pretty sure Kai was the only one getting where I was going. I could tell, because he was shaking his head.

"No, Grace. You'd have to be too close to Coco to eavesdrop on the conversation."

"I can be a lot farther away than any of you."

"I agree with Kai," Emma said. "It's too risky. Plus, remember what happened the last time you hung out in an animal's head for too long?"

I didn't, exactly, because I'd passed out.

When I didn't say anything, Belinda looked around the group. "Somebody going to fill me in?"

"I blacked out."

"For, like, twelve hours," Emma added.

"How close do you have to be to an animal to get into its head?" Belinda asked.

"It depends. Fifty feet?"

"Would be pushing it," Kai said, crossing his arms over his chest.

"Okay," Belinda said. "Less than fifty. That's doable."

"What are you thinking?" I asked her.

"We'll go incognito."

I smiled but shook my head. "It worked in the Quarter but I don't think costumes would be incognito in this neighborhood."

"Who said anything about a costume? I'm talking about leather chaps, baby. For me, anyway."

Belinda walked over to a small coat closet near the laundry room, opened it, and pulled out a bright green futuristic-looking leather jacket. It was padded at the elbows and shoulders with what looked like hard plastic.

I didn't get it, but I was the only one.

"You have a bike?" Emma asked.

"A Harley Wide Glide." She winked at my sister. "What else?"

"Sweet."

I peered out the glass-paned door into the courtyard where the bicycles were parked and noticed for the first time the tarp-covered object in the far corner.

I looked back at the jacket, finally recognizing it as the motorcycle gear that it was.

Belinda handed me the jacket, turned, and reached into the top of the closet.

She pulled out two helmets—one continued the green and black theme of the jacket, while the other's graphics were less . . . stylish.

"Whoa," Emma said, coming to stand next to me. "Very—"

"Rainbow Brite," I said.

She shook her head. "Rainbow Brite didn't have a unicorn."

"Yes, she did," I countered.

"Nope." Emma took the helmet from Belinda and turned it this way and that, admiring the rainbow that swept over its surface and the leaping unicorns on either side. "Starlite was a talking horse. No horn."

"She's right," Belinda said. "He was the most beautiful horse in the universe. But you . . ." She reached out and slid the iridescent, mirrored visor into place. With it down, it would be impossible to see my face. "Will be incognito."

Kai was not overly enthusiastic about the plan, but even he had to admit it was the best we were going to come up with on such short notice.

Basically, we'd mapped out four points around Veronica's apartment that would allow us to see Anya's approach and departure.

Each of us would take up our positions and communicate via a group phone call.

Fifteen minutes before Anya was due to arrive, everyone was in place.

Emma had the easiest post: seated with the Pomeranians at a coffee shop a block from the apartment. Anya had met my sister, which meant she was also incognito. Belinda had covered my sister's shoulder-length dark hair with a long, wavy auburn wig and given Emma a crocheted, forest green, slouchy hat to wear.

That, along with a pair of giant sunglasses, did the trick. Even I wouldn't have recognized her if we'd passed on the street.

It hadn't been as easy to come up with reasons for everyone else to be loitering.

We'd decided Hugh would drive Bluebell, drop Kai, Emma, and the dogs at their positions, then park several blocks away. He would then use one of Belinda's bicycles—easy to transport in Bluebell—and ride to his position across the street from the apartment.

Hugh pretended to be repairing a flat tire. Kai stood near the corner and talked on his phone.

Belinda and I were waiting on the opposite side of the block, where I was going to try to connect with Coco and hopefully overhear something useful.

When Anya decided to leave, Belinda and I would follow, keeping the rest of the crew informed as to our location until they could get to Bluebell and join in the pursuit.

You know what they say about best-laid plans?

Yeah, things started to unravel about two seconds after Hugh spotted Anya.

You see, there's one thing you can't know in situations like this. The variable. Which, of course, was Anya.

We could neither accurately predict nor influence her behavior. And none of us saw what was coming.

As a group, we were able to communicate via an app

that allowed conference calls. Emma had a set of ear buds connected to her phone and was pretending to listen to music.

Kai acted like he was having a conversation, while Hugh, crouched next to his bike, used an old-school wireless earpiece.

Belinda and I had it easy. Both helmets had built-in audio. We could both talk and listen without pretense.

"I see her." Hugh's voice sounded in my ears. "Across the street from my location. Headed toward the apartment."

I wondered if we should all say 10-4 or something. Kai answered my question by saying, "Copy that."

"Me, too," Emma said.

"Hang on—she's still walking. She passed the apartment. Kai?"

"Stand by," Kai said. "Okay, I have a visual. She turned the corner at the end of the block. Emma, she's headed your way."

I tensed.

"I see her," my sister said. "Walking right toward me."

I wanted to tell my sister to run, but knew that would be the worst thing she could do.

"Stay calm, Emma," Kai said. "She probably just wants a coffee or something."

Seconds dragged by.

The leather of Belinda's jacket squeaked in my grip.

The Bluetooth speakers gave me nothing but random ambient noise.

Almost without being aware of it, I started to reach out to connect with the dogs. But stopped when I heard my sister say, "Come here, precious." Her tone was saccharine and she'd turned up the drawl of the light, Southern accent we share to mimic that of Paula Deen. I could hear her making kissing sounds and the happy panting of one of the Pomeranians.

It would've been funny, picturing my sister smooching a dog, if I hadn't been so worried.

"I'm clear," Emma breathed, finally. "You were right, Kai, she went inside."

Belinda and I let out a collective sigh of relief.

"Keep your head down, Emma," I said.

"I've got Elvis in my lap. When she comes back out, I'll pick him up again. She won't see my face."

"Should someone go over there?" Belinda asked. "Just in case?"

I was thinking the same thing. I knew Emma could handle herself. I'd seen her face off against a psychopath with nothing but a roll of duct tape and win. But still . . .

"Em?" I asked.

"No." Emma's voice was quiet but calm. "I'm fine. Everyone stay where you are. We can't risk making her suspicious."

"You got this, Emma," Hugh said.

"Of course I do." Her voice changed abruptly. "Yes. Cuz you're a good puppy, aren't you?"

The sudden switch in my sister's tone was the only indication we had that Anya was on the move. After a few giggles—yes, really—I heard my sister say, "She's headed your way, Kai."

"You're sure she didn't spot you?" I asked.

"She didn't recognize me, but she sure gave me a disgusted look when Elvis was licking my face. I have to say, I completely understand. Belinda, do you brush his teeth? Even Moss—"

Kai's voice interrupted my sister's lighthearted ramble. "Anya just turned the corner. She's moving toward the apartment."

Hugh followed with, "I see her." There was a long pause. "Okay. She's walking through the gate to Ronnie's place."

"That's my cue," I said.

"Grace, don't try to talk to us while you're in Coco's head," my sister warned. "It's too much of a strain."

"Got it. I'll see you on the flip side."

My whole life, I've been dealing with mental interlopers. I learned early how to shield myself from an animal's thoughts and feelings. After all, I can't help a panicking cat if its fear overwhelms me.

The reverse is also true. My nerves were still freshly abraded by the close call with Emma and I knew I'd have to calm down before jumping into Coco's head.

I've also learned to compartmentalize and isolate negative emotions. I took a second to compose my thoughts and tried to marginalize my own anxiety, locking it away in a little imaginary room with a big metal door.

Once the door was secure and my mind was calm, I reached out to the cat.

It was a bit of a reach, like standing on tiptoe to get a jar off the top shelf and feeling your fingertips brush the side. You have to gently, carefully nudge the jar closer before you can get a grip on it.

That's what I did with my mind. Reach. Touch. Gentle pull. Gotcha!

Coco. I spoke to the cat over the threads of our mental connection.

The cat perceived my presence and looked around to see where I was.

I'll come see you soon. But right now I need to stay put. Okay?

Stay?

Coco was lounging on the kitchen counter, waiting for the faucet to be turned on. She loved standing in the sink and drinking from the long, thin stream of fresh water.

Yes. Stay there and I'll come turn the water on for you in a little while.

It can be tricky to express the idea of a future event to an animal. Their concept of time is completely different from a human's. With such precise internal clocks, why would they want to understand hours and minutes?

Anyone with a dog who's tried to take advantage of the extra hour of sleep during daylight saving time will understand what I mean. I can express the feeling of something happening in the future or ask about the past but it was hit-or-miss whether the critter in question was going to get it.

Luckily, Coco did, and was happy to hang out and wait. With Coco on board to stay on the counter, I slipped a little more deeply into the cat's head.

Being inside an animal's mind can be very weird, to say the least. Everything is different. Vision is both heightened and muted. I can hear everything. And smells—well, there's a lot of stuff I'd rather not experience olfactorily, but in for a penny . . .

A rhythmic vibration caught Coco's attention. I knew, because Coco did, that someone was walking toward the stairs.

Moments later I could hear the footsteps as they climbed toward the second floor.

Coco watched as the door opened and Anya stepped inside.

The woman looked around, noticed the cat, frowned, and looked at her phone. Probably checking the time and getting aggravated that I was late.

Anya began to pace while intermittently looking at her phone and taking a sip of her to-go coffee. This went on for an indeterminate amount of time. I couldn't be sure, as I was in Coco's head.

Finally, Anya lifted the phone and made a call.

"She is not coming," she said a moment later.

With my Coco-enhanced superhearing I could understand most of what was said on the other end, and I was pretty sure it was Barry. "You're sure?"

"Yes. I told you she was lying. This has been a waste of time."

"Maybe you should wait—"

"No, I'm not going to sit here. There is too much to do."

Hanging up, Anya turned to Coco.

"Do you know something, kitty cat?" she asked as she walked into the kitchen. "You have not helped us at all."

Setting the coffee on the counter, Anya began stroking Coco's uniquely patterned fur.

"I do not tolerate things that are of no use."

Anya stepped back to regard the cat, then reached into her jacket and calmly pulled out a gun. I watched, horrified, as she pointed it at Coco.

"They call you a bull's-eye tabby, don't they?" Her blue eyes glinted as they swept over Coco's coat. "Bull's-eye. A perfect name."

Anya would have to be off her rocker to pull the trigger. Not just because she'd be shooting a sweet, innocent cat, but because she'd be discharging a firearm in a place where someone was sure to hear the gunshot.

Logic aside, the look on her face told me she really wanted to do just that, and I wasn't about to take any chances.

Digging in as deeply as I could into Coco's mind, I urged the cat to get ready to move.

Coco responded by gathering her feet under her. But she still wasn't sure where we were going.

Speed would be the key. I needed to light a fire under Coco's relaxed kitty butt.

Turning my focus back into my own mind, I grabbed the big, metal door holding my fear at bay and yanked it open.

I shoved all of my fear, all of my panic, into the cat. At the same time I ordered—*Run!*

Coco didn't hesitate. She launched herself off the counter, hit the ground, and was out the cat door like a rocket with fur.

I didn't want her to be so frightened that she ran into the street, so I eased back.

Easy. It's okay, Coco.

Coco made a beeline up and over the back fence into the neighbor's yard and in less than a second was crouched under a large azalea bush.

"Grace? Hey, you still with me?"

"What's going on, Belinda?" I heard Kai's voice in my ear and I realized I'd started to slide off the motorcycle.

"I'm okay," I said. "Sorry."

"You sure? You went all loosey-goosey on me."

"I'm good," I said, relieved to discover it was true. Other than a slight headache, I was fine. "I can tell you this, though. Anya's got a screw loose. Big-time."

I shivered at the thought of her and Barry working together.

"What happened?" Belinda asked. "What did you see? Did Anya say something?"

"We'll have to go over that later." Hugh's voice interrupted the rapid-fire questions. "Anya's on the move. Headed back the way she came."

"I'm on it," Kai said.

The plan had been for one of the group to trail Anya to wherever she'd parked, as the rest of us got ready to follow. Because Belinda and I had the motorcycle, we were up first.

"Belinda, you ready?" Kai asked.

"I was born ready." She started the bike and its engine thundered to life. Cackling as we pulled away from the curb, she said, "I've always wanted to say that."

"We're going east on Camp Street," Kai said.

"East?" Belinda asked. "Oh, you mean toward the CBD. Got it."

"What's the CBD?" I asked.

"Central Business District. There's no east and west in the Crescent City. But I follow. I'll head that way."

"Take your time," Kai said. "If she goes west—I mean . . ." He waited for Belinda's correction.

"Uptown," she said.

"If she heads Uptown," Kai amended, "and you have to do a U-turn, she might notice."

We drove to Camp Street and turned. When we could see Kai and Anya, who was walking along the sidewalk almost a block in front of him, Belinda turned onto the next street.

She used a driveway to do a three-point turn, pulled up to the corner, and puttered to a stop next to the street sign.

"She can't have parked too much farther away," Belinda said as we waited.

Sure enough, a few seconds later Kai said, "Anya's getting into a white, paneled van."

"Of course she is," I muttered. "What else do kidnappers drive?"

"She's pulling out," Kai reported. "Turning toward the CBD."

Belinda made the turn, and we saw the van immediately. She kept our pace slow. Traffic was extremely light and we had to hang back to avoid being spotted.

Thankfully, Belinda knew the city and its various construction projects and was able to predict bottlenecks that might jam us up and let Anya get away.

One of those bottlenecks, which consisted of concrete dividers, a floppy chain-link fence, and a very confusing set of orange cones, was our undoing.

We, with our much smaller vehicle, were expected to maneuver around the larger cars. At least according to the motorcyclist behind us.

He honked and, when we didn't move, honked again.

It was the second honk that did it.

I could see Anya's face in the long, driver's-side mirror. She glanced over to see what the commotion was about.

"If you don't pull up," I said, "she's going to get suspicious."

"But then we'll be right next to her," Belinda whispered.

Even knowing she couldn't see my face, I wasn't keen on the idea, either. "Pretend you can't get into gear or something."

Belinda started fiddling with the handles and shaking her head. I turned and shrugged at Mr. Happy Honker.

The guy made a couple of exaggerated gestures to express his frustration.

Traffic started moving again and we breathed a sigh of relief.

"Hang back as much as possible," I said to Belinda. "Kai, where are you guys?" It would be nice to have our backup in place.

"Trying to catch up. Hang in there—we're on the way."

"She's turning," Belinda said, and gave the rest of the group the details.

We slowed to a stop at the corner Anya had taken and looked down the street. The van was nowhere in sight.

"Maybe she turned again."

Belinda drove around the corner, sped to the next street, slowed, and looked both ways.

No van.

"Damn!" I said. "We lost her."

"Ah—no, we didn't."

"What's going on?" Kai asked.

I leaned over to check Belinda's side-view mirror. The white van was backing out of a driveway, *rapidly*.

"She's behind us."

CHAPTER 9

Tires squealing, Anya jerked the van into a turn and lurched toward us.

"Get out of there," Kai ordered, unnecessarily.

Belinda was already moving. "Hang on, Grace!"

Another redundant order. I was clinging to her like a frightened baby lemur.

We rocketed forward, then screeched around a corner, only to have to brake at an intersection. A moment later we were charging down the road, but again, had to slow for traffic. Each interruption in our forward progress allowed Anya to slip closer.

Even though my dad's a master mechanic and I grew up around all kinds of vehicles, I don't know that much about motorcycles. One thing I was pretty sure of—if we could get on a straightaway, we could outrun a van.

Belinda seemed to be thinking the same thing, kind of.

What I'd had in mind was getting on the highway, but it appeared my pilot had other ideas.

We reached St. Charles Avenue and Belinda turned, not onto the road but onto the dirt-lined streetcar tracks that ran along the center of the avenue.

I glanced back. Anya, too, maneuvered the van onto the tracks.

"She's still coming."

"Where are you?" Kai's voice came over the speakers.

"Um . . . on St. Charles, sort of."

"Sort of?"

"We're in the middle."

"On the railway tracks?"

"It's the only chance we have to outrun her," I said. A car horn blared as we barreled through an intersection.

I looked back, hoping Anya would be stopped by the traffic.

She careened through the cars and kept coming, in fact—"Um, we need to speed up, Belinda. She's gaining on us."

"I can't," she said. "The dirt is too loose here. I can't get enough traction, and if we have to brake . . ." She trailed off, leaving me to fill in the rest.

"We crash."

"Right."

Crap!

"Belinda." My sister's voice was calm and soothing. "You just focus on driving. Grace, we need to know where you are. Give us a cross street."

I peered over Belinda's shoulder to look for a sign.

Mistake.

We were headed right for an oncoming streetcar.

Gritting my teeth, I squeezed my eyes shut and attempted to mute the scream that would no doubt hinder Belinda's concentration.

I was not completely successful but figured the guttural "errrrh," was better than, "AAAAAH!"

I felt the bike tilt slightly without slowing, and I opened my eyes in time to see a green blur and hear the incongruously cheerful ding of the streetcar's bells as we whizzed by.

I checked behind us. Anya had also avoided a collision, but she'd had to veer wildly and it had cost her some speed.

Not enough, though. I watched as the van started creeping closer again.

"Grace?"

Right, I was supposed to be telling the rest of the crew where we were.

"Hang on," I said, looking ahead for a street sign. Seconds later, we zipped through an intersection. Horns blared, and I clenched my teeth to keep from yelping, then said, "We just passed Eighth Street."

"Going which way?"

I tried to get my bearings. "Heading toward the Quarter, I think."

Suddenly, Belinda asked, "What time is it?"

"Almost two thirty," Kai answered.

"Perfect."

Obviously, Belinda had come up with a plan. She was a native, so I hoped it would be a good one.

She cut over the middle of the grassy road, back into the oncoming streetcar track, then, as we cleared the next intersection, pulled onto the pavement, merging into traffic like we were on a freeway.

I expected her to gun it now that we were on the pavement, but instead she slowed, eased into the right lane, and made the next turn.

This unimpressive maneuver had not thwarted our pursuer.

Anya was so close, I was pretty sure she was going to be able to ram us within seconds.

That was when Belinda proved she wasn't just another pretty face.

After an abrupt right turn we passed through a pair of iron gates set in a tall, white wall. Ornate crypts and mausoleums whizzed by on either side as we sped down the center of what was obviously one of New Orleans's famed cemeteries.

The center aisle was wide enough to accommodate a van,

and a quick glance over my shoulder confirmed that Anya made it through the gates and was bearing down on us.

She was gaining fast, because we were slowing down.

"Um, Belinda?" I squeaked.

"I know. Hang on."

I tightened my hold, tucked my head to the side, and flattened my chest against her back.

The van's hood appeared in my periphery. I braced for impact and felt my stomach do a backflip when we swooped around a crypt onto one of the narrow alleyways leading into the labyrinth of tombs.

Tires screeched behind us. I eased off the death grip I had on Belinda and looked back just in time to see the van slam into the base of a large mausoleum.

Belinda reached the end of the alleyway and slowed to a stop. Planting her feet on either side of the Harley, she looked over her shoulder at the van.

The left side was crumpled against the solid stone. Steam billowed from under the hood.

The van was out of commission. Anya wasn't.

Through the steamy haze I could see her making quick, jerky movements.

"What's she doing?" Belinda whispered.

"The impact must have jammed the door," I said. "I think she's trying to force it open."

"Let's get out of here before she succeeds."

There turned out to be four entrances to the cemetery, one on each side. We found the closest one and slipped out quietly. Or as quietly as possible while riding a Harley.

"Give us an update," Kai said.

"We gave her the slip," I said.

"Well," Emma said, "you better hope you're as lucky with the cops."

As she spoke, I could hear sirens in the distance. "You think they'll stop us?"

"If they're responding to a car chase down the middle of

St. Charles and are looking for two people on a motorcycle, then, yes."

"Easy," I said. "Stop and let me off."

"No," everyone said at once.

I told Kai where we were. "How close are you?"

"Not close enough," he answered.

"At least five minutes," Emma said. "You two created quite a stir. Traffic is bogged down, and everyone is trying to use the side streets."

I spotted a cluster of people on a walking tour. "There." I pointed. "Drop me off with them. I'll blend in and wait for Kai to pick me up."

There were at least twenty people on the tour—it was a perfect cover. It took some explaining to convince everyone the plan would work but, in the end, we agreed.

"Okay," Belinda said. "I'll head through Uptown, circle around the city, and meet y'all back at my place."

She gave Kai directions on how best to find me, and I dismounted and removed my helmet.

"Wait—what do I do with this?" I held up the rainbow-striped, unicorn-emblazoned helmet.

"Stick it inside the jacket. Here, like this." She fastened the zipper, put the helmet over my belly, and with a *ziiiiip*, I went from wanted daredevil to profoundly pregnant.

"Don't forget to waddle," Belinda said before rumbling off.

It felt strange, not just pretending to be hugely pregnant, which was weird enough, but suddenly not being in constant contact with everyone made me feel as if I'd been set adrift.

The tour guide frowned at me when I eased into the group, but, really, who's going to tell a pregnant lady to get lost?

Playing the part, I tottered along and half listened as the guide talked about the different types of architecture found in the Garden District.

A few minutes later I heard the rumble of Bluebell's engine as she turned the corner.

I waddled over and climbed into the backseat next to

Emma. "It was Belinda's idea," I said before any comments could be made.

"It seems to have worked." Kai glanced at me in the rearview mirror before pulling away from the curb.

"You make a cute pregnant lady," Emma teased.

I rolled my eyes and changed the subject. "Have you heard from Belinda?"

"I'm still on the phone with her." Hugh, who was sitting in the front passenger seat, turned to show me his earpiece. "So far so good."

I leaned back with a relieved sigh.

As we rode back to the B and B, Hugh kept tabs on Belinda to make sure she hadn't been arrested.

After decompressing on the ride, I was shaky and almost too worn out to face the idea of going on the hunt for Cornelius.

Oh well. No rest for the wicked. I decided to indulge in brewing a fresh pot of coffee, just to keep the fire burning.

Kai was in the courtyard on the phone with his contact at the NOPD. I tapped on the glass to get his attention and held up a mug. He nodded.

"Anyone else want coffee?" I asked as I poured myself a cup.

"I'll take some," Hugh said.

"Belinda?"

"No thanks, *cher*. Let me finish getting this wig off your sister and I'll make some tea."

Emma was seated at the kitchen table while Belinda worked. She cut her eyes to the side and looked at me. "Grace, can you put the kettle on?"

I nodded and did as I was asked.

A minute later Kai came through the back door and with a smile accepted the mug I offered.

"Well?" I asked.

"There was no sign of Anya in the cemetery. The van

has been towed to the impound lot. I left a message with the crime scene investigator working the case—maybe they'll let me take a look when they finish going over it."

"Do you think they'll get prints from the van?" I asked.

"Anya was wearing gloves today. But they might get lucky."

"Maybe we'll find out who she is," Hugh said.

"Aside from a crazy person?" I plopped onto the chair next to Emma and took a sip of coffee. "I'm telling y'all, the woman is mean. She almost shot Coco just because she was ticked off that I hadn't shown up."

"I agree." Belinda set the wig aside and pulled off the stocking cap holding Emma's hair. "You should've seen her face when she realized she was being followed," Belinda added. "It was like laser beams were coming out of that woman's eyes."

"Grace gets a look like that sometimes," my sister said.

"No, I don't."

"You do. It's this hyperfocused, icy glare. Doesn't really work on me, though." She smirked and ran her fingers through her hair.

"I've seen the look," Hugh said.

"Me, too," Kai added.

"Guys, this was way worse. Believe me. The way Anya talked to Coco, about how she didn't tolerate things that *ver not useful*," I said in my best Russian accent—which was pretty bad. "I'm telling you, she's got zero compassion."

"All the more reason to get going and find Cornelius so we can figure out what he knows about Ronnie," Kai said. "Grace, the monkey showed you a sunset, right?"

I nodded. "Or a sunrise. I can't be sure. And it was just for a split second. The only part of the vision with any color at first was the glittery purple of the float, but just as the image blinked out, I could see the sky through the window."

"I think we can assume he was showing you a sunset, because he wanted food tonight, right?"

"Probably."

"Then we have a timeline to work from." He checked his watch. "It's almost four, so we better hurry."

"Let's say you manage to catch him," Hugh said. "And if anyone can, it'll be you, but how are we going to hold on to him? We can't just walk into the museum with a cage."

"Grace can carry the monkey, can't you?" Emma asked.

My sister often thought I could do much more with my ability than I actually could. I shook my head. "Even if I managed to get ahold of him, I'm not sure I could keep him calm for very long. We need to come up with something else."

"I've got just the thing," Belinda said before turning to walk out of the kitchen.

She returned a minute later with what looked like an oversized purse.

"It's got mesh panels on the sides, see?" She held it up and I saw the words BARK BAG embroidered on the side.

"Is that a dog carrier?" I asked.

"Cute, right?" Belinda said, handing me the bag.

"Will a monkey fit in there?" Emma asked.

"He'll fit," Hugh answered, coming to take a look at the carrier. "The question is, will it hold up if he freaks out?"

We both inspected the bag's zipper and seams.

"Looks pretty sturdy," he said.

"It will have to do."

"The sun sets in an hour," Kai said. "If we're going to find this guy we better get a move on."

"What else do y'all need?" Belinda asked.

"Beignets," I said, suddenly remembering that detail. "Is there somewhere I can get them fast?"

"There's a place around the corner. I'll call ahead—you go. They'll be ready."

"Perfect."

Everyone gathered their things and I gave Moss and Voodoo, who were taking turns batting around one of the Pomeranians' dog toys, a good-bye pat and hurried out the door.

• • •

We made it to the Bon Temps Mardi Gras Museum in plenty of time, but were told the building closed promptly at dark. We paid the entry fee anyway and hurried inside.

Our excitement sputtered out as soon as we stepped through the front doors.

There's a scene at the end of one of the *Raiders of the Lost Ark* movies where the Ark of the Covenant is being secreted away in a massive government warehouse. This place wasn't quite that big, but it felt close.

"This place is huge," Emma said.

"Understatement," I said. The building was gigantic and it wasn't just filled exclusively with Mardi Gras floats. All types of festive paraphernalia were stacked on a towering set of shelves that ran through the center of the warehouse. The shelves bisected the space, leaving two aisles, one on either side. The actual Mardi Gras floats were parked along the outer walls.

"Grace, you getting anything?" Kai asked.

I'd already been scanning the area with my senses, and shook my head. "Not yet."

"Divide and conquer?" Emma asked.

"Might as well," I said.

"Okay." Kai turned to address the group. "Emma and Hugh, you take the right. Grace and I will go left. If you spot the monkey or find the float Grace described, call my cell. I'll put it on vibrate."

"Remember," I added. "This little guy is very good at avoiding being captured. If you see him, keep your distance until I can get there."

"Roger that, boss lady." Hugh winked at me, then handed the dog carrier Belinda had loaned us to Kai. We paired off and headed down separate aisles.

A few overhead lamps buzzed faintly and though the ceiling was dotted with yellowed, corrugated skylights, the dusky sky didn't provide much illumination.

"It's kind of dark in here," I said as we walked. "Hugh and Emma will have a hard time spotting a little capuchin monkey in all these nooks and crannies."

"They would recognize the float, though."

I nodded, hoping he was right.

We continued to walk, scanning the area for any sign of monkey activity. Without the benefit of festive parade lighting, some of the Mardi Gras floats looked downright spooky. The dim light and deep shadows transformed jolly jester faces into manic, possessed clowns. Smiling kings became grimacing giants.

We passed a section of random foam and papier-mâché body parts that had been filed away for use on future floats, and Kai stopped to scrutinize a bin filled with disembodied heads.

I came to stand next to him and looked into the box. A giant chubby-cheeked cherub face peered up at us. The paint on one side of the head had been scuffed off, leaving what looked like a large scar.

"Rather . . . unsettling," Kai said. The fact that a seasoned police investigator would call anything outside a crime scene unsettling says a lot about just how creepy the place was.

I tried to shake off the feeling. I was going to have to bring my A game to get Cornelius to feel comfortable and safe enough to coax him to come to me. Staring at a giant, scarred doll face was not helping in that endeavor.

"Come on," I said. "Let's keep looking."

We continued on and suddenly I felt it. The barest hint of a pulsing vibration.

"Wait." I placed my hand on Kai's forearm to stop him.

He didn't ask questions, just paused to watch me. I focused on the echo of that hum, trying to trace it to its source, but got only a vague direction.

"Man, this little guy is hard to get a bead on."

"At least we know he's here," Kai murmured. "Take your time. You'll get it."

It's funny what words of encouragement from someone you trust can do.

When I felt the distinct vibration again, I closed my eyes and let everything else slide away. It took a few seconds, but I was able to zero in on the monkey's location.

"He's down this way," I said in a whisper. "Once we spot him, hang back and let me try to get close. Whatever you do, don't spook him."

"Got it." We continued down the aisle, past a row of cardboard boxes stacked taller than I am. The boxes were marked MG BEADS.

I thought of the glittering strands I'd seen festooning the trees, fences, and lamp posts of the city and wondered how many other boxes like these were stacked, ready for the carnival season.

As I passed the wall of boxes, I looked to my right and froze.

Cornelius sat high above us on a rafter, but that's not what surprised me. After all, I could sense the monkey's presence and knew he was nearby. What stopped me in my tracks was how specific the little guy had been when telling me what he wanted and where. He must've been staying in the museum for a while to be able to re-create the area around the float with such detail.

Though he'd shown me a different perspective—a view from his eyes rather than mine—everything he'd shown me was exact. Even the sunset was perfect.

Smart little simian.

I really hoped I could talk him into coming with me. If not, at least we might be able to trap him inside the museum and then work with the zoo to catch him later.

"Okay, Cornelius." I held up the tray of beignets and shook it. "As requested, I have beignets for you."

The monkey's gaze darted about for a couple of seconds, then he hopped from the rafters onto the float, disappearing behind the king's crown. He reappeared a moment later on the figure's shoulder and paused to eye the beignets.

I got the feeling he didn't really know what they were. Which was weird, as he'd asked for the fried treat specifically.

"Come on. You hungry?"

Hungry. Want a grape.

I can get grapes for you, too. But you have to come here. I projected the idea to him, sending the image of a bunch of big, juicy grapes along with the feeling of warmth and safety.

Then, with as much gentle urgency as possible, I added, *Come.* It was part request, part command.

Cornelius did as he was bid and came slowly toward me.

I slid my gaze to Kai and said in a low monotone, "Wait until I have him, then, as quietly as you can, come here and hold the carrier open for me."

He nodded.

Just as Cornelius reached the front of the float he squealed in alarm and scurried back the way he'd come and leapt into the rafters.

Crap!

"I told you to wait," I snapped, turning to Kai.

"I did."

"Damn." I couldn't believe he'd slipped away again. "Something spooked him."

"It wasn't me," Kai said. "I swear I didn't move. I don't know what scared him off."

I shook my head to dismiss the topic of who was to blame—it didn't matter.

"Okay, let's try this again," I muttered to myself.

I focused my mind and reached out. I caught the barest hint of the monkey's thoughts and reached farther—but it was no use.

"He's too far away to lock on to."

"Sounds like you're launching a missile."

I ignored his comment, still frustrated. "Maybe I should do this alone. Call Emma and tell them to stay wherever they are. That way, they won't run into us and scare Cornelius off." I held out my hand. "Let me have the carrier. I'll meet you back here once I catch him."

He handed me the bag. "You know, if this were a horror movie, going off on your own would trigger a zombie attack."

"It's not a horror movie and I'll be fine."

He nodded, and as I started toward where I'd last sensed Cornelius was headed, I could hear Kai talking to Emma on his phone.

I found Cornelius high in the rafters toward the far end of the building.

"Hey, little guy."

Slowly, carefully, I reached out to once again connect our thoughts. When he didn't bolt, I gently began to fortify the conduit of our minds.

Oddly, he seemed to understand that I was being careful with our interaction and I got the impression he liked the care I was taking.

Safe?

Yes, you'll be safe with me.

Want a grape.

I promise to get you some grapes. For now, how about a beignet? It's what you asked for.

It seemed to take forever but finally the little monkey eased off the rafter and started toward me.

That's it. Come on.

I held out my hand. Cornelius took a beignet and began eating it daintily.

I wondered how frightened he must have been to be on his own in the cold with people setting traps and jumping out at him every chance they got.

Picturing a bunch of big, ripe grapes, along with the feeling of warmth and safety, I offered my arm.

I'll help you. Don't be scared.

With a sudden leap, he was on my shoulder. The instant we made contact—*Bam!* Everything went dark, then an image sharpened into focus. A woman struggling against restraints. Light flashed off something metallic.

The awful scene played on, flickering like a damaged 8 mm film.

Finally, it stopped. I could hear whimpering. It took a moment for me to realize the sound was coming from me and echoed by the monkey, who had scurried up the nearest float.

"Grace!"

At some point, I'd fallen to my knees.

"What is it? What happened?" Kai asked, rushing to my side.

I sucked in a couple of deep breaths and tried to convince my heart that pile-driving a hole through my chest was not going to help.

The wave of fear had me trembling like I'd been dunked in ice water.

"You're white as a sheet," Emma said. Crouching in front of me, she reached out and rubbed my arms. "And you're freezing. Hugh."

"I've got it," Kai said.

A second later, an oversized jacket was settled over my shoulders.

Kai tucked my hair behind my ear and studied my face. "Do you feel like you're going to pass out?"

"I'm okay," I said, which was utter crap.

"Can you stand up?"

I nodded. Taking his hand, I stood, wobbled, and was caught by Kai, who scooped me into his arms.

"No, really, I'm fine."

"Shut up and let us take care of you," my sister said in a tone that was both stern and gentle.

I felt like an idiot, especially when we passed the ticket booth and walked into the parking lot.

"Okay," I said when we'd reached Bluebell. "Really, I got it from here."

I managed to climb into the passenger seat and waited while everyone else got in.

"Do you need us to stop and get you food or water?"

"No. I'm good, really."

"What happened?"

"I saw . . . something pretty bad." I didn't want to think about it, much less talk about it. "Sorry, let's head back to Belinda's. I don't want to have to tell the story more than once."

CHAPTER 10

Emma had called to let Belinda know we were on our way and that I was not feeling well. This must have triggered some sort of mother hen response in our hostess, because she met us at the door and started asking questions.

"You want to lie down? I put extra pillows on the couch."

"No, I'll just sit. Thanks."

Moss was by my side before I'd made it to the kitchen table. Like always, my dog sensed my distress and was there to offer comfort and, if need be, his teeth. He let out a deep growl of warning as he escorted me to my seat.

Guard.

I'm okay, big guy.

I gave him a reassuring pat as I settled onto the chair.

Moss wasn't buying it—he could feel the lingering effects of what I'd seen and was in the mood to dispose of whatever had caused the problem.

Guard.

I sighed and let him grumble, then leaned over to give him a hug.

Okay?

I'm getting there, buddy.

Voodoo, always keen to take her big brother's lead, leapt into my lap and started kneading my thighs. Her tiny, needle-sharp claws found their way through my jeans and I lifted the kitten to cradle her in my arms. She began to purr and I let the rhythmic waves of kitty contentment wash away the sharpest edges of what remained of my fear.

A couple of deep breaths later and I was feeling much better.

"You've got some color back." Emma ignored Moss's warning glare and came to sit in the chair beside mine.

"Purr-therapy. There's nothing like it."

"Except puppy breath," Hugh said, coming to sit next to my sister.

Emma made a face.

"Don't even try it," I said. "I heard you making kissy noises at Elvis."

"Desperate times." Emma sighed.

"You need to eat," Belinda declared suddenly.

I hated to tell her food was the last thing I wanted. "Actually, I don't have much of an appetite."

"We can fix that," she said, and turned to the cabinet holding the little jars and bottles. "Here." She handed me a small, blue glass bottle with a rubber-dropper screw top. "Three drops under the tongue."

"What is it?" I unscrewed the dropper and peered at the milky amber liquid.

"It will make you feel better," Belinda said.

I raised my eyes to my sister. Emma shrugged. "Can't hurt."

"Maybe you should take it," I muttered.

"Ahem." Belinda fisted her hands on her hips and waited.

It was clear I wasn't getting out of it, so I held my breath and deposited three drops under my tongue.

My eyes started to water instantly.

"Hold it under there for thirty seconds," Belinda instructed. "Then swallow."

"Aht? Irty econts?" I tried to protest but it was hard to

talk with what tasted and felt like hellfire burning a hole through my face.

Belinda ignored my distress.

"How about the rest of you? Hungry?"

The men nodded.

"You don't have to feed us again. This is a bed-and-breakfast," Emma said. "Not a bed, breakfast, lunch, and dinner."

"She's right," Kai told Belinda. "You've done more than enough today."

I swallowed with a gasp and croaked, "Water."

Kai had already poured me a glass. I took it from him gratefully and sucked it down.

"We'll get a pizza or something." Emma was still trying to sell Belinda on the idea of ordering out.

Our hostess was having none of it. Even when Emma posited that there must be a pizza place in the greater New Orleans area that had somewhat healthy food.

"Don't argue with her," I rasped. "She might make you drink something from that cabinet."

Resistance was, indeed, futile.

"I've already got the oven preheated. I just have to throw something together."

She kind of reminded me of my mother, with her steel will and the way she could create food for five people out of thin air.

Within minutes a pan of black bean and sweet potato enchiladas was in the oven and everyone was seated at the kitchen table to learn what Cornelius had shown me. I wasn't looking forward to replaying what I'd seen. I tried to detach and go slowly so I wouldn't have to rehash any details.

"I saw a man holding a woman down. She was struggling, but her movements were sluggish. Like she'd been drugged.

"I could hear her, but the sound was muted. I couldn't make out any words, so I think she was gagged and there was this . . . thing on her face. Actually, it was covering her whole head."

I stopped.

"Everything was so . . ." I paused to search for the right word but fell short. "I don't know, vivid. Not what I was seeing but what I was feeling. It was like Cornelius understood what was happening and was terrified."

"Did you get a sense of where this happened?" Kai asked.

"No. It was like the other memories. The colors were muted except for her dress. It was yellow."

"What about the man?"

"I couldn't swear to it, but I'm almost positive it was Barry. He was wearing an earpiece."

"Like for a phone?"

I shook my head. "It looked more like a hearing aid. A really big one."

"And he was tying her up with ropes or something else?"

"Thick leather straps with buckles. She was being tied down to a metal table."

I didn't want to say it, but knew Kai needed to know as much detail as possible. "Like they use for an autopsy."

Everyone fell silent.

I thought of the image on the tarot card and looked at Belinda. "It's her, isn't it?" I asked. "The woman I'm supposed to save?"

She answered with a grim nod. "I think so, *cher*."

"Who is she?" Hugh asked. "It can't be Ronnie, can it?"

"Why not?" I said. "She's missing."

"But if Anya and Barry have Ronnie, why would they ask you to find her?"

"Technically," Kai said, "they asked Grace to find out where Ronnie got Coco, remember?"

"That would mean they need Grace because, even though they've been torturing her, Ronnie hasn't told them what they want to know." My sister looked like she was going to be sick.

I leaned onto my elbows and pressed my face into my hands. "And I lost the only clue that would help find her. Oh God, I'm such a sucky rescuer."

Suddenly, I was angry. Not just at myself for managing to let Cornelius get away but at the one other person who had information on what was going on.

I pushed back from the table and stood so abruptly everyone jumped.

"Please excuse me for a second. I need to make a phone call."

I turned, snatched my phone from where it sat on the counter, and walked out the kitchen door.

I hadn't bothered with a coat—the chilled evening air of the courtyard was no match for the cold fire burning in my belly.

I called the number from Logan's card and paced as it rang.

No answer.

I called again.

No answer.

"I can do this all night, buddy." I hit send for the third time. After a dozen rings I had an idea. I hung up and sent him a text message.

You need to call me. Now.

No response.

NOW

Nothing.

I mean it, Logan!

A few seconds later the phone rang. I was so startled, I nearly dropped it before I could answer.

"So you are alive," I said.

"Why wouldn't I be?" Logan's voice was a low rumble.

"There was blood in the package you left me."

"Flesh wound."

"Yours or someone else's?"

"Worried?"

"Not about you."

"Then why are you calling?"

"I just saw Barry strapping a woman to a table."

"Where?"

Damn. "Well, I didn't *see* it, see it, exactly."

"Who did? I need a name."

"His name is Cornelius and he's not around."

"Grace—"

"He won't talk to you, Logan."

"Want to bet?"

"I don't know where he is, okay? I wish I did."

Silence.

"Hello?"

"You should leave town, Grace."

"Why? Who are these people? What do they want? I know you're involved, Logan. I saw you with Ronnie."

"Who?"

"The woman you kidnapped."

"I don't know what you're talking about."

"I saw you grab her. And now"—I swallowed hard at the memory—"She was so scared, Logan. Terrified. I have to help her."

"You need to stay out of it."

"Out of it? What if I had stayed out of it when Brooke was missing?"

There were several moments of silence.

I knew how much Logan cared about Brooke. The girl was the closest thing to family he had. I was hoping drawing a parallel between her and Ronnie would inspire him to help. Or at least give me some answers.

It was a wasted effort.

"This time, you need to stay out of it."

"It's too late for that, Logan. They're already looking for me."

"Only because they think you can help them get what they want. Call Anya and tell her you're a fraud. Convince her you don't know anything."

"You know what? Screw you, Logan. I didn't ask you to be my babysitter."

"I don't have time for this," he hissed. I could almost feel his anger sizzle over the phone.

Here's the thing, I was pretty sure Logan scared the crap out of a lot of scary people. Pissing him off was probably not the best idea. But in that moment, I didn't care.

"You listen to me, Ghost Boy. I'm going to find Ronnie. Then, I'm going to find you, and I am going to bring you down."

The dramatic proclamation sounded ridiculous. I waited for the derisive laughter to spill through the phone's speaker. I even had a quote ready from *The Lord of the Rings* about how little people can accomplish extraordinary things. But Logan didn't laugh or threaten or even hang up on me. What he did threw me completely.

"Get out of town, Grace. Please."

The line went dead. I stared at the phone in disbelief.

It wasn't just the word *please*, but how he'd said it. He sounded tired and, unless I was hallucinating, like he actually cared.

First he stood me up and now he was being nice. What was going on with Logan?

I shook my head to clear it. I had enough to worry about without adding Logan into the mix.

When I returned to the kitchen a minute later, drinks had been poured and the enchiladas were on the table. I glanced around when I noticed who was missing.

"Where's Kai?" I asked. "And if you tell me he got mad because I called Logan—"

"He got a call from someone at the NOPD." Emma

motioned toward the hallway with her chin as she scooped enchiladas onto a plate.

I took my place at the table, surprised to find I'd developed an appetite—which was good because the food was delicious.

"Did you get anything from Logan?" Kai asked me when he finally walked into the kitchen.

I shook my head. "What about you?"

"They're going to let me take a look at the van."

"Really?"

"Yep. One of the techs remembers me from when I spoke at a seminar."

"They have CSI seminars?"

"Not everyone thinks what I do is boring."

I hadn't meant it that way, but maybe Kai understood because he pulled his jacket on and came to kiss me on the forehead.

"I'll let you know what I find."

"Wait." I stood up to stop him before he made it out the door. "Do you need to take Bluebell?"

"I'm getting a lift from one of the patrolmen." He looked over my shoulder at Belinda. "Which reminds me, I'll get a ride back, too, but it will be late."

She walked to where a number of keys hung on a row of hooks next to the back door. "You want to take a to-go plate?"

"No time," Kai said.

She held up a key. "See if there's any scuttlebutt about the mysterious bikers involved in the chase today," Belinda said.

"I'd planned on it." Kai took the key and headed out.

I wandered back to the table to sit with Emma and Hugh.

I was bone-tired and my brain was ready to shut down, but as much as I wanted to, I couldn't bring myself to call it an early night and hit the sack. Not knowing what I did.

"I feel like we should be doing something," I said, sinking into the chair.

"You mean, aside from sitting here letting our food digest?" Hugh asked. "I agree, but what can we do?"

I looked from him to my sister, then turned to Belinda when she came to sit next to me. "Any ideas?"

"Not really. Unless you can think of a place to look for Cornelius. He's the one with the information we need."

"We could try the museum again," Emma suggested. "I know it's closed but walls don't matter to you. If he's inside, you might be able to get him to come to you, right?"

"In theory."

"Are you up for it?" Belinda asked. "What if he shows you more of what he saw?"

"Then I'll know more than I do now," I said. "Oh no!"

"What?"

"Coco." I couldn't believe I'd forgotten about the cat. "We've got to get her out of there."

"*You* don't need to go anywhere near that apartment," my sister said. "Anya has had her hands full—she won't be going back to Ronnie's today to hurt Coco."

"What about Ronnie's friend from the Erin Rose?" Belinda asked. "Don't you need to warn her?"

"Belinda's right," I said. "We have to talk to Layla. If she goes to feed Coco tomorrow and runs into Anya . . ."

"Okay," Emma said. "We'll talk to Layla and let her know what's going on."

"Ask her if she can take Coco," I said.

"We will. You and Belinda can head back to the Mardi Gras place and try to find Cornelius."

It was better than sitting around doing nothing.

Belinda, Moss, and I piled into Bluebell and headed back to the Bon Temps Mardi Gras Museum.

Unlike the inside, the exterior was ablaze with light.

After discussing the best approach, it was decided I should walk around the outside with Moss. You know, out for a stroll, just letting the dog lead the way.

It took only one complete circumnavigation of the huge, metal-clad building to know Cornelius was not there.

Shivering, I climbed back into Bluebell.

With Belinda at the wheel, we cruised the surrounding area. I kept my eyes closed and my senses open.

No monkey.

Hoping Emma and Hugh had had better luck with Layla, and Cornelius had found somewhere warm to sleep, we gave up and called it a night.

• • •

I awoke the next morning with a familiar canine at my feet and a kitten tail tickling my nose. I brushed away Voodoo's tail, closed my eyes, and had started to drift off when there was a soft knock at the door. I ignored it. The door swished open.

Emma.

I knew because Moss, though awake, didn't stir. Which meant he'd caught her scent before she'd opened the door.

Whatever his issues with my sister, there was one thing my dog knew—she was safe, and was probably the only person he'd allow to approach me or Voodoo while we were sleeping without at least a soft *woof* of warning.

"Grace?" Emma's voice was almost too quiet to hear. Or maybe I was still half asleep.

I opened my eyes and blinked at my sister. Because she knows and loves me, she was holding a cup of steaming coffee.

Stretching to encourage my limbs to get moving, I yawned, sat up, and took the mug.

Printed in large letters were the words LET'S GET SOME-THING STRAIGHT: I'M NOT.

"What time is it?" I asked, noticing I'd forgotten to bring my phone into my room.

"Around eight. I plugged your phone in for you. It's in the kitchen."

"Thanks."

"Belinda is finishing breakfast. She sent me to fetch you."

Elvis nosed open the partly closed door and trotted into the room.

He stopped at my sister's feet, sat, and wagged his tail.

"Poor Elvis."

"What?" Emma asked, looking down at the dog.

"You're putting him out of work. And he's fallen in love with you."

Emma made a face.

I slipped on the fluffy robe I'd found hanging on the door and followed my sister downstairs. Kai had already headed back to the impound lot to do more supersleuthing with the van, and Belinda was rummaging through the refrigerator when we walked in. "Someone missed a call," she said from behind the door.

Emma lifted her phone off the table. "Not me."

I went to check mine and saw I had a new voice message. "I'm almost afraid to play it. It could be Anya."

"Or Logan," Emma said.

"He always calls from a blocked number."

I hit the message and put it on speaker.

It was the Monteleone, calling to inquire about the bag I'd left in my room.

Crap. I'd forgotten about my backpack.

"Well, you can't risk going to get it," Emma said.

"Get what?" Hugh asked, and he walked into the kitchen.

"Grace has luggage at the Monteleone."

"I can go get," he offered.

I shook my head. "There's nothing in the bag that can't be replaced."

"Call and see if they'll mail it to you," Belinda suggested. "It will be worth whatever they charge if you can avoid going back there and running into one of the bad guys.

"Better safe than sorry, my *mamere* used to say."

"Mamere?"

"My grandmama."

"That's what that means?"

"What's up?" Emma asked, not understanding the significance.

"That's what Coco called the lady with the bunny slippers. Mamere."

"You're thinking Ronnie got Coco from her grandmother?" Emma said.

"It makes sense."

"Does that mean Anya and Barry are really after Ronnie's *mamere*?" Belinda asked.

"I'm thinking that's a definite yes," Hugh said.

"They could want something her grandmother has," I said.

Emma shook her head. "Maybe, but I think Hugh's right. There aren't that many things people will endure torture to protect. And family's one of them."

"We've got to warn her," I said, tension coiling in my gut.

"We still don't know how to find her," Hugh pointed out. "Not without a name."

"We have Ronnie's last name," Emma said. "If it's her paternal grandmother, we might get lucky."

Hugh nodded. "It's something to work with, at least."

"And we'll start working with it as soon as everyone is fed," Belinda declared. "I made a quiche."

The quiche was delicious and we finished it completely, much to Moss's disappointment.

"We'll get you a treat later," I told him.

Treat?

"Don't let him fool you," Belinda said. "I cracked an egg over his food earlier."

"Did you?"

Nice try, buddy. She ratted you out.

No treat?

I shook my head. Dogs.

With a full stomach and half a pot of coffee in my system, I'd hoped to be more awake.

Maybe I just needed more coffee.

We cleared the table and Emma brought out her laptop so we could try to track down all the Preauxs in the greater New Orleans area.

There were a lot.

"Holy cow," I said when we started scrolling through the list.

"Let's narrow it down," Emma said. "Belinda, which are the areas most likely to have wrought-iron railings?"

"Ooh, that's a tough one. You mean the thick, heavy-duty stuff? Like the fence around Jackson Square?"

"Yes." I thought of the would-be dove hunter I'd seen stalking through the fence on the first day I'd arrived. "Something very much like that."

"That narrows it down some," she said. "Let's see. Let me get a map."

Belinda went into the other room and returned with a foldout map of New Orleans. She smoothed it out on the table and began outlining areas with a black marker.

"It's still a lot of the city," I said when she'd finished.

"Can't give up before we've started." She turned to Emma. "Read me the first address."

"Well, the first is for a Charles Preaux. Should we skip the men for now?"

"Good idea."

"Okay, let's see . . . the first woman listed is Diana Preaux." Emma recited the address and Belinda shook her head.

"She's in the Ninth Ward. What's the next one?"

Emma read the next address. Belinda nodded. "That's in the Garden District. Right through here somewhere." She ran her finger along a street.

Hugh used his phone to look up the exact location on the online map.

"Let me see," I said, and looked at the display. Finding the cross streets on the paper map, I put an *x* at approximately the right spot.

Once we got the rhythm of the search down, it took only an hour to go through and mark the names.

There were eight.

"That's still a lot of ground to cover," Emma said.

Belinda checked the time and said, "You'll have to do it without me. I've got a client coming in fifteen minutes."

"We'll figure it out," I told her.

"Yeah," Emma added. "We got this. Go be fabulous."

"No other way to be." Belinda flipped a lock of her wig over one shoulder and sauntered into her shop.

"Maybe we can find out how old these ladies are," Hugh suggested. "We're looking for a grandmother."

"Good idea," Emma said, leaning over to kiss his cheek with an exaggerated smack. "Let's do the math. If Grandma had a child at eighteen and they had a child at eighteen, we're looking at thirty-six years. How old is Ronnie?"

"She works in a bar," I said. "So she's over twenty-one."

"Okay, that puts us at fifty-seven or older, give or take a few."

"Still doesn't help us," Hugh said. "What are we going to do, call and ask how old they are?"

"We can give the list to Kai," I said. "Maybe his contact can look up their driver's licenses."

I tried calling him, but got his voice mail. I left him a message to call me and turned back to Emma and Hugh.

"We could search social media sites," Emma said. "A lot of grannies have Facebook pages."

It was better than doing nothing.

With everyone manning a smartphone or a computer, it took us another hour to eliminate four of the names.

"We're getting there." Emma stood and stretched.

I followed her lead. Moss took this as his cue to be taken out.

Walk?

"Heck, yes. I need a break."

"We all do," Emma said as she took her jacket off the back of her chair and shrugged it on.

"I'm in," Hugh added.

Kai called me back while we were on our walk. I told him about learning *mamere* meant grandmother and explained our hopes that tracking down the Preauxs would lead us to Ronnie's.

"I don't have the last four names with me," I said, "but I can text them to you when we get back."

"There might be an issue with that."

"What?"

"I'm off the case."

"Does that mean no more favors?"

"Not with the crime scene unit."

"What happened?"

"It's an interesting story. I'm not really sure how to answer. I'm on my way back to Belinda's now. I'll fill you in when I get there."

Kai Duncan—master of suspense.

We converged in Belinda's kitchen at almost the same time.

"Well?" I asked Kai as I pulled off my gloves and hat.

"It seems someone broke into the impound yard and contaminated the van by stealing its radio."

"What's that have to do with you?"

"I'm the only variable in the equation."

"Why would someone want a radio from a crappy cargo van?" Emma asked.

"That was my question," Kai said. "No one seemed to have a theory."

"I have one." I looked around, feeling it should be obvious. "It was Anya."

"Okay, but why would Anya want a radio from a crappy cargo?" Emma repeated her question.

"I don't know. But what are the chances someone would break into the police impound where I'm guessing there are plenty of other, more valuable cars—" I looked at Kai for confirmation. He nodded with a slight smile. "And target a beat-up van?"

"Exactly," Kai said. "Which brings us back to the question— why would she want the radio?"

"Maybe she left her favorite CD in the player," Hugh said.

"What kind of radio was it?" Emma asked. "Did it have GPS or anything?"

I looked at Kai, hoping the answer was no. The idea that we could have been so close to being able to track where Anya had gone was too frustrating to contemplate.

He shook his head. "It was nothing fancy. I remember noticing the radio was different—it was retrofitted with mismatched knobs—but I didn't pay much attention to the detail."

"Well, she wanted it badly enough to risk breaking into police property to get it," Emma said.

A contemplative quiet settled on the group. I was sure we were all doing the same thing—wondering what the hell was so important about that radio.

Finally, I said, "I'm still not clear on why you're to blame. The criminal who'd been driving the van came to the impound lot and broke into it."

"There's no evidence that it was Anya," Kai said.

"How is that possible?"

"Yeah," Hugh chimed in. "Aren't there surveillance cameras?"

"They were mysteriously disabled during the break-in."

"Seriously? Someone turned them off?" I asked.

"I didn't get the full story but it boils down to this: I showed up and everything went south—therefore, the best way to reestablish equilibrium is to get rid of me."

"Asinine," I said.

He shrugged.

"You don't seem very upset."

"I get it. I don't like it, but I get it. The good news, for now, is I'm still on good terms with Mike."

"That's the guy Jake introduced you to?" I asked.

"Yeah. He's in a different division, so we're okay for now."

"Good," Emma said. "Because we have a favor to ask him." She walked over to the kitchen table and grabbed the list we'd been working on. Handing it to Kai she said, "We need to know how old these four ladies are."

"You're hoping one of them is Ronnie's grandmother."

"It's a long shot but it's better than no shot."

"You're right. I'll call Mike and see if he can run the names."

Kai stepped out into the courtyard and returned a few minutes later with the information we needed.

"Two Preauxs match the race and age we're looking for." He handed me the list and pointed at the names. "Judy and Sylvia."

"Hugh and I could go to one address while you go to the other and have a look around," Emma suggested.

"Grace is the only one who would recognize anything."

"He's right. There's no point in all of us going."

"Okay," Emma said. "I had an idea when we were looking at the map earlier. You guys go and I'll see if I can get it to percolate into something useful."

Because Moss had not had adequate exercise in the last few days, he insisted on being included in our outing.

We stopped at a deli for a quick lunch and pulled up to Sylvia's house just after one. At first glance, it had all the right stuff. The foliage looked similar, as did the fencing. But one thing made me cross her off the list. "Brick pavers," I said to Kai. "Ronnie's grandmother was walking on brick pavers. This is all concrete."

We moved on to Judy Preaux.

I studied the wrought-iron fence as we pulled up. I couldn't be sure, but it was a close match.

"Are there pavers?" I asked, straining to see the walkway through the landscaping.

"Yep."

"Okay. Let's go talk to Judy."

Moss had gotten to share some of Kai's lunch and was happy to nap in Bluebell while we went to knock on the door.

The woman who answered didn't look old enough to be Ronnie's grandmother, but I asked about her anyway.

"I don't know anyone by that name," Judy said. "There are a lot of Preauxs around, though. You said she's missing?"

We both nodded.

"That's just awful."

I glanced at Kai. I wasn't picking up any deceit from the woman, but people weren't my forte.

"Thank you for your time, ma'am," he said, which told me he didn't think Judy was hiding anything, either.

I hadn't really expected to find Ronnie's *mamere*, but still felt deflated that we'd reached another dead end.

As we turned to go, there was a crash from somewhere inside the house. For a moment I thought we had been right and Anya or Barry was bursting through the back door, until I heard the barking.

Three Yorkshire terriers came charging out onto the front porch. They zipped around us, a whirlwind of jumping, yipping energy.

"Oh!" Judy exclaimed. "They must have knocked down the puppy gate again."

She managed to grab one of the dogs and scoop him up into her arms, but when she reached for a second puppy, he darted away.

Kai had more luck with the Yorkie bouncing around his feet. He caught the dog easily and we were left with one hyperactive canine to capture.

"Banjo, come here!"

The dog ignored his owner—he was having too much fun to stop the game.

Judy tried to grab the little whirling dervish but she was no match for him. I, on the other hand . . .

"Banjo." I spoke the name softly, but mentally added a dose of calm, dominant energy.

The dog paused, both intrigued and a little confused. He didn't know what to make of me.

"Come here." I squatted down. Banjo obeyed without hesitation and let me pick him up.

Judy stared at me in surprise. "How did you do that?"

"I have a way with animals."

Kai's phone rang. He handed the dog he'd been holding to Judy, excused himself, and walked down the porch steps to answer the call.

I headed inside with Judy, who couldn't carry all three dogs, and got them settled in their puppy play room.

As soon as I set Banjo on the floor, he began jumping at the gate.

"Behave, Banjo," Judy scolded gently.

She shook her head and murmured something under her breath that tickled the edges of my memory and made me ask, "What did you say?"

"Oh." She shrugged. "I called him some names. He doesn't speak Cajun so it doesn't hurt his feelings."

"*Possédé*," I said, suddenly remembering what Layla had called Ronnie. A *possédé* Preaux. I'd forgotten to ask Belinda about the word.

"*Possédé* means *crazy*," Judy said. "Well, maybe *naughty*'s a better word." She eyed Banjo. "Like a naughty, misbehaving *chien*."

"Would it be used as a nickname?"

"Maybe, but not a very nice one."

I wondered if the fact that Ronnie had been a *possédé* Preaux was significant. I asked Judy if she'd heard the phrase. She hadn't but offered to call some relatives to ask about Ronnie.

I gave her my card and headed out the front door just as Kai was ending his call.

His brows were knit, though I couldn't tell if he was angry, worried, confused, or none of the above.

"That was my contact from NOPD."

"What happened?" I asked. "Mike didn't blacklist you, did he?"

"No." Kai turned and started down the paved pathway. I walked next to him as we headed toward Bluebell. "He widened the search for information on Veronica, AKA Ronnie, Preaux."

"And got a hit?"

"It turns out she's from a small town about an hour south of here named Gallous."

"That's good, isn't it? We know where she's from. Maybe someone there will have information that can help us."

"Maybe. Her name came up because she was listed as a person of interest in a murder."

That stopped me. "What?"

Kai paused and turned to face me. "Her uncle, Sean Preaux, was killed."

"And she was a suspect?"

"The case is still open. Mike didn't have much information. If we want to learn more, we'll have to talk to the detective in charge of the case."

"In Gallous?"

He nodded. "What do you say? Are you up for a trip to Terrebonne Parish?"

CHAPTER 11

I called Emma to let her know Kai, Moss, and I were heading to bayou country and urged her to take the night off and do something fun with Hugh. She agreed a little too easily, which made me wonder if she'd actually do as I'd suggested.

As I steered Bluebell toward I-10, Kai called the police department of Veronica's hometown to make arrangements to meet with the detective who'd handled the investigation.

I was so focused on navigating around the Superdome to get to the on-ramp, I didn't hear his side of the conversation and was lost when he hung up and said, "Looks like we're headed into the swamp. Literally."

"What?"

"Detective Besson just retired. He's staying out at his fish camp, which, according to the deputy I spoke to, is in the boonies."

"Did you get directions to these boonies?"

I glanced at Kai. He was typing a number into his phone. "Nope. You can only get there by boat. But I set up an appointment to meet with the detective who took over the case."

We headed west on the interstate, and not far past the airport we turned onto highway 310, headed south. Instantly, the scenery changed. Apartment buildings and strip malls were replaced by marshland and cypress trees. The late-afternoon sun bathed the swamp in golden light and made the barren branches of the trees less stark.

We skirted bayous, passed plowed sugarcane fields, and drove through small, rambling towns with places advertising frog legs, turtle meat, and hog cracklin'. Moss sat up and sniffed. Bluebell's windows were closed, but that didn't matter to his canine nose.

Treat?

"No way, man."

"What?" Kai asked, looking over his shoulder at my dog.

"Moss wants to try some of the local cuisine."

"You never know—it might be tasty."

Tasty treat, Moss agreed.

"We'll get food on our way back," I said.

"I've noticed several gas station–casino combos," Kai said. "I bet one of them has a restaurant."

"We can get gas, play poker, and try some cracklin'?"

"When in Rome," he said.

After a while it was clear we were nowhere near Rome. Nor were we close to Gallous, Louisiana.

I can't say we got lost on our way to Ronnie's hometown, because we knew where we were, but here's the thing—knowing where you are and having a way to get where you want to be are two different things.

Which is a lot like life, come to think of it.

In any case, we ended up on the wrong side of the bayou. The detour added an hour to our travel time, which meant we were late arriving at the police station. I parked Bluebell under a huge oak tree and took Moss to stretch his legs and have a quick potty break. After loading him back into Bluebell, I lowered the windows enough for the nippy breeze to ruffle Moss's fur when he stuck his twitching nose out of the crack.

"I'll be back soon," I promised.

Knowing Moss would be fine until we got back, Kai and I headed inside for our delayed appointment. Detective

Bryant didn't seem too put out once Kai apologized and explained we'd gotten turned around.

"Easy to do, in these parts," the detective said as he showed us to his office.

The man was whip thin except for a perfectly round paunch that made him look about eight months pregnant. The guy hadn't given up on his receding hairline, though, and what was left of his dark hair ringed his skull like a furry horseshoe.

"Have a seat," he said as he walked around his desk to take his own chair. "I was told you're with the Jacksonville Sheriff's Office."

"I'm with the crime scene unit," Kai confirmed.

"And you?" He looked at me.

"I'm a consultant." It was true. I'd handled sticky animal situations for the JSO in the past.

Bryant focused his attention back to Kai, clearly waiting for confirmation that I was telling the truth. He nodded.

With a last glance at me, the detective asked, "You want to know about the Sean Preaux murder?"

"Informally," Kai said. "We're looking into another matter involving his niece Veronica."

"I heard she left town. Moved all the way to Florida, huh? Can't say I'm surprised."

"Why's that?" Kai asked.

"After all the trouble she stirred up . . . But that's what you're here to talk about, isn't it? Well, I'll tell you this—Ronnie and her brother Max are murderers, and that's a fact."

"You think they killed their uncle?" I asked.

The detective frowned at me. Maybe consultants were not supposed to ask questions.

"Ronnie knew where to find the body. Took us right to it," he said smugly. "What does that tell you?"

"Can you give us an overview, from the beginning?" Kai asked.

Bryant leaned back in his chair. "Sean went missing. After a few days, Ronnie came here, saying she knew her uncle was dead. When we asked how she knew—she wouldn't say. Every time we tried to get her help, she refused to cooperate."

"But if she was involved with the murder," I said, earning another frown from the detective, "why tell you about the body? It just makes her look guilty."

"I've been at this job awhile. And I can say this—criminals aren't half as smart as they think they are. And that's a fact."

"She just incriminated herself for no reason?" Maybe I was giving Ronnie too much credit, but it was hard to believe. Yes, criminals could be stupid, but still . . .

"Oh, there's always a reason. In this case, it was money." He gave Kai a you-know-the-story look. "Sean Preaux had an insurance policy for which his niece and nephew were the beneficiaries. What they didn't know was that if someone just disappeared, they'd get nothing. At least not until a death certificate was issued."

"She told you where the body was to make sure the terms of his policy were met," Kai said.

"Precisely."

"Where was he found?" Kai asked.

"In the bayou, fifty miles from nowhere."

For a moment I wondered if Nowhere might be the name of a town or if he was attempting the use of hyperbole.

"And her brother, Max," Bryant continued. "That boy has been arrested more times than I can count. And that's a fact."

"What was the COD?" Kai asked.

I'd gotten used to hearing Kai talk about cases and knew he was asking about the man's cause of death.

"The body wasn't in the best condition so it was hard to tell. But the coroner concluded it was drowning due to blunt force trauma." The detective looked at me. "Somebody hit him in the head and he drowned."

I could understand him wanting to speak in layman's terms for my benefit, but something about the way he said it made my hackles rise.

"Why weren't Ronnie or her brother ever charged?" Kai asked.

The detective's lips twisted in distaste. "She's got some hotshot lawyer boyfriend. Works for the district attorney. He's got a lot of connections. We gave them all the evidence we had—"

"But the DA decided not to file charges," Kai finished.

"You know how it goes."

Kai nodded. "Well, thanks for your time, Detective."

"Wait," I said. "Quick question—have you heard the name Anya Zharova?"

"No, why?"

"How about Dr. Barry Schellenger?"

He looked at Kai. "Is this about the Preaux murder?"

Kai answered, "No."

I said, "Possibly."

Looking somewhat miffed, Kai took out his phone and brought the photo of Anya up on the screen.

The detective studied the photo and shook his head, then did the same with Barry's picture. We thanked him a second time and headed out of his office.

"What?" Kai asked when he saw me shaking my head.

"That guy is a goober."

"Grace . . ."

"And he's full of himself. Which is a bad combination."

"Ahem." A man who'd been standing in the doorway we'd just passed said, "'Scuse me, miss."

I turned, ready to eat crow from some deputy who'd taken exception to my assessment of his boss, but the man standing in the doorway held a mop and was rolling a bucket of soapy water into the men's restroom. The name embroidered on his overalls was Walt.

Before speaking, he glanced down the hallway in both directions. "You should talk to Detective B if you want to know the truth about that Preaux business," he said.

I studied the janitor. Gnarled hands gripped the wooden

mop handle, and his wispy gray hair lay like a cobweb over skin as specked as a robin's egg.

Walt was no spring chicken, but intelligence radiated from his watery eyes.

"Detective Besson retired to a fishing camp," Kai said.

"He did, for true. But if you want to know what happened, you need ta find 'im."

"We'd have to have a boat," I said, remembering what Kai had told me about the remoteness of the fishing camp.

Walt shook his head. "Not just that. You'd need a guide. T. Paul's Swamp Tours. He'll get you there." Walt glanced down the hall and said more loudly, "I should be finished here in a few minutes, sir. Just have ta pass a mop over dese floors."

"That's okay," Kai said. "Thank you."

Walt nodded and set to mopping the floor. Before turning to follow Kai, I glanced over my shoulder and saw what had prompted Walt to cut our conversation short.

Detective Goober had stuck his head out of his office and was watching us.

I gave him a casual nod and bent to take a sip from the water fountain. I pressed the button, lips pursed and ready for the arcing stream of water. Nothing happened.

"It's broken," Goober said. "All the water fountains were disconnected after Katrina."

I straightened and nodded an awkward farewell, then turned to catch up with Kai.

"You could never be a spy," he said as we walked to where Bluebell and Moss were waiting.

"What are you talking about? I'd be a great spy."

"No, because the second someone told you, 'Don't look now!' you'd look, and that would be that. Cover blown."

"Whatever. I can talk to animals." I stopped to unlock the passenger side door and looked up at him in challenge. "Beat that."

He shook his head. "You can't do it from far enough away and you're prone to passing out afterward."

"I'd just need a partner to catch me."

"You've already got that."

I smiled at him and, because I didn't know what, if anything, he was insinuating, I quickly headed around to the driver's side.

Moss gave me a quick sniff as a greeting and wanted to know when I was going to make good on my promise.

Treat?

Not yet, buddy.

No treat?

Later.

With an audible sigh, my dog settled into the backseat.

"What do you think of Detective Goober's version of Sean Preaux's murder?" I asked as I started Bluebell's engine.

"Without looking at the case file and evidence it's hard to say."

"But do you think Ronnie might be one of the bad guys?"

"Detective Goober thinks so."

"Logan did grab her," I said, cranking the heater. "Maybe he had a good reason."

"Like what?"

"Maybe we've been looking at this the wrong way. Ronnie might be in trouble because she is trouble."

"So she deserves to be tied to a table and who knows what else?" Kai said.

"No, but—"

"Is this about you wanting to believe Logan's not such a bad guy?"

"What? No. I know Logan's a bad guy." As I said it, I remembered his words. *"Grace, please."*

"You're not a very good liar," Kai said.

"Maybe not, but I'm getting better." Not wanting to talk about Logan, I changed the subject. "What's the plan? Are we going to try to track down Detective Besson?"

"According to Walt, that's the only way to get the truth."

"Then let's find T. Paul's."

Kai used his phone to try and Google the tour company with no luck, so we stopped at a Frank's grocery store to ask about it. The clerk gave us directions and advised us to follow the gator signs.

Sure enough, we found the turn alongside a hand-painted sign featuring a smiling alligator wearing a straw hat. Under the gator were the words SWAMP TOUR and an arrow.

In smaller letters, crammed along the bottom, was a phone number.

I followed the signs while Kai called to arrange a tour with T. Paul. When he hung up he smiled and looked at me. "Looks like we're going on a romantic tour of the swamp."

"You really know how to spoil a girl."

"I do my best."

We came to a drawbridge and had to wait an eternity for a barge to pass, which meant it was almost dark by the time we made it to the dock where we were supposed to meet our guide.

There was no one in sight. Leaving Moss in the car for the moment so he didn't frighten anyone, we climbed out of Blue-bell and walked toward the mobile home closest to the water.

A woman holding a squirming toddler answered the door. "You the ones called about getting a ride down the bayou?"

"Yes. Sorry we're late," Kai said.

The woman flicked her gaze to me, shifted the child onto her other hip, and turned to call out, "T. Paul! Those people from town are here."

From inside, a man's voice responded in what must have been Cajun French. I didn't catch more than a few syllables, but the woman turned back to us and said, "You can go on around." She canted her head to the side of the house. We thanked her and headed in that direction.

Feet crunching on winter-dry grass, we walked toward the water. As we reached the small dock, the back door of the trailer banged open and a man wearing white rubber boots, overalls, and a faded green sweatshirt clomped down the steps and walked toward us.

"T. Paul?" Kai asked.

"That's me," the man said, and offered his hand. Kai took it, introduced me, and asked if we could still make it out to the fishing camp.

"Mai, yeah, we can try. Be dark by the time we get there, though."

"Not a problem for us, if it's not a problem for you."

"Me—no. You? Well, we'll see." With that cryptic remark, he moved past us onto the rickety-looking dock and began untying the smallest wooden canoe I'd ever seen. Although maybe *canoe* wasn't the right word, because it did have a small motor attached to the back with what looked like zip ties.

"We're taking that?" I asked.

"Water's too low for anything else. We have to take the pirogue."

It wasn't that I was afraid of the water. I grew up swimming in the Atlantic Ocean. But the bayou, though pretty with its cypress knees and moss-draped trees, was not something I wanted to get too close to. Tipping over and into the muddy water would not be fun—especially in January.

T. Paul saw me eyeing the murky water and said, "Don't worry—ain't nothin' in there to be afraid of. Unless you scared of a little ol' gator."

"I'm not afraid of alligators," I replied. Which was true. "But I'm not crazy about the idea of falling in that water. It has to be freezing."

He huffed out a laugh. "For true, it is! So don't fall in."

I wasn't sure if he was trying to be funny or simply poking fun at the city slickers. I imagined a little of both.

I glanced at Kai, who lifted a shoulder as if to say, *What else are we going to do?*

With a resigned nod, I fetched Moss from the car and joined Kai on the dock, where he waited as T. Paul climbed into the boat.

"Great God!" T. Paul jumped when he saw Moss standing on his pier.

"He's harmless," I said. And, except in situations involving his kitten or myself, for the most part it was true.

"Thought he was the *rougarou*."

"The what?" I asked.

"A werewolf."

"Are those common around here?" I asked.

"Some say so." He eyed my dog. "He's big for a pirogue."

"He'll sit wherever I tell him to."

"Put him up front, then."

"You got it." I had the feeling T. Paul was more concerned with keeping Moss as far away as possible than he was with his size.

Kai stepped into the boat and offered his hand to help me. I took it, then paused to let my dog know he was next.

Steady, Moss. You're coming, too.

Safe?

I promise.

With a firm grip on Kai's hand, I carefully climbed into the bobbing vessel.

Moss managed to wait until I was seated before clamoring into the boat, more specifically, my lap.

I let out an "oof" and grabbed him to steady us both.

Stay!

The boat bounced and listed to the side, but we managed to stay on board.

Dizzy.

You're not dizzy, I told Moss. *The boat is. Be still.*

Because he trusts me, he did as I asked and the pirogue settled.

So far, so good.

"You okay?" Kai asked.

I turned my face to the side to avoid getting a mouthful of Moss. "We're good. Let me just get him off me."

Okay, buddy, go this way. I focused on where I wanted him to sit. *Be easy.*

Moss understood "being easy" meant he had to tread

carefully. He took his time and moved to the front of the boat.

I nodded at T. Paul. He started the engine and we were on our way.

As we picked up speed, Moss positioned himself at the bow like a furry figurehead.

My nose and cheeks were numb with cold within minutes but Moss kept his nose into the wind. All the better to revel in all the unique scents of the bayou.

Basking in the glory of smells as only a canine could, he began to categorize each aroma in detail. The nuance of each was too layered and multidimensional for my poor human brain to understand. Rather than try to untangle and interpret his thoughts, I pulled my mental shield into place and tuned him out.

My interpretation was that the bayou was both teeming with life and eroding with decay.

Darkness came on quickly. Only a few minutes after sunset, we were motoring through the murky gloom of the bayou, and I could understand why you would want to avoid getting lost out here in the dark.

The naked branches of the cypress reached out like skeletal fingers. Logs and other debris bumped along the bottom of the small boat. The haunting beauty I'd observed earlier had morphed into my feeling simply haunted.

I shivered, as much from the eeriness as the cold night air.

As if sensing my unease, Kai moved to put his arm around my shoulder and pulled me close to his side. I felt myself relax a fraction. The feeling didn't last very long.

A moment later, the engine downshifted and abruptly cut off.

"Everything okay?" Kai asked.

"We're here," T. Paul said.

Kai and I glanced around. Out of the gloom I could see the vague outline of what might've been a wooden structure.

"Where's the dock?" I asked.

"Got washed away a while back."

The cold kept most of the bugs away, making the evening oddly quiet for a swamp.

We floated toward the fishing camp and, just as we started to push through the reeds, T. Paul stood, pulled a long paddle from the side of the canoe, and started poling through the marsh.

He stopped when the bottom of the pirogue scraped on the shore.

We were still surrounded by tall reeds and I wasn't sure how to disembark. Moss, however, had no problem either seeing in the dark or hopping off the boat. It was a good thing I didn't try to follow because a moment later a shotgun blast shattered the quiet of the cold night.

Before I could do so much as scream, Kai had pushed me to the bottom of the canoe and was lying on top of me.

"Moss!" I cried out for my dog and struggled to get up.

Kai held me fast and snapped, "Stay down."

Rather than waste time arguing with Kai, I opened my mind to my dog and urged him to crouch low in the reeds. *Down, Moss. Get down.*

I felt him comply. But to be sure he was safe, I slipped into his mind more completely and merged my senses to his.

Two things happened at once, neither of them helpful.

I could feel the shock of icy water on my belly. I could also see from his perspective, and though his night vision is much better than mine that helps only if you're not surrounded by a wall of reeds.

Shivering, I eased away from the connection and let his mind slip away from mine like beach sand through my fingertips.

Kai had noticed my sudden onset of tremors. "Are you okay?"

"Yeah, just cold."

There was a splash and T. Paul let out a string of curses. Most were Cajun but I got the gist.

"Nonc Will!" T. Paul yelled. "William Besson! Put that gun away, *couyon*!"

"Who dat?" A deep voice called back.

"T. Paul."

"T. Paul?" The voice I assumed belonged to Will Besson was full of doubt. "T. Paul'd know better. Sneaking up at night."

T. Paul said something else in Cajun I couldn't hope to understand and I tried to get my heart to slow down before it burst through my rib cage.

"I got some folks from town want to talk to you 'bout a murder."

"Murder?" There was a lengthy pause. "This a trick?"

"Nonc, who'd want to do that, eh? Now, put that gun away, or I'll tell Evangeline you tried to kill her favorite nephew."

There was a rustle in the bushes. Kai, who was still shielding my head with his arms, moved and slowly let me up.

I sat up to see an older man, standing spotlighted in the reeds to our left. T. Paul, who was shining the light, was soaking wet, standing knee-deep in the bayou to our right.

"Sorry," the man said. He lowered the shotgun to point it at the ground.

"Could have killed someone." Shaking his head, T. Paul stepped over to the boat and grabbed the bowline. "Hold on," he told us.

We did and he hauled the boat farther up onto the muddy bank.

"Thought you was the *rougarou*," Will said defensively.

Kai planted his hands on the side of the pirogue and hopped over the side.

"What is it with this *rougarou* thing?" I asked as Kai helped me out of the boat. My boots sank into the mud, but not too far.

"The *rougarou* is cursed. Part man, part beast," Will said.

"And it lives in the swamp?"

"It can live anywhere, because it can change shape." He nodded at Moss. "Your dog doesn't look much like a dog."

"He's part timber wolf."

Will nodded but continued to eye Moss suspiciously.

"Take them on up, Will. I've got to tie off here."

We followed as Will trudged through the reeds.

As it turns out, a Cajun fishing camp, at least in Will's case, is basically a cabin on stilts.

The rickety wooden staircase shook as Will started the climb to the cabin, and I took a moment to study him before following. A solid old guy with leathery, scarred hands that looked like they could bend nails, he was big in a way that spoke more of a life of hard labor and good genetics than an overabundance of time at a desk.

He was the polar opposite of Detective Goober.

"Come on in," he said, leading us through a screened porch into the cabin.

T. Paul stomped past us a moment later, muttering something about dry clothes, and disappeared into another room. Will ignored his nephew and continued into the kitchen.

"You can have a seat there." He motioned to a Formica-topped table ringed with three mismatched wooden chairs. We settled on opposite sides of the table, leaving the last chair for our host.

"I was just fixin' some gumbo," he said, stopping at the stove. He lifted a cutting board and used a large butcher knife to scrape chunks of meat into a pot. "Still has to cook though. Y'all want something else?"

"Detective Besson, we came to talk about—"

"A case." The old man waved the subject away. "I know, I heard what T. Paul said. But that boy don't understand. I'm retired. My memory, it's not so good, see."

"It's a fairly recent case," Kai began.

"How about some jerky?" Ignoring Kai's efforts to steer the conversation, the retired detective opened a mint green

Frigidaire that had to be as old as he was—and I was guessing Will was pushing seventy.

"Let's see . . ." he said as he rummaged around. "I got possum jerky. Some nutria." He turned and looked at Moss, then lifted his gaze to me. "Your dog like nutria?"

Treat?

"Probably. He'll eat anything."

"That so?"

Will unwrapped a package of dried meat and took it to the cutting board to chop off a chunk.

Still holding the knife, he turned to look at Moss. "They say you make a *rougarou* bleed it breaks the curse."

I narrowed my eyes.

Kai stood very slowly and took a step forward. The gesture was subtle but its meaning was clear.

If Will wanted to get to Moss, he'd have to go through Kai.

A surge of fluttering heat carrying a slew of unnamed emotions swirled through me. In that moment I knew the answer to Emma's question.

Did I love Kai?

Yes.

Before I could fully process that revelation, I noticed something odd. Though Kai was clearly tense, Moss was not. In fact, he was not feeling the least bit threatened. And it wasn't just the smell of food and his eagerness for a taste of whatever was cooking.

Something wasn't adding up.

"Put the knife down," Kai said. After a pause he tacked on, "Please."

"What?" Will glanced at the knife, seeming surprised to find he was holding it, then set it on the counter. "I don't mean no harm. I'm just telling the story of the *rougarou*."

When Kai didn't sit, Will picked up a piece of jerky, turned, and offered it to Moss.

"For true, I don't. Here. Come see."

Moss trotted forward. I wasn't worried. My dog was

much faster than Will. And I was watching—the slightest hint that he was going for the knife and I'd let Moss know to protect himself.

But Will fed Moss the jerky without incident. Kai relaxed and took his seat, and Moss finished his treat, licked his chops, and sat.

Treat?

"You're hungry, eh?"

Will fed him another bite.

"He'll eat you out of house and home if you let him," I warned.

Will chuckled. "Okay, go on now." He shooed my dog away. "Moss, come."

Reluctantly, my dog obeyed.

"We need to know about the murder of Sean Preaux," Kai said.

Picking up a long wooden spoon, Will stirred the pot of gumbo. "Oh? And why's that? He kin to you?"

"No—" Kai sounded frustrated so I decided to cut to the chase.

"We're interested in his niece, Ronnie. What was her involvement with the murder?"

"A good question, that. We never found out."

"Do you have a theory?" Kai asked, nearing exasperation.

Will didn't answer. In another part of the house, I heard water running. I guessed T. Paul had decided to take a shower.

Setting the spoon aside, Will adjusted the flame on the burner and came to sit at the table.

When he sat down I asked, "What does *possédé* mean?" Thanks to Judy and Banjo, I already knew the answer, but I wanted to see Will's reaction.

"Like *possédé* Preaux?"

I lifted my shoulder in a you-tell-me gesture. He smiled, looked at Kai, and said with a twinkle in his eye, "I like her."

"Me, too," Kai said, which brought a rush of heat to my cheeks and made me thankful for the dim lighting.

"Keeps you on your toes, huh?"

"You have no idea."

His comment earned a wry look from me and a hearty laugh from Will. Then he said, "*Possédé* means *possessed*, but not like you're thinkin'. Mostly, we'd say *possédé* and we're talkin' about a very bad child."

"So people around here think the Preauxs are bad?"

He made a noncommittal gesture. "For that family, maybe a better way to say it is *cursed*. See, every one of them comes into tragic times. Death, accidents, suicide, murder—that family lives under a cloud. Being touched, it comes with a price."

"Touched?"

"You know," he said, twirling his finger next to his temple.

"Crazy?"

Will shrugged. "Folks around here know—it's best to stay away from the Preauxs."

"What happened to Sean?"

"He was what we call a *traiteur*, a healer. He went missing for a few days. Nothing strange about that as he was prone to get the *thracas* to head off into the bayou on his own."

"*Thracas?*"

"You know, like a need or calling you can't fight. Anyways, nobody was too worried. Then, all of a sudden, here's Ronnie coming to the station sayin' her uncle's dead and askin' what we were gonna do about it. We asked how she knew he was dead and she tells us she had a bad feelin', is all."

"You didn't believe her," Kai said.

"Didn't know what to think. Then she tells us she can show us the body. Well, that caught our interest, for true."

"He was in the swamp, wasn't he?" Kai asked.

"Sure was. And Ronnie came very close to findin' the exact spot. There are miles of bayou out here. She got within thirty feet."

"You think she had something to do with his murder?"

"With that family, you just don't know. Ronnie, she's a

sweet girl. Always a little bit in her own world, I think, but no crime in that, eh?"

"So you don't buy into the murder-for-insurance-money theory?" I asked.

"Heh! You been talkin' to Detective Bryant."

Kai nodded. "He seemed to think Ronnie and Max were guilty."

Will made a derisive sound, leaned back in his chair, and crossed his arms over his wide chest. "He didn't tell you what really made his case against them fall apart, did he?"

We shook our heads.

"There was no insurance. None."

"Sean didn't have a life insurance policy?"

"Never even applied for one. And there's no evidence he talked about getting one—to anybody."

"That's quite a screwup on Bryant's part," Kai said.

"Dat man has no business with a badge."

"I agree," I said. "And that's a fact."

Will laughed.

"Here's what I think. It's tradition for a *traiteur* to pass their knowledge on to someone in the family. I think Sean was teaching Ronnie what he knew, and she might have been with him when he was killed."

"You think she was a witness."

Will nodded. "I tried to get her to tell me, but she wouldn't open up. Too scared, most likely."

"That theory works with what we know," Kai said. He took out his phone to show Will the photos of both Anya and Barry.

"These two might be involved. Have you seen them before?"

Will held the phone away, squinted, and stood up. "Need my glasses." Retrieving them, he came back to study the photos. "No. I don't think so."

"Why would someone want to kill Sean?" I asked.

"I asked myself that a thousand times. I don't know."

"Were they into shady stuff?"

"Sean and Ronnie?" He shook his head. "Her brother, Max, that's a different story. But like I said, that family has had a hard time."

Footsteps clomped through the fish camp and a few seconds later T. Paul appeared in the doorway.

"We got to get going soon, yeah?"

Kai nodded, and T. Paul headed out to get the pirogue ready.

"Speaking of Ronnie's family, do you happen to know her grandmother?"

"Josephine Preaux died years ago."

"Preaux. That would be her paternal grandmother, right? What about her mother's side?"

His expression changed slightly, seeming to close off for the first time since we'd arrived.

"I knew her. That woman"—he shook his head—"moved to town round the same time Josephine died."

"By *town* you mean New Orleans?" I wanted to confirm what I'd assumed, listening to T. Paul and his wife.

Will nodded.

I felt a surge of excitement. "Does she still live there?"

"Don't know. She changed her name when she left."

"To what?"

"Don't know that, either."

Damn! Just as we'd come close to learning something useful.

"What name did you know her by?" I asked.

"Why so many questions about her?"

"We think she might know how to reach Ronnie."

He shook his head. "Doubt it. The woman cut the whole family off when she left. Ronnie wouldn't have known how to get in touch with her. But if you want to take the chance, when she lived here her name was Arlise Dulac."

"Can you think of anyone who might know what she changed her name to?"

"One. But I don't think he'll talk to you."

CHAPTER 12

The person Will had been referring to turned out to be Ronnie's brother, Max.

T. Paul informed us the young man could be found in one of two places—jail or the Cat and Mouse Club.

We started with option two. Though it was getting late by the time we made it back to Bluebell, we decided to head to the area's one and only nightclub.

I'd expected a podunk, backwoods watering hole with a dusty parking lot dotted with a small spattering of pickup trucks. The only part of my expectation that turned out to be accurate was the dusty bit.

Cat and Mouse was a real nightclub, complete with beefy bouncers, laser lights, and blaring music.

The delighted shrieks of a dozen women sounded as we weaved our way inside.

After a second, I could see why. There was a male revue going on, and the dancer currently occupying the stage had just ripped off his tear-away motorcycle pants. After a few slow, rolling hip thrusts the dancer spun around, leapt into the air, and landed in a center split.

"Holy cow!" I said, with real admiration. Kai shot me a look. "What? The guy has talent."

"Yeah," Kai said, looking back to the stage where the dancer had moved onto all fours and begun gyrating wildly. "He's a real artist."

Rather than argue the merits of different forms of artistic expression, I decided to focus on the task at hand.

"How are we going to find Ronnie's brother?" The place was packed.

"Well," Kai said, raising his voice to be heard over the noisy crowd and pounding music. "It's about ten to one women to men, so it shouldn't be too hard."

Good point.

We headed to the bar and Kai leaned over to talk to the bartender. "Have you seen Max Preaux?"

"I'm looking at way too much of him right now." The guy raised his brows and looked pointedly at the stage.

"The stripper?" I asked.

"He goes by Mad Max," the bartender said. He seemed unimpressed with the name.

I exchanged a look with Kai and we headed toward the stage. At the steps leading into the sunken seating area, we encountered our first obstacle. A bouncer wearing a T-shirt at least two sizes too small barred our way.

I smiled and waited for him to unclasp the velvet rope separating the two areas of the club. After a once-over he obliged and I walked past. Kai, apparently, didn't pass muster. Before he could follow me, the bouncer reattached the velvet rope.

"He's with me," I told the bouncer—though it was obvious.

"Ladies only," the beefcake said.

"We need to speak to the dancer—it's important." I pointed to the stage. After glancing that way, I saw Max had waded into the sea of screaming women and was accepting tips.

"Ladies only," the bouncer repeated.

Kai reached into his back pocket and flashed his badge at the bouncer.

"Federal Agent Duncan—with the Special Investigations Unit," Kai said. He returned his ID to his pocket before the bouncer could get a very good look. "I need to speak to Mr. Preaux. If you insist on hindering my ability to do so, you will be interfering with a federal investigation."

The man's demeanor changed abruptly. He slid a glance toward Max, who'd noticed us and was watching intermittently as he moved among the tables.

I thought I heard the bouncer mutter something about *possédé* Preaux, but before he could unlatch the rope to let Kai pass, Max turned and bolted.

"Wait!" I yelled, charging after him. "Max, we just want to talk to you."

Ronnie's brother either didn't hear me or didn't care. He sprinted to the left of the stage and disappeared behind a thick, dark curtain. Figuring Kai was not far behind me, I followed. Without slowing down, I pushed through the curtain and ran down a narrow, dark hallway. Max had disappeared. My steps slowed but after a few seconds of indecision, I heard the hollow *thud* of a door slamming closed.

Gotcha!

Following the sound, I picked up speed, rounded the corner, and crashed through the back door. Breathing hard, I took a second to pause and scan the area. Luckily for me, the rear parking lot was well lit and it only took a moment to pick out Max's scantily clad form running along a row of vehicles.

Figuring he didn't carry his car's keys in his G-string, I took off after him.

Max was in good shape—he was fast. He was also barefoot, which gave me a slight advantage. When I reached the row he'd turned down, I called out again, trying to convince him to stop. Predictably, he didn't comply.

Why the heck was he running? For a moment I had a

glimpse of how cops must feel when they want to talk to someone and the person bolts for no apparent reason.

What had Max done? Was he involved somehow with
the disappearance of his sister? It was easy to become suspicious when people acted like suspects.

Speaking of cops, where was Kai?

A quick glance back at the exit door showed no sign of
him. For the moment, I was on my own.

I was going to have to figure out a way to catch Max or
at least get him to listen to me. Trying to anticipate his
trajectory was almost impossible. I didn't know Max or the
area. What I did know was if I could get Moss in on the
chase, Max wouldn't stand a chance. I considered trying to
herd Max around to the front of the building where Moss
(better be) patiently waiting, but I wasn't a border collie.

If you can't bring the mountain to Mohammed . . . I
focused as much of my energy as I could, while still running,
on extending my mind to connect with Moss.

Hey, big guy, can you hear me?

It was a stretch. My dog was on the other side of the
building, which put him at the very edge of my mental reach.
I sensed his energy and zeroed in on his location at the same
time as I projected where I was. I sent him the message:
Moss, come.

Even though our connection was tenuous, I felt his response
immediately. A heartbeat later, help was on the way.

Just when my quarry and I were running out of parking
lot, and I was wondering how far into the darkness we'd
make it before hitting water, Max stumbled. Hissing out an
inaudible curse, he hobbled a few more steps and stopped.

I jogged to a halt a few yards away and took a few seconds to catch my breath. A moment later, Moss charged out
of the darkness.

Steady, Moss. I didn't want my dog to tackle the poor guy.

Moss planted his paws, sending gravel and shells flying

as he skidded to a stop. Head low, ears pricked in readiness, he snarled at the shivering, nearly naked guy in front of me.

"*Arret toi!* I give up! I give up!" Max said, voice high with panic. "See? I stopped. I stopped."

My dog didn't change his aggressive posture. His growl continued to rumble. The cloud produced by his heated breath roiled out from between his bared teeth like smoke from a dragon's maw.

I have to admit, he looked pretty scary.

Max's eyes, round with fear, were glued to my dog's teeth.

I was just about to call Moss off when I realized I was standing at the far, dark end of a parking lot next to a panicked man who outweighed me by at least fifty pounds of muscle.

Good boy, Moss. Guard.

My dog obeyed.

"Stay right where you are," I commanded in my most potent I-am-alpha-bitch voice.

And guess what? Max obeyed, too.

"Ain't that something?" I murmured one of Belinda's favorite phrases.

"Please. Don't let him bite me!"

I glanced down and saw a smear of blood on the shells at his feet. Figuring the guy was no longer capable of escape and wouldn't be fast enough to attack me, I said, "That's enough, Moss."

Good boy.

"Is—is that the *rougarou*?"

I rolled my eyes. What was it with these people and the stupid werewolf?

"What do you think?"

"No?"

"No."

"Please—" Max didn't move, but he finally managed to pull his gaze from Moss to look at me. "I don't know where she is. Okay?"

"How do you know I'm looking for her?"

"She called me. Said she was being stalked by someone and told me if anyone asked about her, to tell them I didn't know anything."

"Is that true? You don't know anything?"

"Hand to God," he said, making the sign of the cross and raising his hand as if swearing on a Bible.

"When's the last time you talked to her?"

"A couple of days ago."

The heat generated from the run must have been wearing off because Max crossed his arms over his bare chest and shivered.

"Grace!" I heard Kai call out from somewhere behind me.

"Over here." I answered without taking my eyes off Max.

"Look, all I know is she told me to lay low."

"And this is your interpretation?" I motioned to his lack of clothes.

He gave me an aw-shucks grin that probably got him out of a number of tight spots as a kid.

Kai finally made it to where we stood. I glanced over at him and frowned. His hair was mussed; he had a smear of red lipstick on the corner of his mouth and another on his neck.

I felt my brows arch as my fingers curled into fists. I didn't like seeing another woman's lipstick on him. Not one bit . . .

Flicking my gaze over the rest of him, I noticed his belt was partly unbuckled.

Moss growled, mirroring my feelings.

Once I got over my initial spike of anger, I realized Kai looked a little shell-shocked.

"You okay, man?" Max asked Kai.

"I think it was a bachelorette party."

"Really?" I asked.

"It was like being attacked by, what's her name? Shiva? With all the arms?"

"Shiva's male," I said, a little more tartly than I'd intended. "So probably not."

Jealousy is not an emotion I've spent much time with. Probably due to the fact that I hadn't dated anyone in years.

The bizarre rush of burning anger made me feel stupid and immature.

Not wanting to dwell on those emotions, I decided to focus on Max.

"Do you know someone named Anya Zharova?" I asked him.

"No."

Kai brought the photo of her up on his phone and presented it to Max.

He shook his head. "Never seen her. And I'd remember— she's hot."

"What about a Dr. Schellenger?"

He shook his head. "Are these the people after Ronnie?"

"Yes, and they are dangerous. If you see either of them, call the police."

I knew Kai's advice would fall on deaf ears.

"Right," Max snorted. "Like the cops give a shit about me."

I could imagine the police investigation targeting him and his sister for their uncle's murder had left him reluctant to trust the police. I'd recently been on the receiving end of some overzealous cop-ness.

It was no fun.

I knew Kai wouldn't like what I was about to say, but Max needed to understand how serious the situation was. "You're right, the cops probably don't care much for you. But I can almost guarantee they don't actively want to hurt you, either. I can't say the same for the people looking for your sister."

Kai took his wallet out of his pocket and started fishing around in it. "I have a friend on the New Orleans PD. Let me find his card . . ."

Something in Kai's wallet caught Max's attention. "Wait—are you a cop?"

"No," I said.

Kai said, "Yes."

Max's face became completely closed off. I could have killed Kai for making such a mistake.

"I've gotta get back to work," Max said. "Getting the frissons out here."

He started to limp away.

"Wait," I called out. "We need to get in touch with your grandmother." When he ignored me and kept hobbling toward the club, I added, "She might be in danger."

He stopped to look at me. "Why? Who'd want to hurt an old lady?"

"Think about it. First, your uncle is killed. Now Ronnie is missing. If someone is targeting your family, your grandmother has to be warned."

I could almost see smoke coming out of his ears from the effort his brain was making.

Finally, he nodded. "Okay. I'll call her."

"What?"

"You said someone has to warn her. I'll go call her right now."

I looked at Kai. It was tough to argue with his logic.

"Good idea," Kai said. "Grace is a doctor. She can take a look at your foot and you can call your grandmother."

Max looked dubious. He didn't trust Kai, but his foot was bleeding pretty badly. "You're a doctor?"

"Yep." Technically, I was a veterinarian but I assumed Kai had a plan to get Ronnie's grandmother's name, so I went with it. "I'll get my first aid kit and meet you inside."

A few minutes later, I'd put Moss in Bluebell, grabbed my first aid kit, and was standing at a door marked DRESSING ROOM.

It opened before I could knock, and a man dressed as a cop—well, if cops wore skintight uniforms—nodded at me and walked past.

I hesitated. I didn't really want to waltz into a men's dressing room. Then I heard Kai say, "Come on in, Grace, the coast is clear." I took him at his word and headed inside.

Max had donned a pair of sweatpants and a long-sleeved

shirt. He was sitting in a folding chair with his injured foot propped up on a stool and was holding a cell phone against his ear. He looked to be waiting for someone to answer.

"Mamere, it's Max." He paused and, with a furtive glance at Kai, continued in Cajun French.

I didn't know if Kai understood anything the man said, but I sure didn't.

Max hung up and said, as if we hadn't noticed, "I had to leave a message on her machine."

Kai nodded and looked at me. "Think you can patch him up?"

"Sure." I squatted to take a look at the wound. It wasn't a deep cut but it was long and jagged. "Well, it's not too bad. But you won't be dancing on this foot for a little while."

"Really?" He bent forward to look at his injury. As he did, he set his phone down on the counter next to him. Out of the corner of my eye, I saw Kai lean toward the phone.

"Yep," I said, pointing at the ball of Max's foot. "See that? You almost cut a tendon."

He hadn't, but I was trying to buy Kai some time.

"Damn," Max said, squinting at his foot.

Kai used the distraction to his advantage and silently tapped the screen on Max's phone. He then used his own phone to take a photo of whatever was on the display. An instant later, he'd turned back to watch me work.

Clever.

I had to bite my lip to hide my smile.

"You got the number?" I asked a few minutes later when we were leaving the club.

"Yep."

We climbed into Bluebell and by the time we were pulling out of the parking lot, he was calling Ronnie and Max's grandmother.

Her name turned out to be Hattie Hallowell, a fact gleaned from her answering machine message. After a call to Mike, Kai's contact at the NOPD, we had her address.

Kai checked his watch. "It'll be close to midnight by the time we make it back to New Orleans. Should we wait till morning or do a drive-by?"

"Drive-by," I said.

"Then we're headed to the Garden District."

* * *

"This is it." I pointed to the fence running along the sidewalk. "I recognize the wrought iron."

Coco had been right about that but failed to mention the creepy factor. Hattie's enormous house looked like it belonged on the set of *The Addams Family*.

"Cut the engine," Kai said.

I did and we sat in the quiet for several long moments.

"What do you think?" I asked. "Should we wake her up to warn her about Barry and Anya?"

"Maybe. Let's take a quick look around," he said.

"So our drive-by is now a stop-by?"

He shrugged. "We're already here."

"Still, I don't want to scare a little old lady by traipsing through her garden in the middle of the night."

"If she's home," he countered. "Max and I both called and got no answer."

"Listen to you. I take you out of your jurisdiction and you're ready to break all the rules."

"Well, not all of them. Come on."

Moss had to water the bushes anyway, so we had an excuse to be walking around. As nonchalantly as possible, the three of us moseyed up the driveway leading to a detached garage at the rear of the property. We paused when we reached the backyard. The house was quiet, without a single light on anywhere. Still, it didn't quite feel empty.

"Maybe I'm just creeped out by this place but I get the feeling we're being watched," I said.

"Stay here with Moss. I'll go knock."

He walked to the back door and pounded on it as only cops can. There was no response. Kai knocked again. Nothing.

He gave up and came back to where Moss and I stood. "Any of Coco's littermates around?"

I cast my feelers out as far as possible. "There's a dog in the house behind us. Other than that, I'm not picking up much."

"How about Moss? He hear anything we can't?"

"I'll check. It might take a minute."

That was an understatement. Because Moss did, in fact, hear plenty of things we couldn't.

In that moment he was picking up a high-pitched beeping sound I guessed was a microwave, the rumbling swish of someone's washing machine, a distant train whistle, and the hollow *ticktock* of a clock. I filtered through everything to the best of my ability, but nothing stood out. Then the creak of a wood floorboard caught my attention.

I was sure it came from inside Hattie's house.

"I think someone's here." I pointed to the third story. "Top floor."

We watched for signs of movement.

Nothing happened. Maybe it was the creepiness of the house or all the earlier talk of the *rougarou*, but the longer I stood there, the more uneasy I felt. Goose bumps rose on my arms and fluttered up the back of my neck.

"I'm getting the heebie-jeebies," I said, unable to suppress a shiver.

"Okay, let's go."

As we emerged from the driveway onto the sidewalk, I noticed a man standing near Bluebell. At first, I thought he was waiting for us, but he started walking away as we approached. I squinted at his retreating figure.

"What is it?" Kai asked when he saw I was staring at the man.

"That guy"—I pointed as he turned the corner—"I swear I've seen him before."

"Where?"

"I don't know. There's something about the way he walks. It's familiar."

"Barry?"

"Too tall. And his shoulders are too wide."

"Logan?"

It was possible. But . . . "No. Moss knows Logan's scent." I double-checked with my dog—I was right, he wasn't the Ghost.

Then it hit me. The way he walked. With a slight hitch in his step.

"It's him. The man Coco saw with Anya. He had a limp."

We scrambled into Bluebell and sped down the block and around the corner.

He was gone.

CHAPTER 13

I fell into bed around one in the morning, fearing I'd dream of haunted houses, werewolves, and mysterious strangers lurking about.

Instead, thanks to Voodoo's purr-power, I dreamt of being cocooned in soft white dog fur and playing tag on an endless staircase with two equally furry, though not as large, friends.

It made for a good night's sleep, and I woke the next morning feeling better than I had in days.

I still needed coffee to get my brain working.

As I was dozing, and wishing for a cup of java, there was a knock at the door.

I opened my eyes to see Emma enter the room. She held a mug of what my nose told me was coffee in one hand and had Elvis tucked to her chest with the other hand.

I sat up to accept the cup.

"Belinda said you'd be awake."

"From now on, we're only staying at bed-and-breakfasts owned by psychics."

"Fair enough."

"I see Elvis is still working his charms on you."

Emma gave me a flat look. "I'm afraid I'll step on him if I don't pick him up."

"Uh-huh." I winked at my sister. "Keep it up, buddy," I said to Elvis. "Her resolve is weakening."

Elvis tried to lick Emma's chin but she angled her face away.

Kisses!

Atta boy.

Emma set Elvis on the bed and dusted off her hands. "We got a lead on the monkey."

The little dog hopped over to greet Moss.

"Yeah?" I sat up, suddenly feeling more awake.

"Well, it's not a lead. More of a workable theory," Emma said. "I remembered you telling me about the homeowners' association president who was complaining about the monkey so I decided to give him a call—"

"You talked to the crabby old dude?"

"I did."

"How much did he remind you of Mr. Cavan-ass?" I asked, referring to our crotchety old neighbor back home in Ponte Vedra.

"Brother from another mother," she said.

"Didn't I tell you they could be twins?"

"Anyway," she continued, "it turns out he was keeping track of all the monkey sightings. From the very beginning."

My sister seemed to be waiting for me to get where she was going, but I wasn't caffeinated enough.

"Meaning?"

"Come on, you need more coffee. Then I'll show you what I'm talking about."

I looked at my mug. Empty.

"This mug has a hole in it," I told my sister as I climbed out of bed.

She made a dubious *mmmmm* sound.

I picked Elvis up as Moss hopped off the bed and trotted to the door.

Walk?

Moss was talking to my sister.

"Yeah, I guess I can take you out," Emma said.

"Hey, you're getting good."

"It doesn't take a psychic to know he's got to pee. Come on, fur face."

I grabbed a quick shower and got dressed while Emma took Moss out. Drying my hair always took forever, so by the time I made it downstairs, they were back and breakfast was on the table. My sister and Kai were the only ones in the room.

"Where is everyone?" I asked as I poured more coffee into my mug.

"Belinda is getting ready for a big group reading this morning at the casino. Hugh went to stretch his legs. I think the idea of spending the morning reading through all the monkey sightings and looking at a map gave him cabin fever."

"I can help with the monkey map," I said, taking a seat at the table. Belinda had made pancakes and I forked a couple onto my plate. "But first, I'd like to go back to Hattie's place. If she still isn't home, we can leave her a note or something." I turned to Kai. "Maybe that guy from last night will show up and we can get a good look at him."

"What guy?" Emma asked.

"There was a man in front of Hattie's house," Kai said.

"It was the same guy I saw the other day near Ronnie's apartment," I added.

"How can you be sure, if you didn't get a good look?" Emma asked.

"When Kai and I went to Ronnie's, I asked Coco about Anya. The cat didn't tell me much, but she did show me Anya walking around the apartment. Just as she was leaving I saw this guy meet up with her."

"What happened?"

"Coco was inside, watching out the window, so I couldn't hear what they were saying."

"You think he might be working with Barry and Anya?"

"I think it's likely," I said.

"I've been wondering—why is everyone so interested in Ronnie and her family?" Emma asked. She held up her hand and began counting off names with each finger. "We have Logan, Barry, and Anya, and now this mystery guy."

"Uh-oh," Belinda said, breezing into the room. "We already have a mystery monkey, now there's a mystery man?"

I smiled when I got a good look at what she was wearing: jeans, high-heeled black boots with fringe, and a bright red sweater adorned with a pair of sequined lips on the front. Her lips were as red as the sweater and today's blond wig was only half as high as the red one from the day before.

"What you grinning at, *cher*?"

"You're going casual today?"

"Ain't nothing casual about Belinda. But I do have to tone it down for some parties."

"Just remember," Emma said, "you can turn it down, but you can't turn it off."

Belinda high-fived my sister and went to the fridge. Opening it, she pulled out a smoothie container and took a sip of what looked like green mud.

"What is that?"

"Superfood. I like to keep my body clean before a big reading. Now," she said, coming to sit, "what were y'all saying about a mystery man being after Ronnie?"

"We think he's working with Anya and Barry," I said. "And when we went to Gallous, we might have found out why they're after her."

"It's possible Ronnie witnessed her uncle's murder," Kai said.

We took turns telling them what we'd learned from Will and the not-so-sharp Detective Bryant.

"That explains why they'd want Ronnie, but what about Hattie?"

"I've been thinking about that," Kai said. "It's possible that Ronnie went on the run, found her grandmother, and gave her something that implicates Barry and Anya in Sean Preaux's murder."

I nodded. "They might plan on killing Ronnie, but first they have to make sure Hattie's not a threat."

"Okay, I understand that, but why kill Sean Preaux?" Emma asked. "According to the retired cop, he mostly kept to himself, right?"

"Right," I said as another question occurred to me. "And how would they have gotten involved with one another? Anya's Russian. Until recently, Barry worked out of state. Something has to have brought them together."

"Ronnie's brother, Max, seems to be into some shady stuff," Kai said. "I'll call Mike, my contact at NOPD, and ask him to check him out. See what he's been involved in."

I let out a slow breath. "It seems like all our questions lead to more questions."

"At least you found out who Ronnie's *mamere* is," Emma said. "That's one less thing to worry about."

"Was it one of the Preauxs from the list?" Belinda asked.

"Not a Preaux at all. Her name's Hattie Hallowell."

"Hattie Hallowell?"

"You know her?"

"There used to be a psychic who went by that name."

I looked at Kai. No one had said anything about Hattie being psychic.

"What do you mean 'used to be'?"

"I'm not sure what happened but she closed up shop years ago. One day she's the toast of the town, the next, she becomes a recluse."

"I wonder what happened," I said.

"And if it has anything to do with what's going on today," Kai added. "Maybe the reason the family's being targeted doesn't have anything to do with Max or Ronnie and everything to do with Hattie."

"Let's go see what we can find out." I looked at Emma. "You okay working on this?" I gestured to the foldout map.

My sister nodded. "Hugh has promised to help go through the reports and cross-check the sightings. If we have a breakthrough, I'll call."

• • •

Hattie's place wasn't nearly as spooktacular during the day.

Instead of looking haunted, it simply looked run-down.

I've never had my sister's artistic eye, but even without any aesthetic prowess, I could see that with a coat of paint and a little—okay, a *lot*—of fixing up, the house would be a showplace.

We rang the front doorbell and waited. Then rang it a second time.

I tried to peek inside through the front window but couldn't find any gaps in the curtain.

Kai tried the door handle. It was locked, of course.

"Let's try around back," he said.

That door was also locked.

Kai reached up and ran his hand over the top of the door's casing. "We might get lucky and find the key."

"Again?" I doubted Hattie was as careless as her granddaughter when it came to spare-key hiding, but started looking anyway.

Then I thought of something.

"If you witnessed a murder and knew people might be after you, would you put your key outside like Ronnie did?"

"No, but the landlord might. I had one once who required you keep a spare key outside."

"Really?"

"He also charged you a hundred bucks if he had to come unlock your apartment."

"Sounds like a nice guy." I returned to the search for a key. After ten minutes of turning over every clay pot, loose brick, and anything else that might hide a key, we gave up.

"There might be a side door that's unlocked."

We traipsed around the enormous house and found not only a side door, but an attached greenhouse.

The windows of the glass structure were coated with grime. Ivy climbed up and over the roof, engulfing it in a nebulous mountain of green.

Brushing the vine out of the way, I tried the glass-paneled door and shook my head. Locked.

"There," Kai said, pointing to the lower outside corner of the greenhouse.

The glass pane at the very bottom was missing.

We looked at each other for a long moment.

It was one thing to find a door open and walk inside, but crawling through a missing window took things to another level.

"Maybe you shouldn't be doing this," I said. "I'm sure the Jacksonville Sheriff's Office frowns on its investigators breaking and entering."

"Whoever Cornelius saw on that table was being tortured, right?"

"Right," I said, understanding his point. "I'll go through and see if I can unlock the door." I squatted down and, careful to avoid any stray shards of glass, ducked under the metal frame and crawled into the greenhouse.

It took some doing, but I managed to turn the rusty lock and force the door open.

"Let's hope those are unlocked," Kai said.

I looked at the set of French doors leading into the house.

"Cross your fingers," I said, and grasped the handle. It turned easily and swung open with a gentle creak.

From the outside the house looked abandoned. On the inside it just looked . . . preserved.

The doors from the greenhouse led to a large room that looked as if it had been used as an extended pantry–garden shed combo. A large farmhouse sink sat to one side, flanked by rows of shelves stocked with every size of canning jar imaginable. On one wall there was a long wooden table stacked with a variety of clay pots.

"Hello?" I said as we moved through the room and stepped into the main house. I doubted anyone was there, but didn't want to frighten Hattie if she was.

"Miss Hallowell?" Kai called out. His voice carried a lot more than mine and I felt sure that even if Hattie was hard of hearing, she'd know we were there. We listened, but there was no answer. No sound at all.

"Maybe she got Max's warning and took off," I said as we walked through the dim interior.

"Maybe," Kai said. "But I get the feeling Hattie's not the taking-off type. Look at this place."

I did. Everything was tidy, with only a light layer of dust, but somehow it felt like nothing in the room had been used for years.

We moved through a formal parlor and library and finally, into the kitchen.

"If Hattie isn't here, where is she?" I wondered aloud.

The most obvious answer was that we were too late.

"Someone's been here," Kai said after opening the refrigerator. "The produce is still fresh."

"So either Hattie very recently left or was very recently taken."

Kai used the sleeve of his jacket to lift the lid on the garbage can. "Look at this."

"It's a broken plate," I said.

"That used to hang on that wall." He pointed to the far end of the kitchen.

"And?"

"These old platters are heavy. People usually use heavy-duty hangers to put them up." He walked to the wall and studied it.

I followed his lead but didn't see much more than a vague outline of a large platter, no nail or hook of any kind.

"How was it on the wall? I don't even see a hole where a nail would have been."

"These walls are plaster. A lot of people use a picture rail to hang things," Kai explained, pointing to a piece of trim running along the wall about a foot below the crown molding.

I remembered seeing it done before in older homes. "Right—they use a cord and a special hook."

"It would take a good bit of force to send a platter swinging far enough to dislodge the hook."

"Maybe Hattie was moving the platter and dropped it," I suggested.

"It's possible but I don't think so." Kai leaned close to the wall and angled his head to look at it at a more acute angle. "See this?" He pointed at a smudge in the paint. "It looks like the platter impacted the wall and then was scraped sideways."

I nodded, understanding the scenario he was seeing. "If you're Hattie, and you're running away from someone coming in the back door, and you stumble . . ." I mimed the movement as I spoke. "You could have crashed into the platter."

"Exactly."

I didn't like the idea of someone chasing a grandmother in her own home, but it made sense.

"Let me record this, in case we need it later." Kai took out his phone and began taking a video. Every once in a while he'd say something technical out loud—clearly for posterity and not for my benefit, because I had no idea what he was talking about. It looked pretty official so I stayed out of the way and kept quiet.

When he finished he turned to me and said, "Let's check upstairs."

We went through the house room by room. Only one bedroom looked like it had been used in the last decade. Finally, we made it up the stairs to the third floor, but were stymied by yet another locked door. Kai used the flashlight on his phone to inspect the doorjamb.

"The dust is pretty thick here. So are the cobwebs," he said. "No one's been up here in a while."

I thought about the feeling I'd had the night before—that strange instinct that I was being watched from somewhere on this level of the house—but decided it was probably just nerves.

"Now what?" I asked as we headed back downstairs. I'd really been hoping our expedition would give us something to work with.

"We head back to Belinda's and try to get a lead on Cornelius."

"You think my sister's map idea will work?"

"I think it can narrow down the area to search. Most of the city is a grid. It will take time, but if we can section off a few pockets where Cornelius might be, we can drive the grid and might get lucky and find him."

"I keep wondering what I've missed. Cornelius has obviously found a warm place to sleep at night. I keep thinking that's how he stumbled on Barry and Anya's House of Horrors. But he never showed me anything that will help us figure out where. I just wish his memories weren't so difficult to make out."

As we reached the bottom floor Kai stopped and faced me.

"Grace, listen. I know you believe Belinda's reading is true, and I'm not disputing it, but you can't put too much pressure on yourself. You're doing everything you can to help Ronnie and Hattie."

I pulled in a slow breath and nodded. I hadn't realized until then how much stress I'd been putting on myself.

"Okay, let's find the Mystery Monkey."

• • •

Kai dropped me off in front of Belinda's and went to park Bluebell in the lot. I stepped through the courtyard door into the kitchen, expecting Moss or, at the very least, one of the Pomeranians to greet me. But I found Emma sitting at the kitchen table alone. She looked up from the monkey map. "Hey, any luck?"

I shook my head, shrugged out of my borrowed jacket, and hung it on the back of one of the chairs.

"You?" I walked to check the coffeepot, hoping for some steaming brew. There was some left—yay!

"I'm making progress," Emma said.

I poured the remaining coffee into a mug and went to look at the map.

"Heck yeah, you are," I said. There were a number of red and black dots all over the paper.

"I decided to number the sightings starting with the earliest and color-code them. Red is a confirmed sighting. Black is a maybe."

"Em, this is great." I could see three areas on the map with a distinctly higher number of dots clustered together.

"What's this?" I asked, pointing to a black triangle to the far right of the map.

"That is possibly the very first sighting."

"It's nowhere close to the others."

She nodded. "I looked it up on Google Earth—there's not much in the area aside from some swamps and the interstate."

"Then who reported seeing Cornelius?"

"It was a 911 call from a motorist. Here—the cop working the case sent me a copy of the audio." She hit a few keys on her laptop to bring up the file and pressed play.

"Nine-one-one. What's your emergency?"

"Hi . . . Um . . . This is gonna sound weird, but I'm on the I-10 and I swear I just saw a monkey run across the road in front of me."

"A what?"

"A monkey."

"Okay, sir, you're saying you saw a monkey in the road?"

"Yes, ma'am. Around mile marker . . . I'm just passing two forty-seven and it's been a couple miles back east."

"Okay, sir, we will send someone to check it out."

When the call ended, my sister said, "On the plus side, the guy doesn't sound drunk or crazy but . . ."

"It could have been anything running across the road. What time did the call come in?"

"Just before nine p.m. Which is why I'm not able to put this as a confirmed sighting."

"It was dark."

"It did make me wonder, though," Emma said.

I thought I knew what she was going to say and my heart sank. "Someone could have dumped him by the side of the road."

"Poor thing, can you imagine?"

I could. Sadly, people could be pretty heartless when it came to animals. I thought about Anya and how she'd been ready to shoot Coco just to slake her frustration.

"Did you ever hear back from Layla?"

"Yep. She's got Coco at her place and is steering clear of Ronnie's apartment."

I blew out a breath and felt a little less tense. One animal safe. Now I just had to find a monkey and save a woman, and probably her grandmother.

I straightened, took a sip of coffee, and focused on the map.

"Looks like the hot spots are in Uptown," I said.

"Yep," my sister said. "Here and here"—she pointed—"and possibly here, in the Garden District. I say 'possibly' because there are a lot more 'maybes' than confirmed sightings so far in that area."

"I thought Hugh was helping you go through the reports."

"He was. He took the dogs for a walk. Though now that it's past noon, I'm guessing he's using them as an excuse to go to Fay's Fried Chicken."

"Again?"

"The man has a problem."

"Maybe Fay adds crack to the breading."

Emma shook her head. "It's cooked in bacon fat, which is pretty much the same thing."

I wouldn't know, as I didn't eat chicken or bacon. My elementary school class visited a petting zoo when I was seven. Since then, I've been reluctant to eat things I can have conversations with.

I opened the fridge and froze when I saw the container of baby kale and carafe of homemade dressing. Eyes wide, I turned to my sister. She was grinning. "You're making the kale salad?"

"That's what Belinda had to go get. I forgot to grab organic sunflower seeds when I went to the store earlier."

My sister, who tended to use as many organic ingredients as possible, was trying to get me to nix processed foods—like doughnuts.

I can tell you this—if anything could get me to eat healthy it would be this salad. It was that good.

The chimes on the shop's front door sounded. I knew it wasn't Hugh and the dogs, since I would have sensed the canines, or at least heard Moss's tags jingle.

When Belinda didn't appear in the entry to the kitchen, Emma said, "Better go see if it's a customer."

She stood and hurried into the shop. A moment later I heard my sister say, "I'm sure Belinda will be back any minute. If you want to have a seat or look around, I'll bring you some coffee."

A man's voice replied, "That would be great. Thank you."

I winced inwardly, because I'd just swallowed the last of the coffee.

My sister walked into the kitchen as I was lowering the cup from my lips.

"Sorry," I said, setting the mug on the counter. "I can make more."

Emma nodded. "I'm going to take him some scones. Just bring the coffee out when it's ready."

I did as she asked. Thankfully, Belinda's coffeemaker

was pretty quick and let you remove the carafe without spillage. As soon as I could, I poured a cup, grabbed the cream and sugar containers, then tried not to drop anything as I hurried into the shop. The man was standing near the bookshelf. Emma stood to his left and was saying, "Belinda is very good. I promise you'll be glad you waited."

"Fresh coffee," I said.

The man turned, saw I was juggling three ceramic containers, and took a few steps toward me to take the mug.

I froze.

He was limping.

I shot a wide-eyed glance at my sister. Emma frowned at my expression, her eyes narrowing as she watched him move. She raised her gaze to meet mine and mouthed the words, "Is this the guy?"

I started to nod but something under his jacket caught my attention.

I shouted, "Gun!" and tried to fling the coffee in his face, but he managed to sidestep, and everything, including the cream and sugar, went flying past his head.

The guy was too fast for me, but he wasn't so lucky with Emma.

Before he managed to do much more than look surprised, my sister had taken him to the ground—hard.

He let out a grunt but recovered quickly. Shifting his weight, he tried to roll onto his back, but Emma was ready.

Moving like an octopus she wrapped her legs around his waist and snaked her arm around his neck.

"Say good night, sweetheart," she said quietly in his ear.

He couldn't, of course. The pressure on his carotid artery and vocal cords prevented anything more than a strangled gasp.

There's a reason it's called a sleeper hold. In seconds, he was out. Emma released him slowly and he slumped, motionless, to the floor.

That was when the shop's door chime sounded.

I turned, ready to spin an elaborate lie for whatever

customer was unfortunate enough to have stumbled upon the aftermath of our skirmish and heard, "Sweet Holy Mary Mother of Jesus, what is this?"

"Belinda, it's you!" I said. The wave of relief hit me so hard I was almost giddy. I realized I was smiling like a deranged lunatic and tried to calm down. "This is the guy."

She turned, and for a moment I thought she was going to bolt, but instead she engaged the lock on the shop's door and flipped the sign to read CLOSED.

"We'll explain in the kitchen," Emma said. "Grab his legs."

I'll give her this, even though she looked scared out of her wits, Belinda hesitated for only a moment before hurrying to do as asked.

"I didn't see this coming," she muttered as we carried our burden down the hallway. "Why didn't I see this coming?"

"Put him on the chair," Emma directed once we'd made it into the kitchen. "We need something to tie him up with. I don't want to have to hold him while we talk."

"Got it." Belinda rummaged through her ginormous purse and pulled out two silk scarves and pair of fur-lined handcuffs.

"What?" she asked, seeing my arched brows.

"Nothing."

Emma took the cuffs with a shrug, and I worked on tying his ankles to the legs of the chair.

"Somebody tell me what's going on before I have a heart attack," Belinda said.

I went through what happened as quickly as I could.

"A gun?" Belinda looked horrified. "I do not like guns. Where is it?"

She looked like the idea of seeing a gun might make her faint.

"It was under his jacket," I said.

Emma checked and shook her head.

"It must've fallen out." I hurried into the shop and stopped when I saw what was on the floor. "Crap!"

"What is it?" Emma called from the other room.

I walked back into the kitchen and said, "Um . . . I may have jumped the gun a little. No pun intended."

"A cell phone?" Belinda's eyes widened as she stared at what I was holding in my hand.

"Grace . . ." Emma blew out a slow breath and closed her eyes.

"Sorry. But look at it. He's got to be a bad guy with a phone case like that." I handed her the phone. It was encased in a bulky, brushed aluminum frame with black rubber trim.

"It looks like the grip on a Smith and Wesson, right?" I said. "If you turn it, kind of to the side."

"Really?" Emma held up the phone to illustrate how much it *didn't* look like a gun.

"Hey, he's in cahoots with Anya. My assumption was justified."

"Mother Mary, did we just tie up an innocent man?" Belinda asked.

"No," I said adamantly. "He's been following us, or at least looking for Ronnie. And I saw him with Anya."

"You're sure it's him?" Emma was studying the man carefully, her eyes narrowed.

"Yes, one hundred percent."

"You hear that?" She nudged the man's shin. "We know what you've been up to, so stop pretending to be out of it and start talking."

The man's eyes slid open. He regarded us coolly, then said, in a surprisingly calm voice, "I'm going to enjoy seeing the three of you—"

"Nope!" Belinda stepped forward and stuffed part of a silk scarf into his mouth. "I can't listen to murderous bad-guy talk. I just can't."

"You got that?" Emma said to the man.

He glared at her.

"That was a question. Do. You. Understand?"

He nodded.

"Good." She pulled the scarf out of his mouth. "Watch the attitude. Now, tell us who you are and what you want with Ronnie."

"I could ask you the same question," he snapped, anger sparking in his dark eyes like a flame.

"You could," Emma said. "But you're the one who's tied up, so . . ." She spread her arms in a gesture that was both casual and callous.

Damn. My sister could be scary when she wanted to be. We waited.

He glared, then finally said, "My name is Jason Broussard, and Ronnie is my friend. I'm looking for her because I'm worried about her."

He didn't sound worried. He sounded pissed.

"Malarkey," I said. Definitely not as scary as my sister.

"It's the truth," he growled. "I've known her since we were kids."

"Yeah? Then why were you talking to the people who want to hurt her?"

"Who?"

I walked over to the counter and returned with the photograph Kai had taken off Veronica's fridge.

"This woman."

He blinked at the photograph. "I don't know her. Wait—I do remember talking to her the day I went to Ronnie's apartment. She asked me if I lived there. Said she was interested in renting a place. I told her no and that was it."

I tried to remember exactly what Coco had shown me.

"Grace?" Emma asked.

Slowly, reluctantly, I said, "It's possible."

The courtyard door opened and Hugh and the dogs clamored inside.

"Whoa," Hugh said when he saw our captive. "What did I miss?"

I exchanged a glance with my sister, then looked at Belinda. None of us seemed to know where to begin.

Jason took care of that. "These women attacked me and are holding me against my will."

"I can see that," Hugh said. "I'm wondering what you did to deserve it."

Emma beamed at him.

"Nothing." Jason grated out the word through teeth clenched so tightly, I thought they might crack.

Kai opened the door a moment later. His reaction was not as flippant as Hugh's.

"Grace, what's going on?" he asked, eyes scanning the scene.

"I'm being kidnapped," Jason snapped. "That's what's going on."

"This is the guy we saw last night." Kai didn't seem impressed with that explanation so I added, "I thought he had a gun."

"Which I didn't," Jason said.

"How was I supposed to know people carried around giant phones in aggressive-looking cases like this?"

I held up the phone like I was presenting evidence.

"Please tell me you're not insane like these idiots," Jason said to Kai.

"That depends," Kai said, dragging a chair over to sit in front of him.

"On?"

"How well you answer my questions."

"I'm an officer of the court. Check my wallet." He gestured at me with his chin.

Reluctantly, I handed the wallet to Kai.

"Assistant DA Broussard," Kai said, studying the ID.

"Yes."

"Let's confirm that. Emma"—he handed the ID to my sister—"a quick search on Louisiana's State Attorney Office website should do the trick."

She turned to her laptop and started typing.

"While we wait on that," Kai said, "explain how you know Veronica Preaux."

"I already told these lunatics—we grew up together. I've been looking for her because I'm worried."

"Not according to his bio," Emma said. "He's a DA but it says here he's a native of New Orleans, born and raised."

Jason shook his head, seeming exasperated. "Yes, I was born here, but I spent my summers in Gallous with my grandparents."

"We're going to have to have more than that," Kai said.

"Fine. Look at the messages on my phone—there's one from Ronnie."

I'd heard this song and dance from Anya. "Let me guess," I said. "Telling you she'd be waiting where she got Coco?"

"How did you know that?"

"Anya, the woman you claim not to know, showed me the same message."

"What?" Jason sounded bewildered.

"Not exactly the same." Kai handed me the phone. "Look."

I read the message. Then read it a second time.

"What?" Emma asked.

"He's telling the truth," I said, passing the phone to her.

"Finally. Now untie me."

As Kai freed Jason from his bonds, Emma read the message aloud.

"This is going to sound crazy, but I need your help. You remember where I got Coco? Meet me there tonight at eight. Don't tell anyone about this message. Make sure you're not followed. I'll explain when you get here. Please, Jase, I don't know who else to ask."

"I should have all of you arrested," Jason said as he stood and took the phone from Emma.

"I think we can all agree this has been a big misunderstanding," Kai said.

"Why didn't you go to her?" Belinda asked quietly.

"What?" Jason said.

"You knew where she was, didn't you? You knew she'd gotten Coco from her grandmother's house."

Jason crossed his arms over his chest. "Yes."

"Then why didn't you go?"

A muscle in his jaw twitched as he looked at her.

Instead of answering her question he said, "Save it."

"Excuse me?" she asked, brows arching.

"Don't act like you know something about me, because you don't," Jason said.

"I have an idea," I said, aggravated by the way he was talking to Belinda. Sure, the guy had good reason to feel a little temperamental, but that was no excuse to be rude.

"Maybe you didn't show up to meet Ronnie because she's just a *possédé* Preaux. Don't the folks in Gallous steer clear of that family?"

"Superstitious nonsense."

"Then what happened?" I asked. "Why didn't you go to Hattie's?"

"I didn't get the message in time. I went as soon as I saw it. Ronnie wasn't there."

"Did you see anyone else?" Kai asked.

Jason shook his head. "No. I started to leave her a note but wasn't sure if I should. She was so cagey in the message, telling me to make sure I hadn't been followed. I didn't know what to think."

"And she didn't call you again?" Kai said.

"No. I tried sending her messages and called a dozen times. Nothing. I've been by her apartment. I talked to her friend Layla. She'd talked to Ronnie, but had no idea where she was or when she'd be back."

"You didn't report her missing?"

"Why would I? She left on her own. And I know how Ronnie can be."

"Meaning?"

"She's got a short fuse and doesn't always think things through. I was going back to see if she'd been to her place the day I saw you two go in with the key," Jason said.

"That's why you started following us," I said.

He shook his head no. "I tried to but thought you'd spotted me."

"Why not just ask us if we knew where she was?" I asked.

"And expect you to tell me the truth?"

It was a good point.

"You weren't following us last night?" I asked.

"Not until after I saw you at Hattie's," Jason said.

"How?" I asked, remembering that he'd run away.

"I waited in my car until you passed then tailed you here."

"Weren't you worried when Hattie didn't come to the door the night you went to meet Ronnie?" Emma asked.

"She takes her hearing aids out at night, so no."

"You know Hattie pretty well then?" Kai asked. "Have you been to her house often?"

"Often enough—why?"

"She's missing," Kai said.

I'll say this for the guy, he might not have had much going for him in the sympathy department until then, but the look on his face when Kai told him Ronnie's grandmother was missing made me feel sorry for him.

"I'd like you to take a look at something if you don't mind." Kai pulled his phone from his pocket. "We took a video of the kitchen earlier today while we were at Hattie's. Someone who's familiar with the house might see something I've missed."

While Kai and Emma worked on uploading the video to her computer so it could be viewed on a larger screen, I asked Jason, "What happened in Gallous? Why did Hattie change her name?"

"I don't really know the whole story. There was a falling-out in the family. Ronnie and I were just kids. I was about thirteen at the time. I didn't ask. I got the impression Hattie moved to New Orleans to start again."

"Can you think of anyone who would want to hurt her?" I asked.

"She hardly ever leaves her house," Jason said. "Who would want to hurt her?"

"Maybe the same people who wanted to hurt Ronnie's uncle," Hugh said.

"You think this has something to do with Sean's murder?" Jason asked.

"Can't be a coincidence, can it?" Hugh said.

Jason was quiet for several seconds as he considered the possibility. "I don't know what the connection would be."

"Did Ronnie ever talk to you about her uncle's murder?" I asked.

"No. Except to tell me that it was one of the reasons she came to New Orleans. She doesn't have family in Gallous, aside from her brother—and he's . . ."

"We met Max," I said.

"Then you know what I'm saying."

I nodded.

"Ronnie came here and asked if I could help locate Hattie. Though at the time we still thought her name was Arlise," Jason said.

"They hadn't been in contact?" I asked.

"Not for years."

"Her uncle was a healer, right?"

"A *traiteur*, yes."

"And her grandmother is a psychic. What about Ronnie?"

"What about her?" Jason asked.

"Does she have any ability?"

"Ronnie? No."

Belinda nodded. "You might be onto something, Grace."

Jason looked back and forth between us. "You've lost me."

"I was just thinking that it's possible Barry and Anya might be going after family members who claim to have some sort of psychic ability," I said.

"Well, Ronnie doesn't." Jason shook his head. "She would have told me."

"You sure about that?" Belinda asked. "Forgive me for saying so, but you don't seem too open to the idea."

"She would have told me," he said firmly.

"It's not always that easy." Belinda's lips curved into a sad smile. "A lot of times, you don't understand it yourself. And trying to tell someone else, especially someone who wouldn't be open to what you're telling them . . ." She shrugged.

I turned my attention to Jason. "You said Hattie hardly leaves the house. Why not?"

"I don't know."

"Maybe she was afraid of someone," Hugh suggested.

"I can believe it," Belinda said. "If you're not careful, this gift can turn on you."

"What do you mean?" I asked, ignoring Jason's eye-roll.

"The first time I knew something I had no business knowing, I walked up to my mother and said, 'He doesn't want you, not like you want him.' It was at a party. My mother loved her parties," Belinda said.

"My father, who was standing next to her, laughed and said, 'Boy, you know I love your mama.' I looked at him and told him, 'Not you, Daddy, the other man.'

"I was five. I'll never forget the look on his face. Ever. My father was a good man. He adored my mother. Showered her with gifts. Brought her flowers . . . He was devastated. I had devastated him."

"No." Emma, who'd finished helping Kai with the computer, came to stand at Belinda's side. Her voice was somehow both gentle and vehement. "You were a child. The blame falls with your mother and her lover—not you."

Belinda patted the hand Emma had placed on her arm. "My point is—this gift? It's not something you choose. If you're not careful, it can cause a lot of pain. You might not even realize you've hurt someone until it's too late."

"This could be about a reading Hattie gave someone," I said. "Some secret she revealed."

"Or," Hugh said, "something she missed."

It was an angle to consider. Though I wasn't sure how it would help. Without talking to her we couldn't know if Hattie had made an enemy during her career.

Kai waved Jason over to watch the video of Hattie's kitchen, and Belinda walked over to open one of the upper cabinets. I noticed her nails weren't painted as she took out a bottle of aspirin.

I wondered if she was spending too much time helping us and not enough time being Belinda.

"You okay?" I asked her. "I know this has been a lot to take in."

"It's not that. I just got a terrible headache out of the blue earlier. I hate taking this stuff, but I'm out of magnesium tea."

I thought about how surprised she'd been at not having known something was off earlier when she walked in and saw we'd taken Jason out.

"Your headache," I said. "Do you think that's why you didn't feel the Tingle?"

"I'm not sure. I've never had this happen before. It's like my head is stuffed with cotton balls. I've got a client lined up later and I don't even feel like doing my nails."

"Maybe you should go lie down. Voodoo is always ready for a snuggle."

"That's a good idea." She nodded and tried to smile but it fell short of her usual mischievous grin. "I've got an hour before my appointment. Maybe I'll go rest my eyes until then."

I did a mental search for my kitten.

"Voodoo's already napping on my bed if you want to grab her on the way to your room."

"Thanks, *cher*, I'll do that. If you need anything, holler."

"Is she okay?" Emma asked after Belinda had gone upstairs.

"Headache. It interfered with the Tingle and she seems pretty stressed about it."

I moved to where Kai and Jason were watching the video for a second time.

"Stop," Jason said.

Kai clicked the button to pause the video.

"Ronnie's there."

"How do you know that?"

"Chocolate." Jason pointed at the screen. "See the wrappers? This is her favorite brand. She eats it when she's stressed."

"We looked all over the house. She's not there," Kai said.

"Did you check the attic?"

"We tried but the door had been locked for years."

"There's another way in. Come on, I'll show you."

CHAPTER 14

Emma and Hugh stayed at the B and B to continue working on the monkey map. And Emma had promised to keep an eye on Belinda.

Sometimes caretakers need care, too.

We took Jason's car—a sporty SUV that made Bluebell look like the vintage tank she was—to Hattie's. Jason hadn't put up a fuss when I told him we were taking Moss with us. If Jason failed to get into the attic, my dog could at least tell us if he smelled someone.

We got out of the SUV and Moss took a moment to mark a tree or two. Jason walked to where the garden hose spigot sprouted from the house's brick foundation. He grabbed the brass faucet and pulled. The spigot, and the brick it was attached to, slid out, revealing a hollow spot in the brick below.

"Really?" I asked and looked at Kai.

He lifted a shoulder in a half shrug.

"This place has all kinds of hiding places," Jason said as he reached into the hole and retrieved the key.

We entered through a mudroom and then went into the kitchen. Jason paused to look around.

"I remember the plate," he said, pointing to the wall where Kai thought the broken platter had hung.

Moss walked over to where the plate had smashed to the ground. He paused, sniffing the area. A ripple of unease fluttered through our connection. Sometimes, energy lingers. Intense emotions felt in a place leave their mark. Like a never-ending echo animals are tuned in to.

Easy, Moss. It's okay.

Okay?

Yeah, we're looking for someone, though. So keep your ears pricked.

Moss listen.

Good boy.

Jason led us out of the kitchen, down the hall, and into the library. I watched, with a growing sense of disbelief, as he walked to the bookcase and scanned the shelf.

"If there is a hidden passageway behind that bookcase, I give you permission to drop the mic and walk away," I said when he put his hand on a large copy of *War and Peace*.

Jason looked over his shoulder with a half smile. "The house used to be part of the Underground Railroad."

Tilting the book out released some sort of latch and a section of the bookcase shifted, the edge popping out a couple of inches.

"How did I miss this?" Kai said, walking over to study the faux book.

"To be fair, you weren't looking for a secret room," I said.

Jason gripped the edge of the bookcase and swung it into the library, revealing a small staircase. Jason took the lead, Moss and I followed, and Kai brought up the rear. The staircase was so narrow, both Jason and Kai had to walk with their shoulders canted to the side.

We reached the top landing and followed Jason as he headed down a short hall that opened up to the attic. Just as he stepped through the doorway, a loud buzzing cut through the silence. It was accompanied by a rapid, electric *tick-tick-tick!*

I froze, startled, and Kai bumped into me from behind.

I recognized the sound. I had my own stun gun tucked under Bluebell's front seat. Something I'd forgotten about until that moment.

Jason let out a garbled cry and crumpled to the ground. Kai shoved me behind him and reached toward his gun holster for a weapon that wasn't there. Moss stayed silent but readied his stance for action.

Guard.

Before any of us could react further, a woman's voice said, "Jason? What the hell?"

"Jesus H. Christ, Ronnie." Jason was barely able to choke out the words, but they held considerable heat. I guess the guy might have been irritated by being bushwhacked twice in one day—and by women, no less.

Kai eased forward and I could see from the hall landing into the dimly lit attic.

Ronnie stood over Jason. She was holding the stun gun and looking pretty pissed.

Answering his attitude with a bit of her own, she demanded, "What are you doing here?"

"Looking for you, you crazy Cajun!" Jason rolled onto his hands and knees, then sat back on his haunches. Wincing, he sucked in a pained breath, then let out a string of what I was sure were a lot of Cajun curse words.

"How was I supposed to know it was you, eh?" Ronnie jammed her fists on her hips.

"You told me to come," Jason fired back.

"I sent you that message days ago. And I didn't think you'd bring friends." She motioned toward where Kai and I stood and noticed Moss. "A wolf?"

I eased around Kai and said, "I'm Grace, that's my dog, Moss, and this is Kai—he's with the Jacksonville Police Department." I turned and gave him an expectant look, and he slowly removed his ID badge and held it up so she could see.

She squinted at the badge. "Jacksonville, Florida?"

"We can explain what's going on from our end if you'll tell us what you know."

"Well, for starters, Mamere has been kidnapped." She directed this comment to Jason, who was slowly climbing to his feet.

The anger on his face drained away instantly. "I know, *cher*." He reached out and tucked a loose curl behind her ear. The gesture was so intimate and at odds with his behavior a moment before, it took me a second to adjust.

Ronnie's shoulders dropped, and tears sparkled in her eyes.

"Come here." He pulled her into a hug and kissed the top of her head.

"Um, am I reading this wrong," I murmured to Kai, "or are they more than friends?"

He shook his head with a bemused smile. "I knew that the second she tased him."

"Really?" I hated feeling like I was always a step behind when it came to reading people.

Now that there wasn't any drama unfolding in front of me, I had a chance to look around the attic.

The space was huge, running the length of the entire house. There were stacks of boxes and other things you'd expect to find in an attic. The area closest to the backyard had been cleared of the typical storage detritus, and there was a small bed and bedside table with a lamp.

Ronnie had a nice little hideout here. With strategically timed trips downstairs to the kitchen and bath, she'd rarely be exposed to any neighbors or prying eyes.

Jason released Ronnie and stepped back to look her in the eye. "We're going to find Hattie, okay? These folks have been looking for you. They have information we might be able to use."

Ronnie nodded, brushed the tears from her cheeks, and turned her attention to us.

Kai brought up the photos of Anya and Barry on his phone and asked Ronnie if she recognized either of them.

She shook her head and I exchanged a look with Kai. Obviously, Ronnie wasn't the woman Cornelius had seen being strapped to a table. The next logical assumption was it had been Hattie.

"Does your *mamere* have a yellow dress?" I asked.

"I don't know, why?"

"We think—"

Kai interrupted before I could explain further. "Let's not get ahead of ourselves, okay?"

I frowned at him. He met my gaze and shook his head. Obviously, he didn't want to tell Ronnie that her grandmother might be enduring some sort of torture at the hands of a nutjob. Maybe he was right. Upsetting her wouldn't help anyone.

"What's going on?" Ronnie asked, looking back and forth between us. "Who are those people? Are they the ones who took my grandmother?"

"The only thing we know for sure is that they're looking for you," Kai said. "Why don't you tell us what happened and we'll see what we can piece together."

She looked at Jason, and he nodded—indicating that she could trust us, I suppose.

"I got a call from her the other night," Ronnie said. "I was on my way home from work. She sounded really upset and told me I had to leave town right then. She wouldn't say why. Then she told me not to use my phone."

"Your phone? Why?" Kai asked.

"I don't know."

"Did she say anything else?"

"Just that if anything happened to her she wanted me to know that she loved me. She believed in me."

Ronnie's voice dropped to a raw whisper on the last

words. She pressed her lips together and tried to blink away a sudden rush of unshed tears. It didn't work. The tears spilled over and she impatiently wiped them away. "That's all she told me before she hung up. I tried to call her right back but the line was busy."

"Then you came here?" Kai asked.

Ronnie nodded. "I don't have a car so it took me at least fifteen minutes. By then, she was gone."

"Did you call the police?" he said.

"No," she said defensively.

"I'm only asking because there was a 911 call from this house on that same night."

"There was?"

"The caller hung up before the dispatcher picked up. It was written up as a crank call."

"Stupid cops," Ronnie said, which invoked a frown from Jason.

"They didn't even look around?" Jason asked.

"They did," Kai said. "The officer reported the house was locked and there was no response to his knock and no sign of a problem."

"Yeah, no problem," Ronnie scoffed. "Except that she's missing."

"So why *didn't* you call the police?" Jason asked.

"I called *you*," she snapped. "I knew the cops wouldn't do anything."

"When you got here," Kai said, "did you see anything unusual?"

"I knew something had happened because the platter from the kitchen had been knocked off the wall. I didn't know what to do. I was so upset I forgot Mamere told me not to use my phone and sent Jason a message. You didn't come," she said, looking up at him. "I don't know, I kind of freaked out. I thought something had happened to you because of the text I'd sent, so I trashed it."

"What? Your phone?" I asked.

She nodded.

"But you called Layla, too." I saw Ronnie's surprise that I knew this, and so I explained. "We tracked her down. She's safe. So is Coco."

Ronnie relaxed a little. "Good. I was more careful when I contacted her. I used the phone at the coffee shop down the street."

"I did come," Jason said. "It was late, but I was here."

Her face softened as she looked up at him. "It must've been while I was at the coffee shop. It was so weird not having a phone. At first I kind of panicked."

"I understand, believe me," I said.

"But then it was sort of liberating. No one knew where I was. I could try to figure out what had happened to Mamere."

She turned and walked to the other side of the room, stopping at a desk made up of two steamer trunks topped with an old door. Standing on tiptoes, she reached up to turn on a utility lamp clipped to one of the beams. The light revealed a large map sitting on the table next to the gable window. The map covered most of the table's surface. It actually reminded me a lot of our monkey map.

Next to the map Ronnie had taped notes and a few newspaper clippings. Kai immediately walked over to study the display.

Ronnie watched him for a moment, then turned to face me. "You were here last night."

I nodded. "I guess you saw Moss?"

I glanced at my dog, who'd decided it was time to inspect something on Jason's pant leg. Or rather something on his leg that Moss could smell through his jeans.

Liniment of some sort. I wondered what had caused his limp, but decided it wasn't important. Jason glanced down at Moss and did something unexpected. He held out his hand and said in a quiet voice, "Hey, boy." After a few seconds

Moss gave a swish of his tail. Jason returned the friendly gesture with a pat on the head.

Well, darn. I might have to learn to like the guy.

I looked back at Ronnie. She'd angled her head and was studying me intently. Then, something strange happened.

The air didn't stir, but a wave of subtle heat pulsed over me. Like a dream of a desert breeze.

"What was that?" I asked her.

She shifted her gaze to Jason, shook her head, and started to turn away. I reached out to touch her arm.

"Ronnie, what was that?"

She stared into my eyes, a little crease forming between her eyebrows. Then she said quietly, "You can't hear me?"

I arched a brow at her. "Of course I can hear you, you're standing two feet away."

With another quick glance at Jason, she motioned for me to follow her toward the far end of the attic.

"What are you?" she asked in a whisper.

"Huh?"

She reached out and grabbed my hand. "I can feel it. You're a telepath, right?"

Whoa.

"Uh—yeah. How did you—"

She talked over me. "Then why can't you hear what I'm thinking?"

"Oh, it doesn't work with people." She looked completely confused, so I added, "I talk to animals."

"Seriously?" I was having a hard time interpreting the look on her face. She either thought it was the dumbest thing she'd ever heard or thought I was kidding.

"I need a chocolate," she said abruptly, walking back to where the men were standing. "My stash is in the kitchen. Do you guys want anything?"

She didn't give them a chance to respond. "Grace, why don't you help me grab some drinks?"

With her hand firmly clamped on my wrist, she dragged me down the secret staircase. Moss followed on our heels, wondering why we were suddenly rushing around.

Go?

Nope, just following a crazy girl.

Once in the kitchen, Ronnie opened the fridge and grabbed a chocolate bar. Tearing open the wrapper, she broke off a piece and popped it in her mouth.

I recognized the brand. Organic, 73 percent cacao, non-GMO . . . It was one of Emma's favorites—which meant it was expensive.

"A pricey habit," I said.

"We all have our vices." She offered me a piece and I accepted.

I have to admit—it was pretty delicious.

Never one to be left out in such situations, Moss came to sit in front of her.

Treat?

"Chocolate's bad for dogs," she said, but turned back to the fridge. "Can he have a piece of cheese?"

Cheese!

I sighed. "Sure, why not."

Ronnie took out what looked like the remnants of a block of cheese and fed it to Moss. He inhaled the cube without hesitation and looked up at Ronnie.

Treat?

She raised her eyes to me.

"I feed him. Really."

"Uh-huh."

"What's going on, Ronnie? Why did you really drag me down here?"

"Jason doesn't know."

"About?"

"You know," she said as another piece of chocolate disappeared into her mouth. She talked around the food. "Have you told him?"

"Told him what?" She was losing me fast.

"That you're telepathic."

"Actually, it hasn't come up. Ronnie, tell me what's going on. Why did you drag me down here?"

"Jason doesn't buy into the whole psychic thing."

"I got that impression," I told her. "But I'm not sure I understand. He's known Hattie for years. He just thinks she's a charlatan?"

"Pretty much. But in a sweet, grandmotherly way."

"You're kidding."

"Nope, and she hasn't done readings in years and never talks about it in front of anyone. Out of sight, out of mind."

"So you do have an ability," I said.

She nodded. "My *mamere* was helping me understand how to use it. It's not easy. What I can do is unusual."

I thought about what Will Besson had said about her uncle's murder, and it clicked.

"You can find things," I said. "That's how you knew where your uncle's body was. You didn't witness the murder—you were just able to locate him."

She nodded. "It was the hardest thing I've ever had to do."

I could only imagine. "I'm sorry, Ronnie."

She lifted her shoulder. "I thought if I found him, the police would be able to catch who did it. What a joke. All they did was hassle me and my brother."

"You can't really blame them, at least for wanting to know how you knew where to look for the body."

Ronnie glared at me and I decided to switch topics. "You said what you can do is rare. Is it hard to locate things?"

Relaxing, she took another bite of chocolate. "It's called remote viewing. And I can only do it sometimes. But that's not uncommon. Lots of people can find things. What I'm really good at," she said, leveling her gaze at me, "is sensing psychic abilities in others. It kind of runs in the family."

"Really?" I'd never heard of any other telepaths in my family, but then again, I'd never thought to ask.

"Back in the early 1800s one of my great-aunts could do the same thing. People from all over the parish would bring their babies to her to ask if the child was touched."

"Neat."

"You might think so, but after a while, people were scared of her. One of the babies she sensed was psychic was dumped into the bayou by its father."

I stared at her, horrified.

"He thought it would turn into a *rougarou*," Ronnie explained.

"What is it with the stupid werewolf?"

"People can be superstitious. Especially Cajuns."

"And you really think Jason won't believe you? Even if we back you up? Kai knows what I can do—he'll talk to Jason."

"Jason's not like your boyfriend," she protested. "He doesn't get it."

"It took some doing with Kai, too, I can promise you."

"He'll think it's a giant waste of time."

"Who cares what he thinks?" Obviously, she did, but I was betting she cared about her grandmother more. "Listen, if there is even the slightest chance you might find Hattie, shouldn't you try?"

"That's just it," she said. "I've already tried dozens of times. I can't get a read on her. At first, I thought it was just something wrong with me. The stress was messing with my head, or something. But when you showed up the other night, I knew without a doubt that you were like me."

"See? Then you should try again. I have a friend who knows a lot about this stuff. We can call her. See if she can help."

"Yeah?"

"Yeah," I said. "Listen. We can figure out a way to get rid of Jason if you really want to. But for the record, I think you should tell him the truth."

"Tell me the truth about what?"

Crap.

I met Ronnie's eyes and hoped she could read the apology

in mine. I tried to think of something diffusing to say, but one look over my shoulder at Jason told me that wasn't going to happen.

"Jason . . . I—" Ronnie stopped and glanced at me. I gave her what I hoped was an encouraging nod. "There's something I need to tell you. I want you to hear me out, okay?"

He crossed his arms over his chest and waited. Not the most open posture, in my opinion, but maybe he'd listen.

"I'll let you two talk," I said, and started out of the room.

"No. Grace, please stay." Ronnie looked desperate so I did as she requested.

She turned back to face Jason. "You know how Mamere's a psychic?"

Jason arched a brow. "Yeah."

"Well, so am I."

"You're what?"

"I'm a psychic. Grace is, too," she hastened to add, as if that would help her case.

"Ronnie, what are you talking about? You want to read people's fortunes?"

"No, that's not what I can do." Ronnie looked at me for help.

"She's not talking about pursuing a career, Jason," I said.

"You mean you're psychic, like, really psychic."

"Yes," Ronnie said.

He laughed, though there was no humor in it. "Okay, then, what am I thinking?"

"I'm not that kind of psychic. But I do know what you're thinking."

"Yeah?"

"You think I'm full of it."

"Well, look at that, maybe you are psychic."

Kai appeared in the doorway. He looked around at each of us, clearly picking up on the tension. "Everything okay in here?"

"Yeah," Jason said. "Everything is perfect. Ronnie here has decided she's a psychic."

Jason had said the word *psychic* like someone might say *fairy godmother*.

Kai looked at me, then Ronnie. "I see. To be fair, I'm not sure it's something you decide."

"Don't tell me you believe this happy hog shit," Jason said.

Kai didn't cross his arms but he leveled his gaze at Jason and held it. "I do, because it's true."

"This is ridiculous. Hattie's missing and you're wasting time with this?"

"It's not a waste of time," Ronnie snapped.

"Great. If you're psychic, then where is she?"

"I don't know."

"Because you're not that kind of psychic, either?"

"Actually, I am that kind of psychic but I just can't get a good read on her."

"This is crazy. Okay, fine, you're psychic. Great, let's move on to something useful."

"Don't you patronize me, Jason Broussard. You know I wouldn't lie about this. Not now."

"You know something, Ronnie? I don't think I know you at all."

"See?" Ronnie looked at me. "This is pointless."

"Hang on," Kai said. "Everyone take a breath, for Hattie's sake."

Though she looked like she was ready to spit nails, Ronnie pulled in a couple of deep breaths and said, "Okay."

Jason nodded.

"Good," Kai said. "Jason, you don't have to believe Ronnie or us, but you can agree that we want the same thing, right? We want to help Hattie. And to do that, we have to work together. Everyone brings something different to the table."

"I'll say," Jason muttered.

Ronnie shot him a withering look.

Kai plowed on. "I have a few questions about a couple of unsolved cases that might be connected. Why don't we talk about those? Grace and Ronnie, you work your angle."

I noticed Kai was careful not to say the word *psychic*, which was probably smart, given Jason's bad attitude.

I agreed, but didn't know how much help I would be.

"I've got some notes upstairs. We can start there," Ronnie said.

Moss and I followed her up the hidden staircase to the attic.

"I've tried to keep notes, but it's really hard to focus on what I'm seeing and try to describe it on paper at the same time." Ronnie's frustration was evident on her face.

"What about using a tape recorder?" I asked.

"That was my next option. I used to have an audio memos feature on my phone but . . ."

"Right. No phone."

I thought about Logan's sudden case of sticky fingers when it came to my phone and wondered if he'd taken mine to protect me.

There was a way to track people with a phone, wasn't there? Had Anya or Barry figured out a way to hack into my phone?

I shook off the scary thought. I'd think about it later, when a grandmother's life wasn't in danger.

"Did you manage to make sense of anything you saw?"

She shook her head. "Not really. It all just seems completely random. Here," she said, opening the drawer of the bedside table and taking out a notebook. "I'll show you."

Ronnie set the notebook on the table and opened it. "These are just impressions, really. It felt like I could never get a firm grasp on her energy."

I looked over the notes. Basically there were a bunch of words and doodles. Things like *dark road* and *chain-link fence* along with a lot of question marks.

"What's this about diamonds?" I asked.

"I don't know."

"Like the shape or the gemstone?"

"Gemstone. I saw a bunch of loose diamonds sparkling—but that's all."

"Does that mean your grandmother is somewhere where she can see diamonds? Or is that some sort of a metaphor?"

"I don't know." Ronnie's voice was strained. "My *mamere* knew a lot about all this stuff. I've been trying to learn but . . ."

"Hey, remember the friend I told you about? I'm going to call her. I'm sure she'll be able to help."

I called Emma, who put Belinda on.

"You found her?" Belinda said. "You found Ronnie?"

"We did. She's been hiding out in the attic of Hattie's place."

"Then who was the woman Cornelius saw?"

"Hattie, maybe, we're not sure. Listen, Belinda, we need your help." I explained the situation.

"Damn. I've got a client coming any minute. They're persnickety, too. I can come when I finish up. Maybe forty-five minutes?"

"We can come to you," I said.

"No, it would be better if I could get a feel for Hattie in her own space. And we'll be able to find some personal items to use as a focus."

"Okay, we'll see you soon." I hung up and looked at Ronnie. "Help is on the way."

We settled in to wait, but Ronnie started pacing after about fifteen minutes, even though I'd explained that Belinda had a client.

"You know," I said, "Belinda did mention something about needing some of Hattie's personal items. Maybe you could grab a couple of things so they're ready when she gets here."

"Yeah, good idea." Ronnie went down to the second floor, but my quest didn't keep her busy for long. Ten minutes later she returned to the attic with a shoe box. I looked in the box. There were a couple of items of jewelry.

"Why are you smiling?" Ronnie asked.

"I thought you might bring bunny slippers."

"How do you know about her bunny slippers?"

I explained that Coco had shown me a well-worn pair and referred to the woman wearing them as Mamere.

"She loves those bunny slippers. They're not here, so she must've been wearing them when . . ."

Thankfully, Kai walked into the room then and Ronnie's tears were stopped before they'd gotten started.

"Is Belinda here?" I asked.

"No. Actually I was just coming to see if you've heard anything."

"I'll check with Emma," I said.

"She's still in with her client," my sister said when I got her on the phone. "The reading must be running late."

"Okay, thanks." I hung up. "She's running late."

"I'm going stir-crazy waiting around," Ronnie announced.

"I'm sure Belinda will be here soon."

"I need to go for a walk or something," Ronnie said.

"Not alone, you're not," I told her. "Moss and I will go with you."

"Hold it," Kai said. "Neither of you are going anywhere alone."

"We won't be alone," I said. "We have a guard dog." I waved to where Moss was sitting at the door, ready to go.

"Make that two," Ronnie added, pulling the stun gun out of her pocket and waving it in the air.

"Okay, fine," Kai said. "Just remember Barry has a gun and if he's pointing it at either one of you and you zap him with that thing, he could pull the trigger and kill someone."

"We'll be fine," I assured him. "Call me if Belinda gets here before we get back."

With a quick peck on the cheek, I left him to hold down the fort.

CHAPTER 15

The dreary, sunless day and bracing wind made me wish for a parka.

Moss, of course, was happy as could be in the cold. His wolfy roots always put a spring in his step on crisp days.

He'd probably go bonkers in the snow. The thought made me promise myself to take him to play in it someday.

Ronnie didn't seem to mind the cold, either. I suppose her worry and impatience was keeping the fire within burning hot. That, and her argument with Jason.

I hated talking about touchy subjects so instead I said, "Kai's right, about the stun gun."

"Don't worry, I won't sic my electric guard dog on anyone who's holding a gun."

"Good, because I don't feel like getting shot." I shivered and picked up the pace.

"Do you really think we're going to run into one of the bad guys?"

"You never know," I said.

"I almost hope we do, now that I have backup." She pointed her chin to Moss.

"Don't even say that."

"Think about it. If we could grab one of them, maybe we could make him tell us where my *mamere* is."

"Really?" I said. "With what? Your stun gun?"

"Or your guard dog."

I stopped. It took Ronnie a second to notice, but when she did she faced me.

"No. These people are way out of our league, Ronnie. If we see them, we run."

She held up her hands in surrender. "Okay, got it."

We continued down the sidewalk, and I took a second to admire some of the homes in the area.

"Hattie's house is pretty amazing," I said. "She must've been a really successful psychic."

Ronnie smiled. "That, and she had a very wealthy lover."

"Really?"

"Actually, more than one."

"Go, Grandma," I said.

"She's coy about it, but I can tell. You want to know how she got the house?" Ronnie asked.

"Of course."

"A man came to her for a reading. She told him he couldn't trust his business partner and advised him it would be better to invest his money in a company with fruit as a logo."

"You're kidding."

"It's true. All that Apple stock has paid off."

"I bet. Belinda said she was the talk of the town."

"She was, until my mom died," Ronnie said.

Okay, so much for avoiding touchy subjects.

"What happened?" I asked.

"She saw it happen. Standing at her potting bench one morning, she got a flash of her daughter dying. And there was nothing she could do to stop it. I don't know why I'm telling you all this," she said with a sigh. "I'm usually a lot less candid. But I feel totally comfortable with you. Maybe it's the psychic thing."

"Odd birds of a feather flock together?"

"Makes sense, doesn't it?" she asked.

"Maybe," I said, remembering how at ease I'd felt talking to Belinda when we'd first met.

Could there be a connection that went beyond the shared experience of being misunderstood or even disliked because we were different? Something more fundamental about the way our brains were wired that created a kinship?

"I'd never met another psychic, before Belinda," I said.

"Yeah? My family's full of 'em. And you know what?" she said with faux enthusiasm. "Every single one of them that's had some sort of sensitivity or whatever you want to call it, ended up crazy or dead. Except my *mamere*."

The sadness in her voice made me itch for Emma's knack for saying the right thing at the right time to cheer someone up. My sister knew when to sympathize, when to reassure, and when to just listen.

I typically got the signals crossed and made things worse, so decided it would be easier on us both if I asked about someone else in her family.

"What about Max?" I said. "Does he have any special ability?"

"My brother?" she scoffed. "Yeah, he has the ability to cause trouble, get into trouble, and make trouble for everybody he knows. The idiot." Though the words were harsh, the way she said them made me think she was not as critical of her brother as she let on.

"He's a good dancer," I said with a half smile.

"Oh Lord—you saw him dance? When?"

I told her the story of chasing him through the parking lot, and she was actually laughing by the time we made it to the coffee shop.

Maybe I was learning a thing or two about cheering people up after all.

Ronnie started up the entry steps but I was stopped by a sign posted on the door that read NO DOGS. NO EXCEPTIONS.

"Hang on, Ronnie." I pointed to the note when she turned to look at me. "We'll have to wait out here," I said, shivering.

Ronnie looked at the sign with a frown. "We can go somewhere else. There's a place a few more blocks away."

I hesitated. I didn't really want to spend that much more time out in the open where we could be spotted, or in the cold. My nose was already numb.

"Dad, look!" The child's voice was accompanied by running footsteps. "A wolf!"

I turned to see a girl, maybe ten years old, headed toward us.

"Anna, don't—" The girl's father was right behind her and looked a little worried about the fact that his daughter was running full tilt toward a giant canine.

I smiled to reassure the man and, when Moss let out an excited whine, urged him to be gentle.

Easy, big guy.

Friend?

Yes, but be easy, she's a kid.

Moss understood the concept of kids versus adults and usually instinctively knew who he could roughhouse with, but it never hurt to reinforce the idea.

He wagged his tail and let his head drop low in his best I-mean-no-harm posture.

"You can pet him," I said, loud enough for the girl and her father to hear. "He won't bite. He might lick you, though."

The girl squealed in delight when Moss did just that.

"I'm sorry," the dad said. "She loves animals. Is he really a wolf?"

"Not completely, but his mom was a timber wolf. He takes after her," I said, looking over my shoulder at Ronnie, who was still halfway up the steps waiting for me to decide what to do.

"I can order and we can sit outside," she suggested. "Though you look like you're freezing."

"You can leave him with us while you go in," the girl said. "Right, Dad?"

"Ah—sure," he said. Any resolve he might have had melted at his little girl's wide-eyed plea. "But only if it's okay with his owner."

"We'll take care of him," she said, turning her big, doe eyes to work their magic on me. "Really. I'll hold his leash and won't let him go anywhere."

I wasn't going to break it to her that if Moss decided to go, he would. With or without her permission.

Moss? You want to stay out here with your new friend while I go inside?

Stay.

He sat, for emphasis.

"Okay," I said to the little girl and her father. "But if you get tired of petting him or you need to go, come get me."

"He's so beautiful," she said, enraptured. "Can I brush him? I have a comb in my backpack."

Moss, beautiful. My dog looked up at me, with a smug expression on his face.

"It's your comb," I said, and looked at her dad.

He shrugged and held out his hand for the leash. I handed it to him and he squatted down to partake in the petting.

"You're not worried they'll try to steal him or something?" Ronnie asked.

"Moss is undognappable," I said. "Believe me, he's not going anywhere."

We made our way inside and I immediately saw the reason for the ban on canines.

A pair of long, lanky Siamese cats lounged on a cat tree in the corner. One was gazing out the window at Moss with unveiled disdain.

His tail began to twitch rapidly as he eyed my dog.

I knew, without having to be telepathic, that given half a chance, the cat would attack my hundred-plus-pound wolf-dog.

I shook my head and walked to the cat's perch.

"Not the best idea, kitty cat," I said. At the same time, I tried to calm his agitation with thoughts of friendship.

Swat! was the cat's reply.

One of those, are you?

Swat! the second cat added.

Oh well. I shrugged off the twin felines' attitude—it wasn't important enough to pursue. Moss was staying outside, thrilled to be fawned over by the little girl. The cats could hold dominion as they pleased.

"That's Ming," the woman working behind the counter said with a rueful smile. She was older, plump, and looked like she should be baking a pie. "The other one is Thing."

"Ming and Thing." I glanced back at the cats. They were both focused on Moss. Thing had begun to growl softly.

"I wouldn't try to pet them with a dog around. They get hissy."

"I'll take your advice and try the coffee," I told her, turning to look at the menu items listed on the wall.

Ronnie ordered a large mocha cappuccino. I decided to follow her lead and got the same.

We sat at a booth by the window where I could keep an eye on Moss. Removing my gloves, I cradled the cappuccino in my frozen fingers and let the warm steam tickle my nose for a moment, then took a sip.

Heaven.

After a second, bigger sip, the hot coffee started working its magic, warming me from the inside out.

I set down the mug with a sigh.

"Better?" Ronnie asked.

"Coffee makes everything better."

"Exactly how I feel about chocolate."

"Different strokes."

I'd been so focused on warming up, I hadn't noticed the man who'd entered the coffee shop until he broke away from the two women he'd been holding the door open for and headed in our direction.

"Ronnie!" I hissed out her name in warning, but it was too late.

A heartbeat later, Barry was sliding into the booth next to me. Without pausing, he lifted his arm to rest around my shoulders and pressed close. The movement was punctuated by the sharp jab of what I knew was a gun barrel being pressed to my ribs.

I suppressed a wince, but could tell from Ronnie's expression she knew what was going on.

His eyes roved around the room in that unsettling way I'd noticed before. Finally, he said to Ronnie, "So glad to finally meet you, Veronica."

I was trying really hard not to panic.

"How did you find us?" I asked, hoping if I got him talking for long enough I'd be able to calm down and start thinking clearly.

"I found you and followed you, of course," he said dismissively. "Now, we're going to chat politely for a few minutes, without making a fuss. Aren't we?"

He pressed the gun harder into my side.

I gritted my teeth.

"Yes," Ronnie said hastily.

I pressed my lips together and nodded.

"Good. I'd hate to hurt an innocent bystander."

An instant later his threat was amplified when the plump, pink-cheeked woman who'd served us our coffee stopped by the table and smiled at her new customer.

"Can I get something for you, sir?" she asked Barry.

"A regular coffee, please," he told her.

"Coming right up." She smiled cheerfully and bustled away.

"You took my *mamere*." Ronnie spoke the words with quiet calm but there was enough acidity in her tone to let Barry know what she thought of him.

"Miss Hallowell is with us, yes."

"Why? Why are you doing this to my family?"

"You must know how special you are." He looked at me

as if expecting me to back up his declaration. When I didn't he said, "What she can do—it's very unique."

"What am I," I said, unable to help myself, "chopped liver?"

Nerves make me babble, and right then, with a gun barrel stabbing me in the ribs, I was feeling pretty darn nervous.

"You?" He looked down his nose at me and I noticed his left eye had started to twitch. "Aside from leading us to Veronica, you've been rather disappointing."

"You wouldn't say that if she had her guard dog," Ronnie said, emphasizing the last two words.

"I'm not worried about that," Barry said. "In fact, I'm not sure Miss Wilde here can do what she says she can do. In any case, she's expendable. Just keep that in mind."

"You'd shoot me in a coffee shop in front of witnesses?" I said incredulously.

"To keep her—yes."

"Why? What's so special about me?" Ronnie asked.

The conversation paused as the woman brought the coffee and set it on the table.

"I'm sure you know," Barry said when the woman left. "You're a remote seer, like your grandmother, but what's more, you can sense others like you."

"And you want to kill me because of it?"

"Of course not." He looked genuinely shocked at her accusation.

"Can't blame her for thinking that," I said in the most conciliatory voice I could manage. "You did kill her uncle."

Ronnie's face displayed several emotions in rapid succession, finally settling on anger. "You killed my uncle?"

"That was a different situation." Barry waved the question off as if it were a bothersome fly.

"Right. Is this where you tell her you won't hurt her if she comes with you willingly?"

"No. This is where I tell her I won't hurt *you* if you *both* come with me willingly."

"No deal," I said, trying to keep my tone blasé. "I know where I stand with you. You'll shoot me and dump me in an alleyway as soon as you get her out of here."

"Very good. Yes, you're right." He smiled at me like a teacher might when a typically dense student gets a question correct in class. Well, if we were at Freddy Krueger's school for the completely crazy.

"I'd rather not, of course. Keeping you both would be ideal."

"Keeping us both for what?" I asked.

"Research, of course. I'd find out soon enough if your ability is real."

So much for Logan's advice.

It wouldn't have mattered if I'd claimed to be a fraud—it seemed old Barry-boy was keen on "research." Yippee.

I heard a buzzing noise and Barry touched his free hand to his ear. Glancing over, I saw something I recognized.

An oversized earpiece, exactly like the one Cornelius had seen on the man who was tying up . . . whom? Hattie or some other poor, terrified woman he believed was psychic?

A woman I was supposed to save.

Suddenly, the coffee I'd so enjoyed a minute ago felt like a glob of molten acid in my stomach. Bile rose into my throat. I swallowed it back.

"You're experimenting on psychics?" Ronnie asked.

"You wouldn't believe the advances I've made."

"So this is all for the greater good—that's your pitch?" I scoffed.

"It's the truth."

"Call me ignorant, but I don't see how murdering people is for the good of anybody." I lifted my hand to stop his reply. "And you can spare me the 'good of the many' *Wrath of Khan* speech. You're not doing this to advance human-kind. You're doing this for you."

The tic in his left eyelid became more pronounced as he narrowed his eyes.

"What have you done with your gift, Miss Wilde? What

good do you spread? You help little puppies and kitties find good homes. Save the occasional traumatized terrier? What a waste of your talent."

"Not to the terrier," I replied.

"Haven't you ever wondered what more you could contribute? There are scientists all over the globe studying any number of animals in an attempt to benefit mankind."

"Yeah," Ronnie said, her tone dripping with sarcasm. "It would be a shame to break out after using that expensive makeup."

"I'm talking about real science," Barry said. "Understanding echolocation in bats or how homing pigeons navigate. Countless hours have been spent on these pursuits when you could go to the source. You can simply ask the bird, 'What do you see? How does it work?' Instead, you contribute nothing."

I was loath to admit it, but he kind of had a point.

"You both have the ability to tune into a frequency most others can't detect." His eyes were zipping around even faster. "Do you know only four percent of the universe is made up of atomic matter? Molecules, air, dust, planets. What we think of as real. The rest—" He paused for effect. "Ninety-six percent, is comprised of dark matter and dark energy.

"It connects everything," he continued. "If we can crack the code, we can tap into the vibration of the universe itself."

Something in Ronnie's expression had changed. She seemed almost contemplative. She couldn't be buying into his nonsense.

Making sure to catch her eye, I said, "And all it costs to climb aboard the crazy train express is your life." I turned to look at Barry. "I'd rather you shoot me now than be strapped to a table and used in an experiment."

His eye twitch intensified.

"It would be short-lived if I'm right about you." He focused on Ronnie. "Am I right about her?"

She looked at me, clearly not knowing what to say.

"It's okay, you can tell him the truth," I said.

"Grace is a telepath."

"You're sure?"

"Yes. I could tell when I touched her."

Bingo. That was exactly what Barry was waiting to hear. And exactly what I needed to make her understand what was at stake.

"Magnificent." He smiled. "We will be able to accomplish so much more now."

"You know why he's so stoked, right?" I asked her. "He's not going to kill you, because he's going to use you to find other psychics. He'll probably use your *mamere* as leverage. Hurt her a little to keep you compliant."

Ronnie's gaze slid over to zero in on Barry.

"Enough." He jabbed the gun into my ribs, and this time, I didn't hide my wince.

"Just like he's doing with me," I hissed.

"I'm losing patience with you, Miss Wilde."

"You can walk away," I told Ronnie. "He won't shoot you. Just get up and walk out of here."

Her gaze flicked back to me. "He'll kill you."

"Not if you find me first."

Barry did something I hadn't expected. He laughed.

"She's not going to find you," he said. "I've made sure of that, at least. So your little show of bravado is pointless. Don't believe me? Try it. Go ahead, try to sense her ability."

Ronnie took a slow breath, licked her lips nervously, and focused on me.

I waited for the burst of heat I'd felt earlier.

It didn't come.

Ronnie's eyes widened, then she winced and brought her hand to her temple.

"Ronnie?" I said.

"It didn't work," she said.

"What did you do to her?" I asked Barry.

He ignored my question. "You're both coming with me. Now."

Ronnie started to slide out of the booth.

Still keeping the gun against my side, Barry grabbed my arm with his other hand and pulled me to my feet.

"Not that way," he told Ronnie when she reached the front door. He canted his head toward the back of the coffee shop. Then in a lower tone he said to me, "I'd hate to have to shoot your dog in front of such a sweet little girl."

I'd kept my mind shielded from Moss for just that reason—if he'd sensed my fear, he would have reacted. I had no doubt someone would have gotten shot, maybe more than one someone.

So I walked past the glass front door and didn't say good-bye to my friend. I didn't even look at him.

Tears pricked my eyes. But I swallowed the lump of emotion thickening in my throat.

What I was about to do wouldn't work with tears streaming down my cheeks. I was going to have to be calm and cold as a glacial lake.

Lucky for me, I've had a lot of practice with bringing on the deep freeze. Emotionally, anyway.

We stepped out the back door into a small parking area. The cars, which probably belonged to the employees, were unoccupied. At least out here, no innocent coffee drinkers would get shot.

"I meant it, you know." I glanced at Barry, but my words were for Ronnie. "What I said before. I really would rather you shoot me now."

Ronnie stopped, her back still to us. I saw her hands were in her pockets.

"Are you sure about that?" Barry asked, pointing the pistol more firmly in my direction.

"Yes."

Out of the corner of my eye, I saw Ronnie start to move.

She pivoted, the stun gun ready. I stepped to the side, spun, and dove for cover behind a pair of trash cans.

An electric *tick-tick-tick* sounded, followed by a gurgled cry and a thud.

No gunshot.

"Ronnie?"

"I got him! Grace, holy smokes, we did it!"

With effort, I detangled myself from the stack of cardboard boxes I'd landed on and stood.

Sure enough, Barry was laid out, facedown on the ground, moaning.

"Should I hit him again?"

Why not?

"Do it," I said.

Ronnie placed the Taser on his calf and zapped him again. Barry went rigid and was still.

"Don't move, asshole!" she said.

"Where's his gun?" I gasped, trying to pull my phone out of my pocket with useless, fear-frozen fingers.

"I think he's on top of it." Ronnie was breathing as hard as I was.

"Secure the gun. I'm going to call Kai."

The sound of tires on pavement made me look up. From around the side of the building, the front of a white van glided into view, like the nose of a great white shark.

Anya.

"Ronnie, we've got to go."

"What?" Straightening, she looked over her shoulder and froze.

Anya had assessed the situation in less than a second. She'd slammed on the brakes and was getting out of the car.

I grabbed Ronnie's jacket and yanked her toward the coffee shop's back door. We tumbled through it and slammed it closed. Ronnie fumbled with the dead bolt for a second before managing to click it into place.

We backed away from the door, both jumping as it rattled

on its hinges when Anya banged against it. We glanced briefly at each other, then turned and ran.

Just as we rounded a corner into a small kitchen, a trio of bullets slammed into the door.

"So much for them not shooting me," Ronnie said.

"I was talking about Barry. I guess Anya's not as much of a humanitarian."

Throughout the shop, there were shouts and confused cries but no more gunshots. I assumed Anya had decided it was time to gather her fallen comrade and get gone.

"Come on." I led the way through the front door and ran toward Moss.

"What was that noise?" the girl's father asked.

"Gunshots," was all I had to say. He handed me Moss's leash, scooped his daughter up, and ran.

"Where do we go?" Ronnie asked.

"Hattie's."

"But that's the first place they'll—" She broke off as understanding dawned. "We have to warn Jason and Kai."

I was already on the move.

CHAPTER 16

I'm not really built for speed, but I run a lot more often than most people and my body knows the drill. Ronnie was in pretty good shape—she could almost keep up. Moss, of course, had no problem running.

We sprinted down the block. I was praying that the fact that Anya would have to deal with a confused and unsteady Barry would give us enough of a head start.

I could have tried to call Kai, but it would have taken about as much time.

Charging through the kitchen door, we thundered up the stairs into the attic.

"Where's Jason?" Ronnie asked between heaving breaths.

Kai caught her arm before she could run back down the stairs.

"He left. He had to sign and fax some paperwork so I could get copies of your uncle's autopsy photos."

"Oh." She nodded.

"What's going on?" Kai asked, looking at me.

"Trouble," I said. "Anya and Barry are on the way. They'll be here any minute. Crap! The bookcase. It's still open."

Ronnie dashed out of the attic into the hall landing. She returned a moment later.

"That was fast," I said.

"There's a lever up here to close it."

"I love this house."

Our discussion ended a moment later when we heard a car door slam.

"They're here," I whispered. As if everyone weren't aware of that.

Kai put his fingers to his lips and lifted a piece of sturdy-looking pipe he'd picked up while I had my back turned.

Ronnie held her stun gun at the ready.

I squatted next to Moss, took a calming breath, and, sinking my fingers deeply into his fur, opened my mind to his.

Moss could hear Anya and Barry far better than us humans, so I urged him to stay quiet and still and asked him to listen.

Moss listen.

Good boy.

I closed my eyes and tried to pinpoint where the sounds Moss was hearing were coming from.

There were two sets of footsteps, as I'd expected. No voices.

The floor creaked and the rhythm of their movement changed. I opened my eyes and looked at Kai, then used my fingers to mime walking up an imaginary staircase, trying to indicate to him that they'd moved up to the second floor.

He nodded and shifted his gaze to Ronnie.

Our pursuers hadn't found the entrance to the hidden staircase in the library, which meant if they made it into the attic, they'd be coming through the door in front of Ronnie.

She nodded her understanding and, face grim, held her ground at the attic door.

I listened as Anya and Barry moved slowly from room to room below us, then heard a man's voice murmur, "They must be in the attic."

No response from Anya. No movement.

My heart was slamming hard in my chest. Moss had started panting a little in reaction to our connection and my fear. The sound seemed unbelievably loud but I knew that was partly that I was hearing through both his ears and my own.

Still, it would be better to calm him down. I focused on regulating my breathing, and after a few moments he quieted.

The sound of a shuffling footstep came from the other side of the attic door.

Ronnie didn't react, and I wasn't sure if she'd heard it or not, but it didn't matter, because I knew she was aware of the doorknob being jiggled a second later.

Silence followed.

Then shuffling feet.

Bam! The door rattled in its frame as someone tried to kick it in. We all jumped. But no one, not even Moss, made a sound.

A second kick slammed into the door.

"What are you doing?" Barry said, no longer trying to be quiet. "Don't you see the cobwebs? That door hasn't been opened in years."

"It doesn't make sense," Anya said. "They did not have time to escape."

"They did if they had a car," Barry pointed out. "Anya, the SUV they came in is gone. They got away."

There was a curse and the sound of footsteps moving down the stairs.

I let out the breath I hadn't realized I'd been holding and saw Ronnie do the same. Letting her eyes drift closed, she made the sign of the cross and whispered a quiet prayer.

None of us moved, even after we heard the back door to the house swish open then slam closed.

"Wait," I whispered. I wanted to be sure it wasn't a trick. I wouldn't put it past Anya to pretend to be leaving and hang out to see if we scared little mice came scurrying out of our hiding places once we thought the cat had gone.

I listened through Moss and could hear two people walking down the back stairs.

When an engine started, I nodded, indicating the coast was clear.

Ronnie rushed to the window.

"They're in that big white van," I said.

Kai hurried to join her at the window. "Can you see the plates?" he asked.

"No."

"Oh God—they're getting away." She turned to me, frantic. "Grace, what do we do?"

I didn't have an answer. There was no way we could make it down the stairs and into the street in time to hail a cab and follow them.

"I need somebody to tell me what happened," Kai said. "How did they find us?"

"Barry followed us here," I said. "Then to the coffee shop." I briefly went over what happened, leaving out the part where I'd said I'd rather be shot than endure torture.

"I'm telling you, Kai, the dude is nuts. He was talking about vibrations of the universe. And how we're connected with black energy or something."

"Dark energy," Kai corrected.

"Whatever. It was crazy."

"I don't know," Ronnie said. "I think he's not too far off, at least with what he was saying about dark matter and dark energy. Max Planck was brilliant. Sure, he was an out-of-the-box thinker, like Tesla, but a genius."

"Are you kidding me?" I asked. "You bought into all that we-are-connected-with-tendrils-of-the-vibrations-of-the-universe stuff?"

"He was talking about Tesla?" Kai asked.

"Not exactly," Ronnie said.

"Did I just step into the twilight zone? You speak science geek?" I asked Ronnie.

"Hey, I read."

I shook my head, then realized something. "Where's Belinda?"

Kai looked at his watch. "Damn it."

"She's really late."

"Call Emma, make sure everything's okay."

I did. "Yeah, she's fine," Emma said when she picked up.

"Are you sure?"

"Still in with that client, but yeah."

"Okay." I explained what had happened as quickly as I could. "We can't risk staying here. We're coming to you."

Kai called a cab while Ronnie and I gathered up the box of Hattie's stuff, Ronnie's notebook, the map, and all her chocolate.

Thirty minutes later we were walking through the courtyard door into Belinda's kitchen.

After greetings, introductions, and a brief overview of our run-in with Barry and Anya, Ronnie asked, "So, where's Belinda?"

Emma pointed to the hall and the closed pocket door separating the shop from the rest of the house. I'd never seen the door closed. Usually, Belinda kept the heavy curtain in place because it was easy to hear people come and go.

I tiptoed up to the door, listened, and heard a faint *meow*.

Voodoo.

Hey, my sweet kitty.

Out.

Just a second.

I thought I could quietly push the door open just enough to let the tiny kitten through without disturbing Belinda.

As the thought entered my mind, Voodoo said, *Gone.*

I paused. *Gone? Who's gone—Belinda?*

Belinda, gone, Voodoo confirmed, and showed me where Belinda had gone and who she'd been with.

"Oh no," I said, my hand still on the door.

"What?" Emma asked as she joined me in the hall.

"They have her," I said. The knot in my stomach tightened into a lump of cold tension.

"What? Who?"

"Belinda." I shoved the pocket door open. It rumbled into the wall and bumped to a stop.

I stepped into the shop and was followed by Emma, Ronnie, Hugh, and Kai. Moss stayed in the hallway to greet his kitten, who'd bolted from the room when the door had opened.

There was a man in the room, standing with his back to us.

I knew who it was before he turned around.

"Logan."

"Grace," he said, ignoring everyone but Kai, whom he acknowledged by making brief eye contact.

"Where is she?" Emma demanded in a menacing tone.

"I don't know."

"What are you doing here, Logan?" I asked.

"I need to speak to you."

"Well, speak."

He just looked at me.

"Fine. Guys, can we have a minute?"

After a pause everyone filed out of the room. Everyone except Kai. I expected him to refuse to go, but instead he called out, "Moss, come here."

Surprisingly, my dog came when Kai called. I cocked a brow at them both.

Giving Moss a pat, Kai said, "Take care of our girl." He walked out of the room and slid the pocket door closed.

I turned to Logan. "What's wrong with you?"

"How much time you got?"

"Not much. So get on with it."

"I came here looking for Anya, but I was too late."

"Yes. And now she has my friend. Can you help us find her?"

"Anya is very good at covering her tracks."

"How do you even know her?" I asked.

He didn't answer.

"Jesus, Logan, you came here to talk to me. Start talking."

"The company I work for used to fund research on people with ESP."

"Company?"

"It's a very big company with many interests worldwide."

"You mean the government?"

His brow twitched—which was answer enough.

"What are you, a spy or something?"

"Or something."

"Seriously?"

It made sense in a weird way.

"What about Anya? Who does she work for?"

"Anya's with SVR. Russian Intelligence. She is highly trained and she is lethal. Barry was one of ours. He's now working with the SVR."

"Barry was in the CIA?"

"He was running a program called Deepfield. The objective was to study and develop psychic sensitivities."

"How can someone develop psychic sensitivities?"

"He'd come up with a way to enhance a person's latent extrasensory abilities."

"Enhance? With what?"

"I'm not clear on the specifics, but I think it has something to do with electromagnetic fields and DNA."

Damn, Barry really was a mad scientist.

"He's a genius. But the work he did was slow. He'd been able to manipulate the DNA of rodents, but there were issues."

"Like what?"

"Again, I don't know specifics. When he didn't make timely advancements, his funding was cut."

"And he was fired?" I'd imagined the CIA having a more permanent solution for disgruntled employees.

"A few months back, Barry went off the grid completely. Vanished. A week ago, intel surfaced that he was in New Orleans."

"And what? They sent you to find him?"

He didn't answer right away. "I volunteered."

"Because of Anya?"

"Anya and I have some things to settle, but, no. I volunteered because of you."

"Me?"

"The agency has always had an interest in the concept of ESP. Since the '40s, standing protocol has been, if operatives in the field encountered an individual displaying any kind of extrasensory ability, we made a note of it in our reports."

I let that sink in. "You put me in a report."

"Yes."

I felt oddly betrayed by the admission.

"You gave my name to a psycho mad scientist."

"I didn't know him. I just followed protocol."

"Protocol." I repeated the word.

"When it became clear what Barry was doing, I asked to be assigned to the op."

"What he's doing," I said, "is killing people. Your agency's protocol has gotten a grandmother kidnapped. And now my friend, too."

"He's worked his way through most of the names on the list. Anya is resourceful. When things get desperate, she'll find a way to get what she wants."

I knew what she wanted—Ronnie.

"I know you're not going to let this go," Logan said.

"Correct."

"I came here to tell you what I know, because it might help you. And to ask for a favor."

"What?" I asked.

"If you find them, call me. I'm not asking you to let me deal with it. I'm just asking that we share information."

"Are you going to do the same?"

He didn't answer.

"Screw you, Logan."

"Think of me as backup. And I'd appreciate it if you kept the details of what I told you about my affiliations between us."

"I'll think about it."

With a nod, he said, "Watch your back, sweetness." And then he left.

I stood there, processing what he'd told me for a full minute. Then I turned to open the pocket door and face what was sure to be a barrage of questions.

My friends did not disappoint.

I managed to edit the conversation down to a few points.

Anya was a deadly Russian agent. Barry, who we already knew was crazy, was working with her. They'd had a list of names they'd been using to find psychics so that they could use them to do research, and make more psychics.

"How does Logan know all this?" Emma asked.

"He and Anya seem to have a beef. He wants me to call him if we find where she's been hiding."

"You're sure he didn't have anything to do with Belinda's kidnapping?" Kai asked quietly.

I nodded. "It was Anya. She pretended to be a client, and pulled a gun. Voodoo saw what happened."

"But I heard voices," Emma said, walking farther into the room. "So did Hugh."

She looked at him for confirmation.

"We could hear people talking," he agreed.

I took a second to think about what Voodoo had shown me. She'd been curled up napping on one of the curio cabinets, which had given the kitten a good vantage point. Anya hadn't noticed her, but she'd seen what happened from the moment the Russian agent had walked into the shop.

"Voodoo saw Anya put something over here on the bookshelf." I walked over and found a mini–tape recorder sitting on the shelf.

"But, how is it possible that we didn't hear a scream or anything?" Emma asked. "We were in the other room."

"Belinda hates guns, remember? She did everything Anya told her to. There was nothing to hear." I noticed something and looked around. "Where are Elvis and Priscilla?"

"I dropped them off at the groomer's when Belinda said she was running behind," Hugh said.

"We have to find her," my sister said.

I looked at Kai. "Can we call the police yet?"

He looked as frustrated and upset as the rest of us.

"Right now, with a cat as a witness and no sign of forced—" I held out my hand to stop him. I knew the drill.

I looked at Ronnie. "What about Jason?"

"He might be able to pull some strings, but I don't know how long that would take."

"Okay." I tried to switch gears and turned back to Kai. "What about what happened at the coffee shop? Is there a way to use that to get the cops to look for Belinda? Or maybe just the van? There were people around. Maybe someone got the license plate."

"I can call Mike. But the plates on the wrecked van were stolen. I'm betting these will be, too."

"Oh God." Ronnie clamped a hand over her mouth. "She was there. Belinda was in the van."

"We can't know that," Kai said.

"I can," Ronnie said. "I felt it."

"You knew Belinda was there?" Emma asked.

"No. It wasn't that specific. But when Anya pulled up I got this feeling. It's the same anytime I'm around other psychics." She turned to me. "I thought it was you. Remember, whatever it was Barry did to block my ability? I thought maybe zapping him shorted it out or something."

"You couldn't have known," I told her.

"Yeah, actually, I could have, if I had thought to focus on the sensation, on where the feeling was coming from. Damn it!"

"Ronnie, it wouldn't have mattered," I said. "Even if we'd seen Belinda being held at gunpoint through the window, we couldn't have done anything. We barely managed to get away."

Ronnie drew in a shaky breath and nodded. Between her and Emma I wasn't sure who looked more stricken.

"Hang on," Kai said. "Go back a second. What do you mean he blocked your ability?"

I hadn't told him about the psychic energy block, mostly because it was a lead-in for the part of the story I didn't want to tell him.

Unfortunately, I hadn't had a chance to explain to Ronnie that we should keep the bit about me offering to be kidnapped, along with the part where I demanded to be shot, between us. I hoped she would realize I'd glossed over those sections of the story before and would follow my lead and do so again.

"Barry wants to use me to find other psychics," Ronnie said. For Emma and Hugh's benefit she added, "I can sense psychic abilities in others and can use it to locate them."

"Like Professor X from the *X-Men*," Hugh said. "Cool."

"No, not cool," Ronnie said. "Because he plans to use me to find other psychics so he can kidnap and conduct experiments on them."

Emma paled. "And now, he has Belinda. She'll be strapped to a table, too. We have to find her."

"Wait." I had a sudden revelation. "What was she wearing?"

"Belinda?"

I nodded. I already knew the answer, because I'd seen it during Voodoo's recounting of the kidnapping. But I needed to be sure.

"A red and yellow print dress," Emma said. "Why?"

"This is too crazy," I muttered. "But it fits."

"What fits?" Kai asked. "Grace, stop talking to yourself and tell us what you're thinking."

"The woman Cornelius saw was Belinda. He wasn't showing me memories. This whole time, he's been seeing the future."

"You're saying the monkey is psychic," Hugh said. "How is that possible?"

"Barry," Kai said.

"Exactly. According to Logan, Barry had figured out a way to alter DNA to somehow turn on a psychic gene."

"Cornelius could be one of his experiments," Emma said.

"Right. Think about it." The idea made more sense the longer I considered it. "Cornelius showed me a snapshot of myself giving him beignets at the museum. He didn't even know what a beignet was. He wasn't asking me to meet him there, he was showing me what was going to happen."

I turned to look at Ronnie. "You know the guy from earlier?"

"Logan?"

"Have you met him before?" I waved the question away and started over. "Has he ever grabbed you?"

"No," Ronnie said, "and I'd remember, cuz that boy's hot."

Kai let out a sigh.

"That means it hasn't happened yet." I looked around at the group.

"Finally, some good news," Ronnie said.

"Getting grabbed by Logan isn't good news," Kai said.

"Why? Who is he?"

"Forget about Logan," I said. "Cornelius is psychic. Which means his vision of Belinda hasn't happened yet, either. We still have time."

"Yeah, but how much time?" Emma asked.

"Not much," Ronnie said. "If you think about how much information Barry gave us when he spilled his guts at the coffee shop, he might be in a rush."

"I don't think so," I said. "He was very confident you wouldn't be able to track him because he's figured out a way to suppress psychic energy."

"He must have done it to Belinda, too," Emma said. "Remember? She said her intuition wasn't working right."

"And she had that headache." I nodded. "He messed with her ability the way he did with yours, Ronnie."

"What exactly did he do?" Kai asked.

"I don't know," Ronnie said. "Grace had figured out Barry's plan to use me. She was telling me he wouldn't hurt me, that I could just leave and use my ability to find her later."

"You did what?" Emma said, turning to stare at me.

"I was trying to get a message across to her." I waved at Ronnie. "I could tell she was thinking about going with the lunatic. I had to show her what a bad idea it was."

Kai hadn't said anything, but he was looking at me in a way that made me want to squirm.

"It worked, too," Ronnie said. "But then Barry started laughing and said he'd figured out a way to stop me from finding her. So I tried to sense her power, but it didn't work. The sensation I get when I know someone's psychic—it was gone. Instead, I got a massive headache."

Kai had finally turned his glass-green eyes away from me and looked at Ronnie. "What exactly did he do?"

She looked at me. "Nothing. At least not that I saw."

"I didn't notice anything, either," I confirmed.

"Do you think he has some sort of ability himself?" Kai asked. "Has he altered his own DNA?"

I shook my head. "I don't think so. When he talked about tapping into the vibrations of the universe, he didn't include himself."

Ronnie nodded. "He seemed almost envious of us."

"Then it must be something else," Kai said thoughtfully. "A device of some sort."

"Maybe it's the radio Anya took from the van," Hugh said. "Or something that looked like a radio."

"That's one way to keep a psychic from finding you," Ronnie said. "Ride around in an ESP-proof vehicle. Only Barry didn't have anything like that with him in the coffee shop."

"The earpiece," I said. "Remember? He was fiddling with it while we were sitting there." I looked at Kai. "Would it be possible for something that small to be effective?"

"At this point I'm starting to believe anything's possible."

"We'll have to worry about that later," Emma said. "Right now, let's focus on finding Belinda."

"Agreed," I said.

"You back online, kid?" Emma asked Ronnie.

"Yeah, I think so, hang on." She took a quick, deep breath and closed her eyes. A second later, a warm sensation washed over me.

"Yep," I said.

"Wait," Emma said, "you can feel whatever it is she's doing?"

I nodded. "It's like walking through a ray of sunshine on a cold day. Except the warmth goes all the way through you."

"Apricity," Hugh said.

Everyone looked at him.

"What? It's a word," he said. "Look it up."

"There's only one problem," Ronnie said. "I'm not very good at this, remember? We were coming here to get Belinda's help because I couldn't get a fix on my *mamere*'s location."

That stopped us for a moment.

"We have to try," I said.

"I'm willing to try anything," Ronnie assured me. "I just don't know any more than I did before. You saw my notebook—there's almost nothing to go on."

"But this is different," Kai said. "Before you were looking for Hattie. Now you'll be looking for Belinda."

"How is that going to help?"

"He's right, Ronnie," I said, feeling a surge of hope. "You just said it yourself: you felt another psychic when Anya showed up in that van. It had to have been Belinda."

"Maybe the issue isn't that you don't know what you're doing," Emma said. "Maybe the problem is your relationship with your *mamere*."

"Wouldn't that help?" Hugh asked.

"Not if she's too emotional about it," I said. "I know I have to shut down my emotions completely sometimes to communicate with animals. If I don't, I get lost and the connection . . . implodes, I guess."

"You think the fact that I don't know Belinda will help?" Ronnie sounded dubious. "But, according to Mamere, connection is the key to finding someone. It only works if I have a link to someone's energy. That's why we use personal items, to form a link."

"Take a look around." Hugh swept his hand over the shop. "There's plenty to choose from."

"That's not what I'm saying." Ronnie paced in a circle and scrubbed her hands over her face.

"You think the link should be stronger because of your relationship with Hattie," Emma said.

"Yes."

"But being close to someone doesn't always help," Emma said.

"Sometimes it makes you crazy." Kai turned to look at me. "Especially when you find out they volunteered to be abducted."

"You think that's bad—" Ronnie started.

"Anyway"—I wasn't about to let her rat me out about telling Barry to shoot me—"I think you'll have better luck trying to find Belinda. So, what do we need? Something personal, right?"

Ronnie nodded. "Like a wedding ring or favorite sweater. Something she had with her a lot."

"How about a hairbrush?" Kai said.

"We're not looking for DNA," I teased.

Kai either didn't think my joke was funny or was still upset that I'd put myself in danger, because he didn't even crack a smile.

"Right," Ronnie said. "I make my connection through it, so it should be an item she's attached to."

"I don't know," Emma mused. "I've had some pretty sweet hairbrushes."

"Let's head into the kitchen," I suggested. "She spends tons of time in there."

We filed out of the shop. I paused at the shrine to Oshun.

"What is it?" Emma said, stopping beside me. "You think something on here would work?"

"No. Belinda told me I could make an offering and ask

for protection. I should have asked to protect her. I just didn't know. Now I don't have anything."

I patted my pockets.

"I do—here." Emma dug into the pocket of her jeans and pulled out a tube of lip balm.

"But it's your favorite, and they don't make it anymore."

"Maybe that will give it extra kick." She placed the lip balm on the altar. "Oshun, please keep our friend safe."

"Emma," Hugh called from the kitchen. "Grace, we found something."

My sister and I hurried into the kitchen.

"A skillet?" I said, looking at the object on the table in front of Ronnie.

"Not just a skillet," Hugh said. "This is Belinda's favorite. She was telling me yesterday how long it's taken her to get it seasoned. And how much she loves to cook with it."

"Think it will work?" I asked Ronnie.

"Let's find out," she said.

Closing her eyes, she placed her hands on either side of the cast-iron pan.

We watched and waited.

"I'm getting something," Ronnie said.

Kai had taken out his phone and was holding it toward her. Obviously recording her words.

"It's dark. There's humming, like an engine. I think it's the van."

I clasped my sister's hand. She squeezed it as we waited for more.

"The road is smooth. And it's . . . that way."

Ronnie pointed.

The entire group looked in the direction she'd indicated, as if there'd be something to see, but we were just staring at the kitchen wall.

"It's foggy." Frowning, she shook her head. "I'm losing it."

We continued to wait in silence for a few more seconds, until Ronnie opened her eyes.

"I couldn't hang on to it."

"That's okay," Emma said. "You did great. At least we have a direction."

"Yeah," she said. "But half the city's that way."

"You said foggy—did you mean actual fog?" Kai asked. "Or was your link becoming murky?"

"I don't know. I'm sorry. That wasn't much help. Let me try again."

Rolling her shoulders, Ronnie placed her hands on the skillet, blew out a breath, and closed her eyes.

After a few minutes she gave up.

"Nothing. It's totally gone."

"I know this is going to sound crazy." I paused to look around the room. "Okay, more crazy than all of this has been so far. But if Barry figured out a way to block us on a small scale, maybe he did it on a large scale, too."

"Like a giant psychic-blocking force field?" Emma sounded skeptical.

"Why not?" Hugh said. "He managed to create a psychic monkey."

"Good point."

"It would explain why you can't get more than a vague location," Kai said, "if it's made to block off a specific place, like a building. You wouldn't be able to access anything inside."

"So we're screwed." Ronnie huffed out a frustrated breath and slumped back against the cabinets.

A wave of inspiration hit me so hard I nearly dropped my glass of water. "I've got it."

"What?"

"For whatever reason, Ronnie can't get a bead on her grandmother or Belinda. Maybe because of some antipsychic force field, or maybe it's something else. Whatever. But what about Cornelius?"

"What about him?" Hugh asked.

"Oh my God—you're right," Emma said.

"What?" Ronnie asked.

"Cornelius knows where Barry has been doing his experiments, because he *was* an experiment."

"It's kind of poetic," Hugh mused. We all looked confused, so he clarified, "You know, Barry flipped the psychic switch on Cornelius and that's what let him escape."

I turned to Ronnie. "Think you can find a psychic monkey?"

"A monkey?"

Kai was nodding thoughtfully. "It could work."

"Not with monkeys," Ronnie said. She looked shocked at the suggestion.

"Why not? The concept is the same, right?" I asked.

"But I don't have anything of his to guide me," Ronnie protested.

And just like that, my big idea deflated like an old inner tube.

"Use Grace," Emma said.

I perked up. "Will that work?"

"I don't know," Ronnie said. "I've never used a person as a link before."

"It's worth a shot, isn't it?"

"Say this works, and we find Cornelius," Hugh said. "How are we going to catch a psychic monkey who can literally predict what we're planning?"

"We won't have to catch him," I said. "We just have to get him to lead us to wherever Anya and Barry are holding Belinda and Hattie."

"It's our only option," Kai said.

"Then I guess we should try it." Ronnie looked at me. "What do I need to do? Think about him or something?"

"Your guess is as good as mine."

"Grace, I think you should try to focus on Cornelius and block out everything else," Kai suggested. "You've had telepathic connections with too many animals. It might get confusing."

"Okay, give me a second." I closed my eyes and pushed

everything out of my head, filling it with white noise and static. Then, I pictured a dot in the center of my field of inner vision. I focused on the dot and brought it closer. The closer the dot got, the more features it developed. I could see a long, prehensile tail. And a sweet face with quick, curious eyes.

"Okay," I said.

I felt Ronnie's hands clasp mine.

"Here goes," she said, and we went.

Lights flashed. Car horns blared. Blurred images lurched in and out of focus. Trees. A rooftop. A barking yellow dog.

In a whirlwind the images flew by, then came to an abrupt halt.

"Holy crap. That was like being in monkey warp-drive," I said.

"Did you see him?" Emma asked.

"I saw a lot of stuff. Ronnie?"

"Yeah, way too much. I got a direction, though." She pointed.

"That's the opposite way from Belinda."

"Hey, wouldn't you want to put distance between yourself and the mad scientist's lab you'd escaped from?" I said.

"Yes, but it's still half the city," Kai said.

"No, it's not." I looked at my sister. "Em, where's the monkey map?"

"Um . . ." She looked at the kitchen table.

"Here," Hugh said. He'd obviously folded it up and out of the way when Ronnie had sat down to try to find Belinda with the skillet.

Spreading the map out on the table, we tried to decide which hotspot on the map was in line with the direction Ronnie had indicated.

"This one." Emma pointed. "In Uptown."

"Let's go," I said.

We loaded everyone, except Voodoo, into Bluebell. Once we got close to the monkey zone, Ronnie and I tried again to locate Cornelius. Holding her hand tightly in mine, I tried to maintain focus as images flooded my head in dizzying swirls of color and light. When Ronnie broke the connection, I was so light-headed that I almost toppled over.

"You okay?" Emma asked from where she sat next to Ronnie.

"Yeah, it's just a wild ride."

"We're much closer," Ronnie said. "Take a right."

Kai, who was driving, did as she asked.

"Somewhere along here," she said.

I nodded, recognizing some of the scenery from her vision. "There's the broken tree limb," I said.

"And the birdhouse." Ronnie pointed. "What were all those boxes? Beehives?"

"Nope," I said. "They're winter boxes. Some people with outside cats or who take care of ferals use them so the cats don't freeze."

"That's nice."

"It is," I agreed.

"So," my sister asked, "you know where to go?"

"Yep. I got it," I said.

I hopped out of Bluebell, glad I'd decided to wear my heavy red coat on such a bitterly cold night, and walked to the second house on the street.

The mailbox was decorated with dozens of paw prints. I'd seen it from Bluebell, which was how I knew we were in the right place.

Stopping at the gate, I focused on locating Cornelius. I found him quickly, but not where I'd expected. I thought he would be curled up in one of the insulated boxes in the backyard, but the clever little capuchin was snuggled up on a cat tree, *inside*.

This ought to be interesting.

The sign on the front door read: CAUTION, CRAZY CAT LADY CROSSING.

Well, at least I could talk to her. Some people might not know this, but not only am I fluent in whale; I also speak crazy cat lady.

I knocked on the door.

A woman in her forties answered a minute later.

"Hey there. I'm so sorry to bother you. I was hoping to ask you about your winter boxes."

"You're not with the homeowners' association, are you?"

"No, ma'am."

"Good. Those idiots with their Fleur-De-Lis la-di-da think they have the right to tell me how to take care of my pets. You know what I say?"

I didn't.

"They can stick it, that's what. What did you want to know?"

I took a card out of my pocket and handed it to her. "My name is Grace Wilde and I'm an animal behaviorist. I'm working on redesigning the boxes we currently use at the Humane Society."

"Well, come on in. I'm Pat." She squinted at the card, then handed it back to me. "You might as well keep it. I can't see a thing without my glasses. I lost them a couple of weeks ago."

"Oh?" I said as we walked into her living room.

"Yep, blind as a bat."

"You don't say." I slid my gaze over to the cat tree and the animal perched there.

Hello, Cornelius. Remember me?

Grapes?

He remembered me.

"Yesterday, I almost took a sip out of a bottle of dish soap," Pat said. "My new glasses should be here in the next few days if you want to come back. I can show you how I built the winter boxes."

"Actually, Pat, I found what I was looking for."

• • •

Cornelius had been happy to come with me—he was getting tired of eating cat food.

Pat had been stunned to learn she had been harboring a fugitive and was grateful I could take the little monkey off her hands.

With Cornelius perched on my shoulder, I climbed back into Bluebell. Hugh turned around in his seat to face me. "I've said this before, but it bears repeating. You're good."

"I am. And I promised him a bunch of grapes. We'll be good for a while."

Cornelius crawled around my neck to sit on the shoulder closest to Ronnie. She smiled and cooed at him.

"Did you ask him where we're going?" Kai asked.

"Not yet. I wanted to get him in the car first. That way, if he freaks out we won't lose him."

Ronnie eased away from the small monkey. "Is there a chance he might freak out?"

"He's been experimented on by a mad scientist," I said. "What do you think?"

She blanched, eyes going wide.

"I'll try to keep him calm, though. Give me a second."

I needed to come up with the least traumatic way possible to learn what I needed to know.

I thought about the little troop of capuchin monkeys I'd seen at the zoo and wondered if, when Cornelius had escaped from wherever he'd lived before this, he'd left any friends behind.

With the concept of family and friendship firmly in my mind I asked, *Where are your friends, Cornelius?*

The answer wasn't helpful. Cages. Darkness. Pitiful cries of pain. And the pressing weight of sadness.

Okay, I can help them.

Help?

Yes, I want to help. I patted the monkey on the flank to reassure him. *Can you tell me where they are?*

I should've known what was coming but I'm telepathic— I can't see into the future like Cornelius.

The world flickered and sputtered. An image formed,

dancing between light and blackness. Suddenly, I could make sense of what I was looking at. The five of us, Emma, Hugh, Ronnie, Kai, and me, along with Moss, stood in front of a chain-link fence, facing an open gate. The colors were faded into sepia tones. Except my red coat—it stood out like a drop of blood.

I still didn't know where we were.

Where, Cornelius? Show me your friends.

That was the wrong thing to ask for.

The image strobed out in a flash, and I was treated to a series of scenes featuring Anya, being indiscriminately cruel to the monkeys.

I squeezed my eyes shut. I couldn't get overwhelmed.

Okay, you're safe.

Friends!

I'm going to help them. I promise. But you have to show me where.

Then it came to me.

He'd escaped.

Show me that, Cornelius. Show me how you got away.

Cornelius started at the beginning. He'd always been a clever little guy. But once he'd developed his psychic ability there was no stopping him. It didn't take long for him to foresee his escape, which showed him *how* to escape.

Thanks to this vision, he knew how to unlatch his cage door. And even knew where to hide in order to slip outside when Barry walked in. From there, it was a mad dash down dark, litter-strewn hallways.

Finally free, Cornelius had shot up the first thing he could climb.

A roller coaster.

CHAPTER 17

"What did you see?" Ronnie asked.

"Too much," I said, trying not to let the need to wrap my hands around Anya's throat distract me from the task at hand. "I have an odd question for you. Are there any abandoned amusement parks around?"

"Yeah, there's one that got destroyed in Katrina," she said. "They used to shoot a bunch of movies there but I heard they closed it down because it was too dangerous and the filmmakers' equipment stopped working."

"Could it be that the same thing blocking the psychic energy is interfering with electronics?" Hugh said.

"Why not? I tossed logic out the window an hour ago," Kai muttered.

The logic didn't matter to me. "How far away is this place?"

"This time of night, twenty minutes, max," Ronnie said.

I kept a comforting hand on Cornelius as we drove. I knew I'd have to put him in a cage when we got to where we were going and worried about his reaction.

Not wanting to upset the little guy, I decided to focus on happy thoughts and memories.

I was shown a few flashes of his favorite toys and a swing, and then I heard a woman's voice.

"Give us a kiss then, eh?" she said.

Cornelius hopped onto the woman's shoulder and kissed her cheek.

The memory faded, and I knew that the woman, years ago, had cared for and loved Cornelius. I didn't know what had happened to her, but I felt his deep sorrow and knew he missed her very much.

Now he wanted to find his new family.

We will. We're almost there.

The amusement park was easy to find. A designated exit led us right to the entrance.

Kai pulled to a stop and turned in the seat to look at me. Before he was able to say anything, light flickered in my vision and my brain went wonky.

Cornelius went still and I knew, when the strobing effect started, he was having one of his visions.

"Grace?" My sister's voice sounded distant.

"He's showing me something," I said.

"Like a future something?" Ronnie asked.

I raised my hand to forestall any more questions.

To forge a better connection to his mind, I closed my eyes, locked on to the monkey's thoughts, and waited for the image to form. When it did, I saw something so shocking I thought my heart might stop mid-beat.

I sucked in a gasp and opened my eyes.

"What is it?" Emma asked in a harsh whisper. "What did you see?"

"I . . . I'm not sure."

"Did it have to do with Belinda?" Kai asked.

I glanced at him, looked away, and shook my head.

"No. It's . . . I can't explain. It's not about this." I waved my hand in a vague reference to the current situation.

I didn't want to think about what I'd just seen so I tossed

the thought into the oubliette of my consciousness and left it there to be forgotten.

With renewed composure I said, "Kai, check under your seat for my stun gun."

After a long, searching look he did as I asked.

"Got it." He held up the foot-long cylinder.

"Good. Now, everyone out so I can get Cornelius settled in his cage."

By the time I secured the monkey and joined the group, I was calm and ready.

We had to park Bluebell on the shoulder of the main road and walk past the concrete barricades blocking the entrance. The weathered chain-link security gate hung askew. The signs warning all who bothered to read them of the penalties for trespassing were faded and tagged with graffiti.

Collectively, we drew to a stop a few feet from the gate. Just like Cornelius had predicted.

The air was utterly still and the night unusually quiet. In the distance, the peaks of the roller coaster rose over the fog like skeletal humps of a prehistoric beast.

"Think they're watching?" Emma asked.

"No question," Kai said.

"What's our move?" Hugh asked.

"We walk in like we don't give a damn?" Emma suggested.

"Ballsy," he said, grinning at my sister. "Psych out the psychos."

"Sounds good to me," Ronnie said.

"Better to act like we have no clue, right?" I suggested.

"They already think we're stupid," Ronnie said.

"For the record, they may be right," Kai said.

"What choice do we have?" I asked. "Belinda is in there with a mad scientist who has a device that will put a hole in her head. I'm not okay with that."

"None of us are, Grace, but we need to think this through."

Emma gently placed a hand on my shoulder and turned me to face her. Her dark, deep-set eyes searched mine. "You okay?" she murmured.

"No, I feel like my flesh wants to crawl off my bones."

"I feel it, too," Ronnie said. "Maybe it's the thing that's blocking the psychic energy."

"I can buy that," Kai said, "but if whatever it is, is doing this"—he motioned to Ronnie's grimacing face—"from this far away, can we ask her, or Grace, to go in there?"

"I'm fine." Ronnie and I spoke in tandem and then shared a wry look.

"Ronnie, you said film crews avoided this place because of the issue with electronics, right?" I asked.

"Yeah."

"Then, how can they be watching us?"

"Good question. Maybe they can't," she said.

"I say we go with Emma's idea. Show of force. They'll either be intimidated or think we're stupid," Hugh said.

* * *

"This place is creepy on a level that takes creepy to another dimension," Emma said as we walked between broken-down old rides.

She was right. It was like we had stepped onto the set of a postapocalyptic horror film. The dilapidated theme park was strewn with fallen leaves and other trash. Graffiti was everywhere.

"My phone doesn't work," I said. *Damn.* I had been about to call Logan.

"Mine either," Hugh said.

Kai turned in a slow circle and pointed. "There."

"Is that a cell phone tower?" I asked.

"Yeah."

"Then why aren't we getting a signal?"

"My guess," Kai said, "is that it's been modified somehow."

"So that's what's scrambling the psychic energy and messing with our cell phones," I said.

"My head feels like an ice pick is being shoved into my forehead," Ronnie said.

"It must be emitting some sort of frequency or generating a specific electromagnetic field," Kai said.

I had only a vague idea what he was talking about, but I knew whatever the tower was doing, it was good for the bad guys and not for us.

"Can we take it out?" I asked.

"We need to," Ronnie said, "or I'm going to be useless soon."

I looked over at her. She squinted at the tower as if it pained her to keep her eyes open. The subtle freckles I'd noticed when we met now stood out on her rapidly paling face.

"Grace?" Emma asked.

"I'm okay," I said, which wasn't exactly true. "My head is pounding, too, but my connection to Moss is fine. Mostly."

"Mostly?"

I shrugged off Kai's concern. "It's intermittently fuzzy, but it's okay."

Ronnie pointed to a large building not far from the cell tower.

"There."

I saw it, too. An almost imperceptible light traced along the bottom of a door.

"Okay," I said. "Emma, Ronnie, and I will head inside, and you guys work on getting that thing off-line."

Hugh pulled Emma close for a quick kiss and said something in her ear.

Kai handed the stun gun to me, cupped my chin, and angled my face up to his. "Be safe."

"You, too."

"Moss," he said, looking down at my dog. "Take good care of our girl."

Guard.

Emma, Ronnie, Moss, and I walked to the building, while Hugh and Kai went toward the tower.

The door wasn't locked. Opening it a crack, I peeked inside. Seeing the coast was clear, I nodded to Emma and Ronnie and, with my stun gun held tightly in my right hand, slipped through the door into a dark hallway. Like the rest of the grounds, the floor was littered with a layer of mostly unrecognizable debris.

We tried to walk quietly, but it was impossible. Every few feet someone would step on a brittle piece of plastic or crunch on a pile of broken glass. Even sure-footed Moss sent an aluminum can rolling loudly down the hall.

"We might as well have a second line with us," Ronnie said in an irritated whisper.

I remembered hearing about second lines but my understanding was limited. I knew it was a type of small marching band and I was pretty sure they had something to do with funerals.

Not the most comforting parallel to draw.

"Just keep moving," I said.

Sorry.

It's okay, big guy.

Quiet?

Yeah, that's the idea.

I thought I'd made it clear to him to be as stealthy as possible, but maybe the energy field was stronger than I'd realized.

I shifted the stun gun to my left hand and fisted my right in my dog's ruff. My fingers barely penetrated his fur but the connection was enough. The interference quieted to an annoying but ignorable thrum.

"We found Cornelius's friends. Look," my sister whispered.

I stood on tiptoe to peer through the little square window in the metal door.

By the light of a lamp on the desk set to one side, I could

see a row of cages against the opposite wall. Three capuchin monkeys sat in separate cages. One rocked back and forth in an unceasing rhythm—neurotic behavior indicating an unhealthy mental condition. Not surprising.

I put my hand on the door but my sister stopped me from pushing it open.

"We can't," she said. "I know you want to get them out of there. I do, too. But we have to find Belinda first."

I didn't like it but knew she was right. Rescuing the monkeys wouldn't be easy or quiet.

Still, I hesitated. I desperately wanted to reassure them, but didn't dare try to reach out to them with my mind. Who knew how upset they might become? Plus, I didn't trust how clear the communication would be with the energy field blocking me.

I nodded to my sister and even though they couldn't hear me, I whispered to the monkeys. "I'll come back for you, I promise."

"Come on." Ronnie's hushed voice was strained with either pain or irritation. Probably both.

We continued down the corridor until we came to a T. Faint light was visible in both directions.

I looked down and touched Ronnie's arm. "Look."

Hundreds of pieces of shattered glass sparkled on the concrete at our feet.

"Diamonds," she whispered.

"Looks like you were tuning in to Hattie after all."

Ronnie gave me a faint smile and turned to survey the hallway in both directions. "We should split up."

"No, we shouldn't," I told her.

"We can't change the plan now, Ronnie," Emma said.

"Fine," she said, relenting. "But which way do we go?"

"You tell us," I said.

"I don't know. My head. I can hardly think."

"This way," Emma said. She headed right and we followed.

The glowing light was coming from an open doorway. Slowly, we peeked around the corner and saw the room was empty except for the occupant of the operating table. Belinda lay unmoving on the stainless steel slab. Her head was free of any contraptions and I didn't see any bandages or blood.

"I can see her breathing," my sister said. "Come on." We rushed into the room as quietly as possible. The knot between my shoulder blades relaxed a fraction when I saw Belinda was semiconscious but physically unhurt. I pulled the IV out of her arm as my sister shook her gently. I checked the bag. It was midazolam, a sedative.

"Belinda, wake up," Emma said.

She didn't move.

"We've got to get her out of here," I said, as if that weren't already the idea.

"How?" Emma asked. "This thing isn't on rollers."

I turned to scan the room. "We need something to counteract the drugs." I tried to think of something that would work on humans. "Look through the drawers for vials of Flumazenil. Smelling salts might even work."

"Grace, look at this." Ronnie was standing next to what looked like a high-tech workstation.

I rushed over, hoping she'd come across something useful.

Spools of wire and bits and pieces of unidentifiable metal and plastic parts were scattered over the table's surface. Ronnie held up something I recognized.

"Barry's earpiece?" I asked.

"I think so, but look at it." Wires dangled from the earpiece like the tentacles of a bionic sea creature.

It was creepy, but it didn't help with Belinda's situation.

"Is this what he's doing? Putting wires in people's heads?" Ronnie's voice trembled with rage.

"Actually, I think he's doing that to himself."

"What kind of a sick freak—"

"Ronnie, listen." I took the Borg-inspired earpiece from

her and set it on the table. "We need to focus on getting Belinda out of here, okay?"

Ronnie met my eyes and for a second, I thought the anger I saw there was going to boil over. Instead, she pulled in a deep breath and nodded.

"Right. Yeah, okay."

"Good." I turned to the drawers and resumed my search. "Help me look through these."

Belinda moaned.

"She's waking up," Emma said. "Hey, Belinda. Can you hear me?"

"No," Belinda groaned.

"It's going to be okay," Emma soothed.

My sister was right—Belinda was waking up, but not fast enough.

I started going through drawers, looking for vials again.

"Where's Ronnie?" Emma said.

I hadn't even noticed that she'd left. I turned to where she'd been standing, seeing only empty space. "If I had to bet, I'd say she went to find her grandmother." It was what I would do.

"Damn. Now we've got to get Belinda out of here and find Ronnie."

"One thing at a time," I said.

Belinda was struggling to sit up. My sister helped her.

"Grace? Emma? Oh, my head."

"Can you stand?" Emma asked her.

"I don't know."

"It's okay. We're going to get you out of here," Emma said.

"I've got an idea," I said, remembering something I'd seen in the room where the monkeys were caged. "There's a rolling desk chair down the hall that we can use as a wheelchair."

"I got this," Emma said with a firm grip around Belinda's waist. "Go."

I squatted in front of Moss.

"I need you to stay here."

Go.

No. Stay with Emma. Keep them safe. I'll be right back.

Go!

No, Moss.

I didn't have time to argue and the stupid energy field stopped me from communicating as easily as I needed to.

I was going to have to be sneaky.

"Stay."

I backed out of the door and pulled it secure behind me. Though I'd moved only a few feet away, I could barely feel Moss's presence on the other side of the door. The farther away I moved, the less I could sense him. It felt very . . . lonely.

Shaking the feeling off, I tightened my grip on my stun gun and tiptoed down the hall as quickly as possible, stopping in front of the door leading to where the monkeys were caged. Placing my free hand on the knob, I muttered, "Please don't be locked."

It wasn't.

With a relieved sigh, I pushed the door open—it swung in with a soft *swish*.

Keeping my focus on the chair and not the monkeys, I stepped into the room. A concussive blast of emotions slammed into me. My stun gun slipped from my fingers, clattered to the floor, and rolled away. Staggering to the side, I barely managed to keep my feet as the storm of images tore through my head. Flashes of light. Screams. The utter chaos of jumbled feelings. I was so confused that it took a moment to realize the information was coming from the monkeys.

Hugh and Kai must have disabled the tower. *Perfect timing, guys.*

Gritting my teeth, I tried to wrestle my mental shield into place, but the tide was too strong.

I'd been linking my mind to animals my entire life—and

I'd never experienced anything like it. Dizzy, with my heart racing, I struggled to get my bearings.

The only thing I could do was try and calm the source of the torrent. I pulled in a breath. Only a fraction of the space in my head hadn't been invaded. I focused on that part and tried to use it to project calming thoughts toward the monkeys.

Damaged.

The word formed clearly in my mind, almost as if someone had spoken in my ear. And suddenly I understood how much devastating pain had been inflicted on the animals in that room.

A sudden, searing rage scorched through me. The monkeys responded to the tide of emotion. Screeching howls echoed in the room. They lunged and banged on the cage doors.

The thing about capuchin monkeys is that they are fast learners. Show them how to open the door to their cage a couple of times and they're good to go. Barry had been careful—he'd blocked the latch from view and made sure it was secured with a clip robust enough to be tough for little fingers to open. But that was not a problem for me.

I rushed to the cages and opened every one.

A loud electric snapping sound came from behind me.

I had just enough time to think *uh-oh* before the pain of many thousands of volts shot through my body.

The monkeys screamed in alarm. My back arched involuntarily. Rigid with pain and spasming muscles, I hit the ground temple first. Red lightning shattered my vision and everything splintered into blackness.

• • •

Getting tased by your own stun gun is an embarrassing, unpleasant experience. Add the face-plant to the equation and when I came to, I was not keen to move or open my eyes.

It turned out to work in my favor because Anya and Barry were in the middle of an argument. Pretending to be unconscious allowed me to listen in.

". . . reset the system," Anya was saying.

"If we reboot now, everything will go off for thirty seconds," Barry answered. "Power, lights, everything. Even this."

I hadn't opened my eyes so I didn't know what "this" was.

"Do you have another solution? Soon, those two will reach the top of the tower. You see that piece of metal he is carrying? I do not think he means to twirl it like a baton."

"No." Barry's voice was a disbelieving whisper.

"Yes," Anya snapped. "He is going to use that to smash your precious machine. Look at what is happening."

I knew they had to be watching some sort of camera feed. Which meant I wasn't in the same room I'd been in when I blacked out. I desperately wanted to open my eyes but kept up the charade. The more freely they talked, the better.

"The monkeys are loose," Anya continued. "The test subject is going to escape."

"Damn it! Why did you leave your post to go after her? She's worthless."

"It does not matter. What's done is done. We must focus on a solution. Before those men reach the top of the tower."

"I have a solution," Barry said.

"What? You think you can shoot them?" Her tone was mocking.

"No. But I can electrocute them."

Oh shit.

"Good. I like it," Anya said. "Get it done and get back here."

Barry's footsteps faded. With him gone, there wasn't a reason to keep playing possum. I opened my eyes to find I was lying on the floor of a large room.

It looked as if it had originally been a pavilion or cafeteria.

Doesn't matter, I told myself. Barry was on his way to electrocute Kai and Hugh.

I needed to get my bearings and figure out a plan. Judging from the state of my clothing and the scrapes that stung the length of my back, I guessed Anya had grabbed me by the ankles and dragged me into this room. Which meant I wasn't far from where I'd left Emma, Belinda, and Moss.

Slowly, I turned my head. Anya was seated in a cheap office chair with her back to me in front of a couple of long, folding tables, similar to the ones you'd see at a family reunion.

There were six monitors sitting side by side on the tables. Three on each. Two were dedicated to the front and rear entrances to the park. Nothing going on there. Another showed the room where the monkeys had been kept and explained how Anya had known where to find me. The desk was in disarray and the cage doors hung open. No capuchins in sight. Good. At least they had a chance.

Given my supine position, and the angle, I couldn't see the monitors on the second table.

I was pretty sure that if she'd wanted to kill me, she'd have done it, so moving wouldn't put me in danger. Plus, I really wanted to get a look at the second set of monitors. I decided it was best to roll onto my side rather than try to do a sit-up.

I made it into the fetal position and had to take a break. Concussed. No question.

"I told Barry we wouldn't have to tie you up." Anya swiveled in her chair to watch me. She held a small pistol in her right hand, but kept it resting on her thigh. "It seems I was right."

She was.

If I could get to my feet, I was pretty sure I could walk. I also knew I wouldn't get far.

I had to think of a way to even the odds.

My scrambled brain kept going back to the reset button Anya had talked about. If I could find it, I could cut the power. No power meant no electrocutions.

Problem number one—even without the concussion, I was no match for Anya. According to Logan, she was a trained killer, with or without the gun.

I groaned as I used my arms to get my body into a mostly upright position.

As I moved, something inside my coat slipped to the floor next to my hip. I looked down at the balled-up piece of paper.

At first, I thought a wad of trash had gotten caught in my coat, then I remembered Marvo.

I was looking at the smoke bomb he'd given me.

I almost laughed in giddy disbelief, but soon realized the bomb would do me no good if I couldn't find the reset button.

Under normal circumstances, a wall of smoke between Anya and me might give me a chance to get away. But injured?

Blinking my blurry eyes, I tried to assess my surroundings.

The monitors on the second table were visible now. One displayed what I'd loosely call the operating room. There seemed to be two cameras in the room, with the picture flashing back and forth between two different angles. I could clearly see my sister and Belinda. When the screen jumped to the second camera, Moss came into the frame.

He paced back and forth in front of the door.

I knew, even without my ability to reach him, that he wanted desperately to come after me, and I was grateful he didn't have opposable thumbs. If Emma opened the door and let him out, he'd head straight for me and run into one of Anya's bullets.

Stay put, Emma, please.

One of the last two monitors displayed a view of the cell tower. The picture jumped between two angles, like the one showing the operating room. Both perspectives showed Kai and Hugh climbing the central column via an affixed ladder.

The other monitor also had two camera feeds. One displayed a long, dark hallway; the second showed a small room with a bunk. On it, a frail form was huddled.

Her face was turned away, but I recognized the silly bunny slippers.

Hattie.

The derelict building and dim lighting combined with

the images on the screens were like something out of a horror flick.

Reset—I reminded myself.

I needed to get to my feet. But before I could do that, I'd have to pick up the smoke bomb without Anya noticing. And she was watching me intently with a strange look on her face.

"What?" I asked her. "Never seen a concussed psychic before?"

"Many times."

"Of course you have."

I placed my palm on the ground next to the bomb and shuffled onto my hands and knees. My head was pounding, but it was manageable.

For Anya, I made sure to let every bit of pain show. Better for her to underestimate me and think I was weaker than I was. Though in reality, if I'd been any weaker I would've been unconscious.

With a groan I didn't have to fake, I wobbled onto my knees. As I moved, I grabbed the smoke bomb, keeping it wadded in my hand and my body angled so it was out of Anya's line of sight. With effort, I slowly got to my feet.

"Why am I here?" I asked once the room stopped spinning. "You could've shot me."

"I recently learned you are important to someone I wish to punish."

It took me a second to understand what she meant.

"Logan?"

"We have unfinished business."

I tried to roll my eyes but it hurt too much.

"Lady, you're turning out to be one big cliché—you know that?"

"You think so?"

"Yep."

"Here is another cliché. The damsel in distress is used as bait to lure her rescuer to his death."

"You can't really believe that's going to work on Logan."

"Logan," she scoffed. "Such a stupid American name."

"What happened? Did he out-spy you or something?"

"No. He murdered everyone I loved and now I will do the same."

Not the answer I'd been expecting.

I knew of only one person Logan loved, if someone like Logan was capable of love: a sixteen-year-old girl named Brooke.

Reset button. I shook my head slowly and tried to think. If I were installing a reset button for some giant, advanced, psychic force field in an abandoned building, where would I put it? Not on the table where something could accidentally be set on top of it. Not on the ground for the same reason. On the wall maybe?

"I think you're overestimating how much Logan likes me," I said. "He owed me a favor, but that's it."

"Yes, you saved that girl, Brooke. She will be next."

"You'll never get your hands on Brooke. Don't you know who her father is?"

"Charles Sartori does not worry me."

"Then you're stupid."

"Accidents happen. These teenagers"—she *tsk*ed—"always texting and driving."

My stomach clinched. Disgust and fear vied for dominance. Man, I really hoped Logan got his hands on this bitch.

Reset!

I needed to find the damn button and . . . then what? Come up with a plan.

"Where is he, then?" I made a show of looking around the room as if trying to find Logan, and searched for the reset button. The movement made my head swim and I had to place my free hand on the corner of one of the tables to stay upright.

"Would you like my seat?" Anya stood and offered it to me.

"No thanks." As much as I wanted to sit, I had to remain on my feet, because my scan of the room had paid off.

Over my left shoulder, affixed to a metal support beam, was the reset button. I knew what it was because below the button was a piece of paper warning—DO NOT PRESS THE RESET BUTTON.

Okay, now, I needed a plan.

The power would be out for thirty seconds. Barry was headed to electrocute Hugh and Kai, who were still climbing the tower. I assumed he intended to use the metal tower as a conduit. If I cut the power now, would it prompt them to climb back down and away from the tower? Would thirty seconds be enough time for them to get clear?

My head was pounding. I was having a hard time thinking.

Maybe I could hit the button and make it outside in time to warn them.

That wouldn't work. I'd have to get past Anya, who was between me and the door.

Think, Grace.

I had thirty seconds to work with. If I could contact Moss, I could send him to stop Barry. With the tower off-line, I'd be able to reach Moss—but he was stuck in the room with Emma and Belinda.

I also had to consider that my dog might not blindly do as I asked until he knew I was okay. As soon as he sensed my pain, he'd try to find me. Even if I was able to warn him about Anya, and he was able to avoid being shot, it would be too late to send him to warn Kai.

I glanced at the monitor to watch Kai and Hugh for a moment, and something on the neighboring screen caught my attention.

Ronnie was moving slowly down the hallway near Hattie's room, looking through the windows set in each door she passed. Out of the darkness, a man appeared. Clamping a hand over her mouth, he grabbed her from behind and pulled her backward out of sight.

Just before the picture switched to Hattie's room, Barry appeared in the hallway and I understood Cornelius's prediction.

Logan had saved Ronnie. For a moment I wanted to surrender to the idea he would do the same for me, but let the thought go. Logan might ride to my rescue, but what about Kai and Hugh?

Barry was on the way to kill them. I needed to forget about Logan's help and act.

Even with my ability restored, it would be useless in this situation.

Just as the thought entered my head, something appeared on one of the monitors. A monkey. Running through the rear entrance.

Cornelius?

How on earth did that little . . . Of course he'd escaped. He'd become an expert.

He was moving fast and was soon out of the frame, but he was headed this way. Coming to help his friends, I was sure.

I couldn't use Moss to stop Barry, but maybe Cornelius could warn Kai and Hugh.

I'd have to get the timing right. I couldn't hit the button until Cornelius was close enough to connect with.

Which would probably be in the next few minutes.

I'd wait, throw the bomb to make sure Anya couldn't see, hit the button, and run. I might not make it very far but at least Anya wouldn't know where I was.

Once I'd recovered my ability, I'd find Cornelius and get him to warn Kai.

Simple.

What could go wrong?

Out of the corner of my eye, I saw Emma and Belinda on the monitor. They'd started toward the door of the operating room.

No.

Moss stood, waiting.

Anya saw what had caught my attention.

"You're worried about your friends?"

I didn't answer.

"They won't get far. Barry will have locked the perimeter doors."

Emma reached out to clasp the handle.

No, Emma.

She opened the door.

Moss was gone in a flash.

"Oh, it looks like the doggy is coming to rescue you, too. I will kill him, like Logan."

A few seconds later, Moss appeared on another monitor. This time, in the room with the cages.

"Look," Anya said. "He is tracking you down."

I wasn't sure how far away Moss was, but I tried to reach out and connect to his mind.

I couldn't. It was like he wasn't anywhere.

"He will come here, next. Yes?" Anya asked like a kid waiting on a prize.

Anya turned to the darkened doorway.

"Too bad you cannot warn him."

I heard the faint jingle of his tags. They grew louder as he drew closer.

Moss, no!

There was no answer.

"Moss, stay!" I yelled.

He kept coming.

"Moss, NO!"

Anya raised her gun.

I threw the smoke bomb as hard as I could at her feet.

There was a tiny *pop!* An instant later, she was enveloped in a solid wall of smoke.

I spun, lunged toward the support beam, and slammed my hand on the reset button.

A heartbeat later, the room went dark.

Disoriented by both the absence of light and my sudden movement, I tried to run around the desks but tripped over a coil of wires and stumbled onto my hands and knees.

I know, with a name like Grace you'd think I'd be graceful, but no.

A sudden surge of protective anger roared to life in my head.

Guard!

Moss!

Grace! His elation at our reconnection soared through me. But I couldn't be distracted by the unexpected rush of joy. Moss needed to understand he was racing toward danger. I knew there was no way to make him stop, so I warned him instead.

Careful! I tried to project the concept, and showed him the image of where Anya stood, pointing her gun at the door.

He got the message at the last second and changed tactics. Instead of biting her leg and holding on, my dog plowed into Anya's shins and kept running.

She got off a shot but missed.

Moss, be quiet.

Okay?

I'm fine, buddy. Stay still and quiet. Okay?

Okay.

Without hesitating, I cast my senses out to find Cornelius. I felt the thrumming buzz of his brain a moment later.

Cornelius! Help!

Yes, help.

To more clearly understand where he was and guide him to Kai and Hugh, I solidified our connection and slid into his head.

He'd found the other monkeys. They were shivering, frightened, and confused.

Grace, help.

He was asking *me* to help *him*.

Damn. I didn't have time to explain my predicament. I had to get Cornelius to Kai.

Kai will help you and your friends. Find Kai.

I sent him an image of Kai along with what I'd seen on the monitor, which gave him a location.

Help?

Yes, hurry!

The little monkey took off. Once I was sure he was headed toward the tower, I pulled back from his mind. All the scampering and jumping was making me dizzier than I already was.

Out of the darkness, I heard the most unexpected sound.

Anya had started laughing.

"Something funny?"

"Yes. You just killed your friends."

I ignored the taunt. She was just trying to psych me out, right?

There was no time to dwell on it. In less than thirty seconds, the power would come back on, which would not only allow Anya to see and, therefore, shoot me and my dog, but would cut off my connection to Moss.

Remembering the emptiness I'd felt when I'd reached out for him brought on a wave of anxiety so powerful, I almost shut down.

From somewhere to my left I heard a low growl.

Moss sensed my sudden surge of fear.

Guard.

Easy, Moss.

Anya didn't try to shoot him, though his growl would have given her a general idea of where he was. She knew as well as I that he stood no chance once the lights were on and was probably just biding her time.

We needed to disarm her. The problem was, it was too dark to see. Even Moss's wolf-eyes couldn't penetrate the darkness.

If I could come up with the smallest amount of light, he could charge Anya and take out the arm holding the gun.

Bite. Moss knew what I was planning and was ready.

Steady, big guy. Wait till I say "Go."

Guard. He protested my plan, but stayed silent.

How could I generate enough light to let Moss see and keep Anya blind?

Distantly, I sensed a surge of emotion from Cornelius. Restoring my connection to him didn't take long.

Kai, help!

The monkey was hopping around Kai and making distressed clicking and whistling sounds.

"Cornelius?" I heard Kai say via Cornelius. "Hey, it's okay."

Cornelius continued to vocalize his need for help.

Unfortunately, Kai didn't speak capuchin.

Hugh, on the other hand . . .

"He's freaked out," Hugh said.

Show them where you want to go, Cornelius. Go down.

Cornelius did as I asked. When the men didn't follow, he climbed back to them.

Help!

"The machine is off," Hugh said. "Do you think—"

Kai squinted at the monkey. "Grace?"

Yes! How to confirm I was sending them a message?

I did the first thing that came to mind.

Give him a kiss.

Cornelius hopped onto Kai's shoulder and, just as he had done with his previous owner, kissed Kai on the cheek.

Still hanging on the rung, Kai glanced at Hugh. "It's her."

Cornelius hopped away and started down the tower.

Follow the monkey, Kai.

"Let's go," Kai said.

I wasted no time coming back to myself. But the head-hopping was taking its toll and it took me a couple of seconds to adjust and locate Moss.

I found him in the most unlikely place.

My dog had his front paws firmly planted on Anya's chest, pinning her down.

I knew this not because I'd jumped into his head, but because I could see them. Or the silhouette of them, in any case.

On the floor a few feet away, a cell phone glowed softly. Anya tried to shift her weight.

Moss's low growl intensified.

"I'd be still if I were you," I told her as I got my feet under me.

She was cradling her arm.

Guard.

Good boy.

Using the table to keep me steady, I searched for the gun. It was near Anya's foot.

I walked over to it. Rather than bend over and tempt my already pounding head to explode, I squatted and picked up the gun.

A second later, the lights blinked on. The hum of machines started as the power was restored.

I saw my stun gun sitting on one of the tables and picked it up. I really wanted to sink into the office chair but was afraid if I did I wouldn't want to get back up.

"Call him off." Anya grated out the words.

Holding a weapon in each hand I turned to look at her.

"No."

"Please, call him off."

"Why should I? I saw your cruelty, Anya," I said. "I know what kind of person you are."

"Oh, and what kind is that?"

"You believe animals are nothing more than property. Shells to be used however you deem necessary. But they can feel, Anya. Want to guess what he's feeling now?"

Moss inched closer to her face. His lips peeled back from glistening, sharp teeth.

Her eyes went wide.

"You won't let him kill me."

"Let?" I scoffed. "He's a sentient being. He makes his own choices."

With that, I walked around her and headed for the door.

"Wait. Please!"

I kept going. I'd walked only a few feet into the hall when Moss caught up with me.

"See? You're a better person than she is," I said, and we continued on.

We reached a dark doorway and Moss stopped and pricked his ears.

I knew someone was standing inside, and after a moment I knew who it was—Logan.

I had a lot of questions for him, but only one mattered. "Is everyone safe?"

"Everyone but Barry."

That worked for me.

Glancing over my shoulder at the room where I'd left Anya, I asked, "Did you really kill everyone she loved?"

No answer.

"She wants revenge."

"I know."

"She knows about Brooke."

Leaving it at that, Moss and I walked out of that awful place into the cold night.

CHAPTER 18

Belinda was at the stove, wearing her colorful kimono, topped with her Hot Stuff apron.

Emma had tried to get her to sit and rest and let her do all the work, but Belinda wouldn't hear of it.

What happens when an irresistible force meets an immovable object?

Pancakes.

I hadn't even bothered to argue when they'd decreed I was to sit and be waited on.

My headache was better, but my brain was not functioning at full power, which was normal for someone with a concussion.

Unfortunately for me, that meant I couldn't shield my mind from the animals I came in contact with. Moss had saved me again. He'd somehow understood how sensitive I was and stayed by my side, maintaining a solid presence for me to connect to.

Staying linked to him helped keep other animal brains at bay.

Even so, sometimes I'd get a blast of telepathic energy so strong that I wished for Barry's mini-anti-psychic contraption. Though neither it nor Barry had made it out of the amusement park in one piece.

"What's the latest on Barry?" I asked Kai, who'd set a plate of pancakes in front of me before taking his seat.

"The police aren't sure they'll be able to charge him, given his condition. The doctors say he'll never recover from what that thing did to his head."

When the power came back on after the reset, the tower had emitted some sort of pulse that had, because of the device implanted in Barry's ear, pretty much fried his brain. It had also somehow short-circuited the monkeys' psychic ability, if that's what you want to call what had been done to them.

"Does that mean he'll wind up drooling on himself in a psych ward somewhere?" Hugh asked as he spread butter over his pancakes.

"Yep."

"Good." Hugh punctuated the word by stabbing a piece of pancake with his fork. Instead of eating it, he lifted the fork into the air to hand off to my sister, who was buzzing around the kitchen like a bee.

She took the bite, handed the fork back to Hugh, and zoomed back to the stove.

A few seconds later Emma came back to the table to set a glass of orange juice next to my plate. She got another bite of pancake from Hugh and used the fork to point at my pancakes.

"Eat."

She gave Kai a sharp look before heading to the refrigerator.

He cut off a piece of pancake for me and held it up.

I arched my brow at him.

"Do I need to make airplane noises?" he asked.

I smiled and opened my mouth.

"I talked to Jason," he said. "He and Ronnie are still at the hospital with Hattie. She's stable and should be released in the next couple of days."

Hattie had been spared the horrors of Barry's lab. As predicted, he'd wanted to use her to control Ronnie, so aside from injuries suffered from her kidnapping and some lingering psychic symptoms similar to the ones Belinda and Ronnie had been dealing with, she was okay.

"Any progress with the fire investigation?" I asked.

"No," Kai said, forking another bite of pancake into my mouth. "I think they're going to write it up as a secondary spark after the one that zapped Barry."

Logan had taken care of most of the evidence of what was going on at Barry's lab by torching both it and the tower, which was good, because now no one else could use his research to do something similar.

No bodies had been found in the charred wreckage. I didn't know if that meant Anya was still running around or if Logan had simply covered his tracks and disposed of her elsewhere. I had the feeling the latter was the case.

I hadn't heard from the Ghost, but figured he'd show up eventually to irritate me with his "help."

Emma claimed to have put her birthday plans on hold until everyone was well enough to attend, but I'd heard her and Belinda whispering and was pretty sure a Mardi Gras ball was in my future.

Oh well, there were worse things, right?

I turned to Hugh. "You talked to Marisa?"

He nodded. "She has the capuchins in quarantine. The isolation has helped."

All the capuchins but Cornelius had suffered what basically amounted to insanity due to the trauma caused to both their brains and their DNA, which Barry had also been playing around with.

The room they'd been kept in had been carefully shielded from the tower's emissions. Which was why, though the device had still been on, I'd gotten a blast of psychic energy from the monkeys when I'd entered their room.

For now, the monkeys' psychic insanity had been reversed,

but no one knew how long it would last. Cornelius was the most balanced, and his presence seemed to help his friends.

The zoo was caring for them until their condition was stable. Hugh was already making arrangements to get them into a good, permanent home.

"Speaking of monkeys," Kai said, "are you going to tell us what Cornelius showed you?"

"When?" I asked, though I knew perfectly well what he meant.

"In Bluebell before we went into the amusement park."

"Oh, um . . . no."

I felt a flash of anxiety. "I mean, I don't really know what he was trying to tell me."

"Not enough detail?" Kai asked.

I nodded.

"Maybe you'll figure it out later."

"Maybe." I tried to mask my unease by taking a swig of orange juice and wound up draining the glass.

"Here, I'll get you a refill." Kai stood and walked to the fridge. I watched him for a few seconds and felt my mouth go dry. Something about the way he was standing, with his back turned, triggered the memory. It rose from the deep recesses of my mind like a ghost.

Kai's back had been turned in the vision, too. I'd recognized him instantly, though nothing else was familiar.

After a moment he'd said, "Don't worry, we'll figure this out."

It had made me wonder who he was talking to and what they needed to figure out.

The first part of my question was answered a moment later when he turned and I could see that he held something in his arms.

The memory didn't carry quite the impact as it had the first time but I still felt a wave of surprise roll through me.

Cradled in his arms, swaddled in a sage green blanket, was a baby.